P9-CZV-566

YOURS,

MINE,

AND

OURS

ALSO BY MARYJANICE DAVIDSON

Me, Myself, and Why?

MaryJanice Davidson

YOURS, MINE, AND OURS

ST. MARTIN'S PRESS
NEW YORK

This is a work of fiction. All of the characters, organizations, and events portrayed in this novel are either products of the author's imagination or are used fictitiously.

www.stmartins.com

Library of Congress Cataloging-in-Publication Data

Davidson, MaryJanice.
Yours, mine, and ours / MaryJanice Davidson. — 1st ed.
p. cm.
ISBN 978-0-312-53118-8 (hardcover)
ISBN 978-1-4299-8808-7 (e-book)
1. United States. Federal Bureau of Investigation—Officials and employees—Fiction. 2. Serial murder investigation—Fiction. 3. Christmas stories. I. Title.
PS3604.A949Y68 2012
813'.6—dc23

2011041099

First Edition: March 2012

10 9 8 7 6 5 4 3 2 1

Dedications are always so boring unless you're the author, or having sex with the author, or gave birth to the author, so I'll speed this up: This book is for my husband, Anthony, who's awesome, in bed and out.

acknowledgments

Again: the boring part, unless you know the author. So, for those of you who know me (and those of you gathering info the better to *spy* on me), here we go.

Many thanks are due to my family, who pay me the ultimate compliment of being unsurprised, yea, even unmoved, by my success. (I've been trying to work in *yea* for quite a while, and lo, opportunity, she knocked! Okay, "*unmoved*" is a little strong, but I saw a chance to jam *yea* in there and went for it.) Thanks for being unsurprised, gang!

Thanks are also (over)due to my friends Cathie and Stacy for putting up with my long absences from planet Earth. I'd tell them where I go or what I do when I disappear from their lives for weeks at a time, but then I'd have to kill them—and not in a "nothing personal" way, but in a "sorry to be so mean" way. And who needs that?

Thanks to the rest of the gang, Andrea and Sara and Vana and Jon and Mike and Curt and all the rest, for same, and for still trying to buy my books. (Stop that. Stop trying to buy them. I have a zillion copies and I know how they all end. Stop it!)

Thanks also to my fearless assistant, Tracy. She doesn't look fearless. In fact she looks quite mild-mannered in a cute-face-cute-figure-sugar-cookie-personality way. But she's fearless, even though she'd be the first to deny it. The things she's heard . . . the things she's seen me do and, more important, tried to prevent me from doing . . . the things she's talked me out of . . . the times she's refused to buy more shotgun shells . . . or Malt-O-Meal . . . anyway, thanks, Tracy, for often saving me from myself. And shrapnel. And thunder thighs from too much Malt-O-Meal.

Many thanks are also due to my tireless editors. Tireless, because I can be exhausting. Editors, because they are my editors. They never question *if* I can do something, they just wonder how. And sometimes why. As in, "How do you come *up* with . . . never mind. I don't want to know." But they've never once told me I couldn't, or shouldn't. And how often in life do we run into people like that? Rare enough so I thank 'em in a book.

Seriously, whether it's teachers or bosses or neighbors or friends (*nice* friends, friends who mean well, friends who don't *want* you to go to jail and truly feel you were provoked) or family members or pets . . . wait, did I say pets?

My point is, we run across people who say "better not" or "the police will have questions" or "they'll deport you" all the time. So much so that we think nothing of it.

So when I run across someone who says "Great idea, let's see it!" I tend to make a note of it. They're always editors. And sometimes children. Okay, usually children. Either way, I'm really, really lucky.

So thank you, all of you. Now I'm off to try something many of you think will get me deported. But *I* think *you're* wrong. But if I'm wrong, hey . . . another book idea!

—MaryJanice Davidson writing from "Carlton Cruise Line: The Ten Worst Jails in the World," Winter 2010

author's note

When *MMY?* came out I held my breath; many entities (*Publishers Weekly*) and people (Mom) were wondering if the concept and writing style I'd put into an all-new series with an all-new publisher was the greatest idea I'd ever had . . . or the most deeply insane. Thus the question: Would readers find it brilliant, or bad? Brilliant as in "Hey, a secretary turned vampire queen, that's different," or "John, Polly, let's go to the Biograph Theater, I'm soooo bored" bad?

I was lucky; most who read *MMY?* found it different from anything else they'd ever read, but also good. (That's the trick, because different and bad is easy.) That was pretty great to hear.

Pretty great, but no big gusty sigh/gasp/wheeze of relief. No, *that* came with messages from nurses, doctors, therapists . . . basically, various members of the mental health community got in touch to tell me a) they liked the book a lot and b) hey, you got it right, not bad for an idiot!

That was critical for me (I've never hidden being an idiot); that was the path to the next book in the series, the tome you're holding/shoplifting/scanning/downloading right now.

Cue swoon of relief, then long nap of relief, then big turkey dinner of relief, then second nap of relief.

The path to *Yours, Mine, and Ours* was through mental health professionals who agreed that I hadn't utterly destroyed the public's perception of DID (Dissociative Identity Disorder). Though many of them told me MPD (Multiple Personality Disorder) is now referred to as DID (Dissociative—right, you remember), so I might want to go back and change that.

To which I said, nuh-uh, you're not the boss of me, mental health professionals, and they were all, you *need* a boss with an attitude like that paired with your crippling immaturity and we should know we're professionals, and I was all, "back off, stupid mental health professionals, no one hit your buzzer," and they were all, "someone should hit *your* buzzer, you skeevy gargoyle," and I was all, "ohhhh nice, mental health pros, you kiss your mother with that mouth?"

Anyway. They said I didn't suck. They said I got MPD/DID/Sybil-ism right. Not bad for someone with no college degree, never mind a nonexistent background in mental health (from the therapist's side, anyway).

So hopefully I brought the same "hey, that didn't completely suck" can-do attitude to this book. And if you disagree, well, I know you are but what am I?

A question for the ages, truly.

(yet another) author's note

I've taken some liberties with the holding cells used by the St. Paul Police Department. So for those of you who have been arrested in St. Paul and noticed my processing and holding cell details are slightly off, sorry about that. Although, for someone who knows what a holding cell looks like from the inside, you're pretty quick to judge, don't you think?

Also, the Land O'Lakes Kennel Club Dog Show does take place in St. Paul, Minnesota, but usually in January, not December. For my own ruthless intent, I willfully changed the dates. Suck it, dog lovers!

I also lived in a trailer park for many years, so Cadence's description of Heron Estates is totally accurate. Unlike people who have never lived in a trailer park, I am allowed to mock trailer park clichés.

The list of unusual deaths was courtesy of Wikipedia and, obviously, isn't complete. But imagine if it was!

Worst of all: the characters in this book make reference to several serial killers. Understandably—the FBI is in the *other* side of the serial killer biz, and by necessity need to know all about them, past and present. But research for that part of the book was easy. Really easy. And I'm sorry to have to say that's so.

It's pretty lame when the world will talk about a murder victim practically down to her ponytail holder, yet lock a teenager in federal prison for stealing stamps.

"It's time for us to call a truce. None of us likes this situation, but if we want to win out we need to unite against the greater enemy."

—William Beardsley, *Yours, Mine, and Ours*

"Curiosity killed the cat, so don't wonder."

—Sybil Dorsett

"I don't think that they had too much of a trial."

—Lorraine Binnicker Bailey, at the murder trial of George Stinney

"Honey, there are a lot of things you've never seen me do before. That's no sign I don't do 'em."

—Nunnally Johnson, *The Three Faces of Eve* (screenplay)

"He was like my idol, you know. He was very smart in school, very artistic . . . We had a good family. Small house, but there was a lot of love. It took my mother a long time to get over it. And maybe she never got over it."

—Katherine Stinney Robinson, on the execution of George Stinney

Fidelity, Bravery, and Integrity.

—FBI Motto, est. 1908

Factious Bitching Inmates

—George Pinkman, Special Agent, FBI

"With every day, and from both sides of my intelligence, the moral and the intellectual, I thus drew steadily nearer to the truth, by whose partial discovery I have been doomed to such a dreadful shipwreck: that man is not truly one, but truly two."

—Robert Louis Stevenson, *The Strange Case of Dr. Jekyll and Mr. Hyde*

"You don't get it, do you, Finch? You're my job. You're what I'm paid to do. You're about as mysterious to me as a blocked toilet is to a fucking plumber. Reasons for doing what you did? Who gives a fuck?"

—Detective Will Dormer, *Insomnia*

YOURS,
MINE,
AND
OURS

chapter one

"—doing in here?"

I blinked at the woman across from me. She was not pleased, not even a teeny tiny bit. Her hair, which was once probably a lovely brunette pageboy, now looked as though the woman had been combing it with a wire whisk. Her face was red and shiny. Her clothes were a mess—a run in her pantyhose, her blouse untucked, one shoe missing—and she was standing ankle-deep in a drift of snow. Her brown eyes were really, really starey.

"Well? What do you have to say for yourself?"

"I didn't miss Christmas, right?" I asked. This wasn't an idle question. The last thing I remembered was December, but hardly any snow—it had been a weirdly "green" winter.

"*That's* your question?"

I wondered if she had a hearing problem. "Um. Yeah. That's my question. I really, really hope I didn't miss Christmas again."

"Didn't you hear me?" the woman croaked. Her voice was hoarse, either because she was ill or she'd been screaming. Probably at me, poor thing. Unless she was hoarse *and* ill. Poor thing! "The cops are on the way! This is . . . it's . . . it's destruction of property! You think I don't *know* that? Everybody knows that! You're . . . you are a destroyer of property! *My* property!"

Well, that certainly sounded bad. I nodded encouragement ("yes, my, sounds terrible, really, just awful awful awful") but it didn't calm her down, not even a little.

I tried to figure out where I was. There were no newspapers around, so I had no idea what city I was in or what the date was. No TVs running with a CNN stream. Windows, sure, but too high for me to see billboards or the Golden Arches or any sort of landmark. (Mmmmm. Arches! Suddenly I wanted a Filet-O-Fish or five.) Nothing indicating the name of the building the poor thing and I were trapped together in. Just barking.

Lots of barking from, I would deduce (being a trained investigator for the FBI, I could do that; I could deduce all over the place), lots of dogs.

Dogs.

Ah.

I looked down and observed that the "snow" I was standing in was actually mounds and mounds of poodle fur.

"Uh-oh."

"That's it? That's *all* you have to say for yourself? After what you did?"

"Um . . . oh, crumbs?" (Profanity was for the unimaginative.) "And . . . I'm sorry?" An apology seemed like the right move. When I woke up in a strange place with enraged strangers who were wearing only one shoe while standing in poodle fluff, it was almost always the right move.

"And there they are!" she shrilled, pointing with a flourish at the approach of two police officers. "You boys! You come over here and . . . and *get* her."

"*Get* me?" I asked, appalled. "But you don't even know me."

"Don't say that like we haven't spent ten horrible minutes together."

Well. *We* hadn't. She and I, is what I meant. She had spent time with my body, but not with me. Don't worry: it's not as depraved as it sounds.

"She committed felony assault on all my show poodles!"

Scratch that. It was at least as depraved as it sounds.

"Ohhhhh, that sounds bad," I said as the officers hurried up. They were St. Paul police, I noted, as I nodded politely and tried to look the opposite of dangerous. Both big and blond and puffy, one with blue eyes and one with brown.

"You called in the assault, ma'am?" Blue Eyes asked.

"I think, yes, Officer," I said, well into helpful mode.

"You shut up! *I* did." She blew a hank of hair off her forehead with a gusty, egg-scented puff. "She committed assault all over everything and I'll lose now and months—months!—down the drain!"

"You should probably arrest me," I agreed. I went to set down my mocha, then realized my hands were empty. No wonder I was thirsty. "I'll come along quietly."

And I did.

chapter two

"Haw!"

I looked up and stifled a groan. My partner, George Pinkman, was standing just outside the holding cell bars, clutching his stomach with one hand and pointing at me with the other. "Oh my God! I thought the police report had been exaggerated. But you really did it. Shaved poodles!" He hee-hee'd for several seconds; I'd rarely seen him in such a good mood.

"You did not think that," I said, appalled. "Cops wouldn't exaggerate on a government document."

"Like I give a shit," he replied, instantly bored . . . the classic mood swings of a clinical sociopath. He eyed the contents of the holding cell, which looked and smelled exactly like holding cells all over the country. I had reason to know, I was sorry to say. "Okay, so, this could still be interesting. My situation can be salvaged."

See that? *My* situation. Like I said. Classic.

He looked up and down the corridor. "So, is there some kind of *Chained Heat* thing going on here?"

"Gross."

"Don't take this away from me," he begged. "I have so little in my life. *Caged?*"

"George."

"Bare Behind Bars?"

"Are you *trying* to make me throw up, or is it just a side effect from talking to you?" Zow! I must be grumpier than I thought. I could usually be a little more civil. "Sorry."

(I was a compulsive apologizer. I saw a doctor for it and everything. I was a get-along girl; if everyone wasn't content I apologized. My sisters hated it. *Hated.*)

"So Young, So Bad? Women In Cellblock 9? Cell Block Sisters?"

"I'm sorry to have to point this out." Really. I was! "And maybe you'll remember I've told you this before, but there's something deeply wrong with you."

He cursed me. "Goddammit. *Reform School Girls*, at least?"

I shook my head. "The terrible things I find out about you when I'm stuck in a holding cell."

"Coffee?"

"No thanks. I'm a cocoa girl."

"I mean *you* should buy *me* coffee, you useless harpy." He yawned and ran his fingers—pianist's hands, surgeon's hands, psycho killer's hands—through his thick black hair. "Goddamned Michaela called me at the crack of dawn, and I had to haul my firm and wonderful ass down here to get you out. On my day off, I had to get up early and rescue your sorry ass!"

"It's two o'clock in the afternoon."

"Shut up. I had stuff to do first." He rubbed his eyes, which were a fine, pure green. "Hey, I said "crack" and "ass" in the same sentence. Let's go."

I turned to the three women I'd been spending time with. Two of them were in the far-left corner. The other one was crouched beside the lower bunk. They were all staring. My, what big eyes you have, cell mates. "It was nice talking to you."

"Please don't hurt us anymore."

"No, no," I soothed. "Of course not. And, um, I'm very sorry." For whatever it was I did.

If I had to guess (and I didn't have to guess; I knew), I'd say my sister, Shiro, had paid them a visit. That was bad, but if my youngest sister, Adrienne, had come, things would have been much, much worse.

Natch, I couldn't remember a thing. This was behavior I was used to, but never cared for. I remember reading *Sybil,* by Flora Rheta Schreiber, years and years ago and thinking *Thank goodness somebody gets it somebody really gets it this woman is writing about me!*

Sometimes I hated the sorry fact that my sisters could hijack my body, make it do all sorts of odd and unacceptable things, and then return the body back to my control . . . usually after they've used it to commit various felony acts.

All that to say, I don't know what nonsense my cell mates pulled, nor did I know what Shiro did for payback, but I was never one to hold a grudge.

"So. Um. It was nice meeting you all."

The gal by the bunk was going to have a gorgeous shiner. As for the other two, the moment I got my body back I'd been able to stop their nosebleeds after a couple of minutes. I'm not one to badmouth, but I really think they blew this whole thing out of proportion.

chapter three

Cadence was right. They blew this whole thing out of proportion.

chapter four

"—she do?" George stepped aside as the duty officer unlocked the holding cell. Officer Crayon (the poor man! what a name), too, was careful to stand far back as I exited.

"Sorry, George? I didn't catch that." Most people would think *Huh, I must have drifted off* or *Golly, guess I wasn't paying attention*. I never drifted off. Stupid fargin' MPD. Shiro must have popped back in the driver's seat, probably to show off by coming up with a silly obscure fact. Less frequently, it was to agree with me.

And again: I was trying to keep my internal whining under control. It could have been worse. There are much worse things than putting Shiro in the cockpit.

"I said—and try to stay in your body for half a minute if it's not too much damned trouble—what'd you do to those poor bitches?"

"Don't call them that!" I was so shocked, if they hadn't closed the door I would have fallen back into the cell. "They are human beings, George Pinkman, and deserve respect."

"They're two whores and a dyke-beater." He turned, walking backward, the better to talk to my former cell mates. "For the record,

I'm into that. Hey, domestic abuse should apply to everyone, not just heteros. So keep up the good work, gals. Hip-hip-hooray for equal rights!"

"You shush your big mouth!" I was frantically waving my arms, trying to hush him up. "They can hear you!"

"You look like a duck trying to take flight when you do that. And of course they can hear me," he said reasonably, with no idea why I was upset. "We're only eight feet away. Now, after we walk through this big iron door and they clang it behind us, *then* they won't be able to hear me."

"You . . . you never get it, do you? And you never will. You look at them, you look at me, you don't see people with feelings. You don't see people at all. Just things to play with. Toys. At *best*." I wouldn't say it. I wouldn't say it! "Sorry."

Rats!

George yawned. This wasn't anything he hadn't heard from any one of his number of bosses, therapists, coworkers, family members, or random strangers. I didn't know why I was wasting my breath. I didn't know why his yucky crapola was getting to me more than usual.

Yes, I did know. I promised my psychiatrist I would make a real effort not to lie to myself so much. "We lie best when we lie to ourselves," he said, which I thought was profound and accurate, though my sister Shiro thought

chapter five

I thought it was obvious, and idiotic. Trust Cadence to be charmed by the yappings of a fortune-cookie therapist.

chapter six

it was idiotic. But Shiro could be strangely close-minded sometimes.

I pinched the bridge of my nose, then rubbed my eyes. The month had barely started (at least, in my head) and I was already tired of it. And tired of George's ickiness.

"—more pathetic than usual. Are you all right? For you, I mean?"

No. Though I appreciated George's attempt to fake empathy. He, too, received regular instructions from a platoon of therapists. But at least in my case, there was hope. George would be out of luck for the rest of his life. There was no cure for sociopathy.

My sisters and I could theoretically be put back together, like a grumpy Humpty-Dumpty, but no one can grow a conscience past, say, the age of five. When George wasn't being a big mean poopie, I felt sorry for him.

"Did one of those bitches get a shot in before Shiro took them out?" He instantly turned on his heel. "Hey! Nobody smacks, taunts, or bruises my partner except me! And maybe a random bad guy! Which one of you worthless cows—"

"Stop it, please. I'm getting a headache. They didn't bother me. Just . . . stop being mean for five minutes. Please?"

"No." His gaze was on me, green eyes narrowed. "If that's true, if they didn't hurt you, then what's your problem?"

"Well . . ."

"Oh, God! You're actually gonna tell me. Christ, I can't believe I'm opening myself up to more whining . . . you don't have to tell me. In fact, I'm officially withdrawing the question."

What was wrong with me was the thing that was always wrong with me. I was tired and scared. I didn't like waking up in holding cells. I didn't like being sprung by sociopaths. Two-thirds of a murderous trio were in the wind. I was expecting my period any second.

Oh, and the bigger problems (yes, bigger than two-thirds of a murderous trio out in the world somewhere plotting against me)? My psychiatrist was trying to kill my sisters. My boyfriend wanted to date my sisters . . . *and* me. My best friend wanted her brother, also my boyfriend, to go away—which, since he was about to close on a house in the area, was problematic. (These weren't two different men! I was a good girl, not some skeevy, sleep-around, icky, yuck-o slut puppy.)

"A day without a lecture on morality from Cadence Jones is a day that is really, really great," George was saying. His yakking was giving me a headache. So was his tie: decapitated goats against a lime-green background. George was not a subtle man. Any stranger could tell after a glance that he was good-looking, smart, deranged, and had odd taste in men's neckwear. "Really really really really really really great."

"Stop that, please. My head is killing me."

"Well, maybe you shouldn't go around *shaving poodles*!" His voice actually cracked on "poodles." He could get pretty shriekey when he wanted. And my head, my head, it was just *pounding*; I could have used about a thousand Advil right then. A million. A billion. This must have been what Zeus felt like right before his daughter Athena popped out of his brain.

I take it back; it couldn't have hurt more than this. My head really

chapter seven

hurt!

Yesyes and the only cure
is the hurt cure the only cure
is to hurt back and George stupid George with his

stupid tie his stupid stupid and who who's holding their head now George who has a headache NOW?

Ha! His head hurts
like a bus
The wheels on the bus
The wheels

And who needs Advil, anyway? Not me and not the geese! The geese are Advil free and so am I I I
I I I the wheels on the geese
go 'round and 'round

and they didn't

you didn't

they didn't hurt me NOBODY HURTS ME I do all the hurting I I I

Ha! Screaming.

Oh, yay.

chapter eight

The only thing worse than waking up in a holding cell is waking up handcuffed to a hospital gurney. (It's dreadful that I know that. It's worse that I've known that since I was fourteen.)

My clothes were torn. My hair, when I reached up with my uncuffed hand and cautiously fluffed it, was sticky. Two of my right knuckles were starting to puff. And there was a terrible racket just on the other side of the curtain.

"Godammit! She attacked *me*, you dumb shits! I'm the one who got tossed through a fucking window like fucking Eddie Murphy in *Beverly Hills Cop*! I'm Axel Foley and you assholes are Victor Maitland and his henchmen!"

George paused, but only to take a breath. "Get these fucking cuffs off me and give me back my shoelaces and get me some coffee and get the hell out of my way and then kindly die screaming! And call my boss so she can fire my numb-fuck partner! *Is anybody listening to me?*"

It really wasn't funny. It was sort of horrible. I mean . . . poor George. Poor, poor George. First Shiro showed up to torment my cell mates, then Adrienne came out to . . . well, I don't know what she did, but not only was it spectacular, it seems as though she'd managed to get George restrained, too.

Which was not funny.

Was *not*.

I cracked up anyway. I guess I'm just weak that way.

chapter nine

Since George was still being forcibly restrained, and would be for a while judging by his enraged shrieks, I used the chance to clean myself up and then trot downstairs to donate platelets. I won't deny I was seriously hoping Dr. Welch, the gentleman who ran the Red Cross sharing space with the hospital, hadn't yet hired his replacement.

Dr. Welch understood things that many other people wouldn't. If the new guy was there and running the show, I'd have to deceive him or her all over again.

Unlike my nutty-bar sister, Adrienne, I hate hate *hated* deceiving people. It made me break out in a clammy sweat and sometimes a rash. *(Dear Gepetto: You should have made Pinocchio get a rash when he lied, because that would be much worse than a growing nose. Most sincerely, Special Agent Cadence Jones.)*

I whipped past the radiology department and the burn unit (oh my good golly goshit those poor poor people!), then cautiously eased through the double doors of the blood bank. I could only see familiar faces, to my relief.

Joey, one of the nurses, spotted me at once (like a T. rex, her vision was based on movement) and called, "Hey, there, Adrienne, where you been all my life?"

Okay, reason number one I *must* donate blood no matter what the consequences: Adrienne behaved herself here. Shiro never came, but Adrienne did, and often. And she was just as sweet as a spring lamb, devouring cookies and watching cartoons while our plasma was sucked out of our arm.

So I suffered myself to respond to her name. It was annoying, but easier.

Reason number two: my sisters and I were universal plasma donors . . . type AB positive. That meant anyone could use our stuff.

Reason number three: my conscience. Only three people out of a hundred donate, which is disgraceful when you think that a lot more than three out of a hundred get hurt and need blood. Every two seconds someone needs blood! Almost nothing else happens every two seconds, except divorces and possibly tax audits. Supply and demand . . . except in this case, it was more like demand and demand and demand.

And reason four, we/I didn't just donate for others. We/I donated for ourselves. (Ugh. I'm getting a headache.) I needed my first plasma transfusion when I was eleven, after Adrienne decided she could fly and jumped off a fire escape in my body.

And do not get me started on how often Shiro charges into a fight and sheds blood like a spring hound sheds fur. Really, who has the time—for the fighting, *or* the recitation? So we had an account at the blood bank.

So there they were, all my clever calm reasons, lined up like ducklings. It was how I justified lying to health care professionals.

But no matter! Here I was. Ready and willing, a favorite with the nurses, chock full of platelet-ey goodness, with a chart full of lies that, I hoped and hoped, were mitigated by my good deed.

It . . . it makes sense if you give it a minute. Really!

"Oh, now . . . look who it is." Wolf, another nurse at the bank, straightened up from his paperwork and smiled at me. "And here it's been so quiet around here. Y'know, Adrienne, you're in the ER so often, they oughta start charging you rent."

"Shush! Don't give Administration any new ideas. Or the billing department. You got a bed?"

"For you, we have a suite. We have five suites. Okay, a cot. A sleeping bag?" Wolf, so called because of his prodigious body hair (it sprang in curly tufts from the V on his scrubs shirt and out of his sleeves, and God only knew what was going on in the places covered by clothes), extended his arm like a maître d' showing a favorite customer the best table in the restaurant. "This way, cookie face."

I didn't want to know how I'd earned that nickname; it was the first I'd ever heard it. I knew he wasn't talking about me. *He* thought he was, and I couldn't say otherwise. Not if I ever wanted to donate for Shiro or myself or a burn patient or a

(*goose*)

kid with a ruptured appendix ever again.

"And hey," Wolf said as I sat on an empty couch and rolled up my sleeve, "you can meet the new chief."

"That's okay," I said hastily. The horror! "I'm sure he—is it a he?—I'm sure he's super busy. Catching up and all. Or she is." Wow. I was *really* bad at this. "In case it's not a he. Which I wasn't assuming anyway." To think, I was a government employee throwing "he" around! What century did I think this was? More PC classes for me, straightaway. Shame, shame.

"Catching up?" Wolf snorted, taking my vitals. "From what? Welch left the place neat as only an extreme Type-A personality *can* leave it. Staggering, y'know? No old paperwork. No filing. No out-of-date charts. I think even the carpet's immaculate in there. You knew the old bugger. Naw, the new guy, Dr. Gallo, is big-time distracted, but not for the reason you'd think."

"Reason I'd think?" I asked, intrigued in spite of myself. Wolf was right about Dr. Welch, of course, and I should have realized. Dr. Welch was old school, Dr. Welch was a type-A, and Dr. Welch would no more leave a mess than I'd run over a cat on purpose.

(*And, ugh.*)

"He transferred here for a reason. His nephew was murdered, and he's out here now helping his sister's family cope and all."

"That's awful."

"More than you know, Adrienne. His nephew was beaten to death, and nobody has a clue who did it. His whole family—they're not doing too well."

Beaten to death?

"Beaten to death?"

"Yeah. Pretty shitty, I know."

"Shitty" was one word for it. "Strange" was another, because despite the inherent violence in our society, "beaten to death" did not typically show up as a COD on a death certificate. How odd, and terrible.

Wolf did the worst part of the procedure, the pinprick of blood from the tip of my right index finger to check my hemoglobin. How lame is it that I hate that worse than anything? They can jam bigger needles into the crook of both elbows and I could hum a tune in response, but that finger stick was the worst.

"I moved here after New York, right?" He was deftly wiping my poor bloodied finger and sticking a Band-Aid over it. "Except for the seventeen-month winters, Minnesota rocks. There are alleys in New York that have a higher crime rate than the whole state put together. I guess it's naïve to be surprised when something like that does happen around here."

"I don't think it's naïve. We're really lucky with the crime rate."

"Sure, but then Gallo finds out his nephew got beaten to death in some kind of—" Wolf glanced over his shoulder, but no one was paying attention to us. "Some weird ritual thing, I guess."

"Ritual thing?" Wow, did that not sound good. At all.

"Yeah, I guess he was beat up and dressed in clothes that weren't his."

"Clothes that . . ." No. No chance.

Really. *No chance.* What were the odds, for the love of Micah?

"His nephew . . . he was a kid? A teenager?"

"Yup. Sicko bastard . . . bad enough to beat anybody to death, but a kid? You believe that crap?"

Yes. I did believe that crap. Odds or no odds, the truth was that I could have told Wolf exactly what had befallen the late nephew of his new chief. I could have told Wolf lots of things, things that would even murder the dreamless sleep of a nurse, which was a good trick given all the guts RNs waded through on a daily basis.

"Is . . . is the new guy . . . is he white?" Aaggh! Through my tidal wave of stress I realized how that must have sounded. First I assumed the replacement was male. Then I asked if he was a *Caucasian* male. Very nice. I will have to double-up on those PC workshops. "Was his nephew white?"

"Uh . . . yeah. Are you all right? You look—"

"Was he fourteen?"

"I don't know. He was just a kid, I don't know how old. A teenager, that's what I heard." Alarmed, Wolf had put his hands on my shoulders as I tried to surge up from the couch. His small black eyes were squinting in anxiety. "Adrienne, stay put. You look like you're gonna stroke out."

"Let me up." I heard a click, and saw that Joey had crossed the room and turned on Nickelodeon, in what I assumed was an attempt to calm me down. "Please let me up!"

"What's wrong?"

"I can't."

"Can't what?" Wolf asked, growing more and more perplexed.

"Can't tell. That's part of the problem, I can't tell." Confidentiality issues. A media blackout. Oaths that were not to be broken, ever.

Worst of all: it was my case. And not only had I not been able to catch him/her despite the trail of bodies, I didn't even have a suspect.

Welch was gone, the new guy came because I was failing at my job, and dead fourteen-year-old boys kept popping up every summer. I wasn't having a headache so much as a guilt-induced aneurysm. Whatever I wanted to call it, it still hurt like

chapter ten

Who lives

I want a pineapple!

Who lives in that pineapple? Under the sea, is it you you you

Dead boys? Who lives with the dead boys
Under the sea?

Spongebob Squarepants!

Who lives with the Wolfman
Under the sea?

he's not a wolf he is a man he is

A pineapple under the sea

I

don't know what to

I came out because her
head hurts it hurts I'm here but

Spongebob is, too! How can I hit
if nautical nonsense be something you wish
Then the wheels on the bus go

'round and 'round
'Round and

'round

Who lives
Who lives in the bus
Going 'round and 'round
'Round and 'round
The sponge on the bus
Goes

'round and 'round
And he's friends with Squidward!

O he's so

Oooooo Plankton I love love love
love love love love love you!

Silly he's so
Smack him with all those arms smack him with that Squidward

'round and 'round
Underneath the sea

The wolf

and the vampires

But the monsters are nice. These monsters aren't geese. They don't know about geese

The wheels on the

Lawn mower Daddy's lawn mower and the blood makes the feathers sticky

The vampires are happy to see me the vampires are always happy because
'Round and 'round

They suck my blood
Suck my blood

And cookies, too!

O Spongebob I love you
'Round and 'round

(i'm so happy)

chapter eleven

I spat oatmeal crumbs out of my mouth. Faugh! I loathed oatmeal in all its wicked guises, even when surrounded by sugar, butter, and flour. Why? Why would anyone ruin a wonderful idea like a cookie by stuffing it with oats? Not even Cadence would do something so asinine.

At first I assumed I had wakened in some sort of modern torture chamber. There were prone prisoners everywhere, tubes and machines pulling the very lifeblood from their arms (and some were pulling precious fluids out of one arm and putting them back in the other . . . fiends!), and several white-coated mysterious figures. And the vile oatmeal cookies, of course.

Then one of the prisoners got off their bed and crossed the room seeming none the worse for wear, sporting a cheery sticker on their shirt: I GAVE BLOOD TODAY!

Faugh again. Worse than a torture chamber . . . a blood bank. And I knew why I was there. Cadence would not tell a lie.

Note I said "would not" as opposed to "could not." One of her many useless affectations. Of course she *could*. But rather than face that, she disappeared. And so I was here in her stead.

"I was wondering when you'd had enough," commented a deeply amused male voice I did not know. I looked to my left and beheld an odd sight: a physician who would have looked more at home pushing meth on a street corner than hovering over a hospital bed.

His eyes. I noticed those first. But several other impressions crowded my brain: the physician had the lean, muscular build of a champion swimmer. He was wearing a pale blue, baggy T-shirt and scrub pants so faded with multiple washings that they looked velvety soft yet fragile, as if they might shred if he moved too quickly.

His hair was deep black and long—past his ears, but not to his shoulders; it was trying to curl but not quite getting there. His eyes were also black—it was difficult to tell where his irises left off and his pupils began. He blinked slowly, almost like an owl. That, coupled with the dense darkness of his eyes, gave him an almost sharklike air.

Predatory but . . . what? Something else, something I could not quite identify. Because if you set his physical features aside, you were only left with his expression, which was oddly expectant, as if he was waiting for the other shoe to drop. Or the other brick. Right on and through the top of his head. How did the song go? *Eyes glazed over in the thousand-yard stare.*

His hospital picture ID read MAX GALLO, M.D. He was scowling in the photo.

In all, a startling-looking male in his midtwenties who had (at least in my perception) abruptly appeared, like a round out of a handgun.

And . . . what had he said? "Beg pardon?"

"The cookies." His voice was deep; his tone, amused. His eyes smiled; his mouth did not. A trick I would have liked to learn, in all honesty. "I can't believe I just sat here and watched you suck down eight of them. We appreciate your donations, but maybe you shouldn't skip meals on platelet days?"

Oh dear God. My stomach goinged noisily and I could taste and feel the wretched oats coating my throat. *Adrienne, you demented wretch, I will make you pay and pay.*

With that vow still clanging like a furious bell in my mind, I leaned over the side of the bed and threw up on Dr. Gallo's sneakers.

chapter twelve

This . . . this was not my day. Not any of our days. After Shiro finished barfing (I couldn't remember the last time *that* happened, poor thing) I sat up. I opened my mouth to apologize, only to hear the doc start to laugh.

I could tell he was really trying not to; he was visibly trying to get hold of himself, so I suppose I wasn't as embarrassed as I could have been. It's tough to stay super-upset on someone's behalf if they are not super-upset themselves. So I let him chuckle while I slid off the bed and searched for something to clean up the mess. Not to whine overmuch, but it was another mess Adrienne started that Shiro made worse that I got stuck with cleaning.

"I've got it, I've got it," he said, taking the bundle of towels I'd snatched and thrust at him. "Don't worry; I used to be an ER resident. If this is the worst I get on my shoes today, it's gonna be a pretty great day."

"I don't know about that," I admitted, "but I'm sure sorry about your shoes."

"It's the perfect end to a disastrous morning." He was smiling at me, but it looked a little startling. His expression was tight-lipped but natural, like he wasn't used to showing his teeth in grins.

He was . . . kind of odd looking. I didn't mean unattractive or off-putting. He was anything but off-putting. He was very on-putting. Really very yummy and on-putting. But the lean body gave him a sharper look, almost pinched, like he'd been hungry a lot and was used to it. And his eyes! Like something you could fall into. And drown in, or be saved . . . on *his* terms.

"And if you didn't want that many oatmeal cookies," the good-looking healer was saying, "why'd you eat them all?"

"I . . ." *Think, idiot! It's a reasonable question!* ". . . lost a bet?"

"With who?"

"Uh . . . God?" Would he buy it? Would he think it was funny, or clumsy? Or that I was devout? Or deluded? It was a bibbidi-bobbidi-boo shame that the one man whose notice I'd hoped to avoid was the one Shiro barfed on. For Dr. Gallo was the new doc running the blood bank.

Then I remembered why he was here, why he'd moved here, why I'd fled and left Adrienne in the hot spot. I remembered the only reason he and I were having any conversation, ever, and *I* nearly threw up. "I can't . . . I just can't apologize enough."

"It's fine; put your anxiety in park. I wanted to meet you anyway, and this was quicker." He dabbed at the last of the vomit. I was kind of impressed he hadn't stuck a nurse with it. "If messier. Says here . . ." He glanced at what I assumed was my chart—well, Adrienne's chart. "You're one of our consistent platelet donors. The bank almost wouldn't be here if not for your efforts."

I could feel my face get warm, which was embarrassing, which made me blush more, which was embarrassing . . . oh, great, now I was trapped in some kind of remorseful circle in Hell. What he said just wasn't true, but it was super-duper-cooper sweet to say, and on next-to-no acquaintance it was surprising, too. He just didn't strike me as the type to waste time saying stuff he didn't mean. "I just . . . it's not even that big—really, it's not."

He looked up from my chart, and his dark-dark eyes took on an amused gleam. "And typical of a lot of our reliably generous donors, you're gonna downplay all over the place."

"I'm not sure how telling the truth translates to downplay, and I don't think I was doing anything all over the place, but thanks anyway." I looked at the clock and tried to looked anxious. It wasn't hard, since I *was* anxious. "Jeepers monkey tracks! I didn't know it was so late. I've got to go."

"And with that, Cinderella vanished." Was Adrienne using yet another alias?

"Pardon me?"

"Probably just as well," Dr. Gallo said, standing. He took a courteous step back, and a good thing, too, because if he hadn't I would have knocked him sprawling into one of the centrifuge machines as I struggled to my feet and galloped past him. "Since you might have the flu. Or a latent oatmeal allergy," he finished, by now actually hollering as I put space between us.

"I'm so sorry!" I managed, then gave him a lame little wave (lame! so, so lame!) and sprinted out the doors.

Nice, Cadence. Niiiiice. You blended so perfectly, Dr. Gallo will likely never give you another thought. He certainly won't be curious about all sorts of things he wasn't curious about an hour ago.

Worst of all: I hadn't actually gotten around to donating.

So I'd—we'd—have to go back.

Calgon, never mind taking me away. Calgon, please beat me to death. Thanks. You're a pal.

chapter thirteen

Here's the truth, and it's a cold truth: I work for the government, and we *are* out to get you. We put in overtime to get you. We are paid to get you. We are rewarded with health benefits to get you. We are given a 401k to get you.

Which is why George and I were at the FBI building in downtown Minneapolis instead of headed our blessedly separate ways.

I'd been able to find him quickly enough, and was too rattled to talk about who I'd met (and who Shiro barfed on with my mouth), so I just sort of scuttled back to the car. George—who'd finally been able to convince the ER attending who he was—had been right behind me.

He was so furious with me (which wasn't fair . . . I didn't do a gosh-darn fargin' thing to him) he didn't even try to torture me by deliberately parking in a handicap space. George's theory was, he was a nut job and had the diagnosis, paperwork, therapists, and neck ties to prove it. "Who needs a crip space more than me?" he'd asked reasonably (for him).

"Anyone else," had been my response. "Gross. Be ashamed." A huge mistake in retrospect. The number one rule for being

George's partner was to never let on which behavior of his bugged you. And also, never put Splenda in his coffee. He swells up like a balloon. And it isn't funny. It isn't. It's not even one little bit funny when his cheeks bulge and his lips swell and his rants are muffled ("Fffgggnnn huckin' nitch! Huckin' hill hoo nitch! Ook ah mah ace!") and he walks into doorways because his eyes are almost swelled shut, and they have to give him a shot and it takes hours and hours for the swelling to go down and the shots make him throw up.

It's terrible for him. And it isn't funny. Right? Right.

chapter fourteen

Wrong. Wrong across the board. But I would never expect Cadence to see it. She hardly sees herself, even in a mirror.

Once, when Adrienne had dosed him with *two* Splenda packets, George almost fell down a fire escape when we were six stories up. We'd been chasing an arsonist through one of the old buildings in the warehouse district. George's muffled, rage-induced hysterics could be heard two blocks away.

The arsonist, caught hauling kerosene, was so rattled by the surreal experience of a puffy, engorged George ("Are you . . . are you the Great Pumpkin?") he not only forgot to fight, but forgot to run.

Where was I during these shenanigans? In the alley, at the bottom of the fire escape. I was waiting to see if George would lose his grip, and deciding whether or not I would help him if he did.

In the end George saved himself, which was convenient for me as I had enough paperwork. Murder and paperwork: they never, ever end.

chapter fifteen

Now where was I? Right. Don't let George get to you; keep all artificial sweeteners away from him.

It was kind of nice, him not speaking to me . . . though the stomping and muttering and glaring were kind of unpleasant. It gave me some peace and quiet in which to mull over Dr. Gallo, recently come to town to help his grieving family. I made a mental note to figure out which victim had been his nephew. Having a family member close by for a formal investigation was wonderful and terrible.

The FBI's BOFFO (Bureau of False Flag Ops) division looks like any office building, complete with cubicles, printers, administrative staff, restrooms, Berber carpeting, and lowest-bid government-supplied furniture.

The only difference was, BOFFO kept a ton of mental heath professionals on staff, and also haldol, Thorazine, clozapine, and other neuroleptics. Oh, and we had to run everything we did by the federal government.

Today, a Saturday, was typical in that you couldn't *tell* it was a Saturday. We staffed all three shifts, business was (sorry to say) good, and for some of us the cubicles were the closest thing we had to a home. And our co-workers the closest thing to a family.

That's not to say I was happy to be here. Nuh-uh. I had to see my boss, Agent Michaela Taro, and it wasn't going to be pleasant. BOFFO policy: If our mentally disturbed shenanigans got us arrested, we had to be debriefed as soon as possible.

She was waiting for us by our desks, not a good sign. Michaela was not one to loiter, but she had someone with her, a woman I'd never seen before. And as we got closer, I realized it was the new girl. Uh, woman. Agent. The new BOFFO agent. She had a pleasant-looking face with a wide forehead, a surgically trimmed nose, and deep brown skin with reddish highlights. Her hair was clipped Jarhead short, but in a weird way it made her even prettier. Emphasized her bone structure or something.

"Agent Jones. Agent Pinkman."

"Boss, you would not believe—" George began, his voice climbing into a whine.

"Yes, yes, I'm sure it was horrid."

"It was!"

"And I'm certain you've never done any one thing in your life to deserve a trip to the ER via the police."

"But—" George's whine was spiraling up and up; soon only dogs would hear him.

"Quiet, Pinkman, I don't have time. Neither do you. This is Agent Emma Jan Thyme; she starts today . . . the Washington office has kindly lent her to us. You two bring her up to speed—"

"Did you really say that? 'Bring her up to speed'?" George wondered aloud. "Nobody says that in real life. Next you'll be talking about birds in bushes and feeling the burn and collaring the perp."

Michaela jabbed a finger in George's direction. It was a dangerous finger, yet beautifully manicured with lavender polish. Our boss was striking. Not she-looks-good-for-her-age striking. *Really* striking, with chin-length silver hair, green eyes, a neat, trim figure, and a squarish face. She was almost always in a tailored suit (she had family money; the government sure wasn't paying for them) and spotless white tennis shoes. Today she was wearing a green Ann Taylor suit a couple shades lighter than her eyes, and a sidearm full of tranks.

I think her brusque manner hid deep affection for us.

I think.

She was still pointing at George. "Quiet, Pinkman, or I'll accidentally arrange to have you shot. So: get Agent Thyme caught up with the murders. Then solve them. Then stop getting arrested and making me talk to the feds about *not* having you put down like rabid dogs."

"That's a big to-do list," I said, and Agent Thyme grinned.

"Uh." George cleared his throat. "Which murders?"

"Which do you think?" Michaela said irritably. "The June Boy Jobs."

"Catchy," Agent Thyme volunteered.

"Yes, it's a rule," I said. "All serial killers must be given a weird yet distinctive yet lame moniker. The Green River Killer. The I-5 Killer. The Cabbage Patch Doll Killer. The Smells Like Bacon Killer. The media loves it."

"Go fight crime, and don't do something silly like get killed in the line of duty," Michaela commanded. "I have far too much paperwork as it is. Cadence, do not for a minute think you and I are *not* going to have a chat about dog shows and holding-cell fights and shaved poodles."

"Wow," Agent Thyme said, her big dark eyes widening. "Your Saturdays sound fascinating."

"They're not," George and I said in unison, then glared at each other like a couple of kicked cats.

"I just can't do it with you *now*," Michaela finished, "being too busy begging Congress for more money, and dreaming about the day I can burn this building down."

"That's okay." It sure was. Yes, indeed! Except for the part where Michaela needed kerosene, or explosives. "Maybe you could just send me a memo."

"Maybe you shouldn't hold your breath." She stalked off. I stared at the trank gun. Sometimes I thought Michaela was more like a zookeeper than an FBI division head. She once told Shiro that was nonsense, that zookeepers were far more humane than she could ever be. Weirdly, that didn't comfort any of us.

"What's up, new girl?" George asked.

"Oh, all sorts of things." I just noticed she had a Southern accent, so it came out "all sortsa thangs."

She stuck out her hand. George and I both shook it, me first because I was just naturally better at social cues than he was.

"Wow, you sound *just* like Paula Deen," he said. "Will you make me some mashed potatoes?"

"Everyone from the South sounds like Paula Deen to everyone in Minnesota." She glanced at his ID and then got an odd look on her face . . . sort of wary puzzlement with a dash of interest and respect.

"George Pinkman? The same Pinkman who tracked down the skinhead gang who pulled a train on that little—"

"No," he said abruptly. "Different Pinkman."

It wasn't.

We just sort of stood there and looked at him while he frantically searched for his coffee so he could leave.

He abruptly gave up the search and almost shouted, "I need coffee and drugs. And drugs! *You* bring the new girl up to speed. Argh. Now *I'm* saying it. 'Up to speed.' Jesus." Then he scampered toward the break room.

I hadn't noticed, but Karen, one of the admin staff, had stopped by my desk to drop off more forensic analysis for the JBJ case. She must have overheard, because just as George fled she asked, "Does 'pulling a train' mean what I'm pretty sure it means?"

"If you mean 'gang rape,' then yeah," I said.

"That's what I thought." Karen looked at Agent Thyme. "It's the same Pinkman. He saved three of the girls and killed all the bad guys. Um. Accidentally."

"Accidentally?" Emma Jan asked, arching dark brows.

"They fell."

"On *what*?"

"Three of George's hollow points," Karen admitted. "In a way that no one could possibly see coming. Because they all died of accidental deaths. Uh, death by misadventure. Tell her, Cadence."

I shook my head. Like George Washington, I was terrible at telling lies. I usually left it to the pros. "You'll have to ask the same Pinkman, Agent Thyme."

"You suck at office gossip," Karen told me, resplendent in her gray flannel penguin jammies. With feet! She looked like a giant baby with a corona of reddish-brown curls. A giant baby who could type 120 wpm. Then she turned to Agent Thyme. "It's funny. Just when I think I can't stand him and he should be gassed, he does something that makes me almost not hate him."

"It's an exclusive club," I agreed, "and you and I are both in it." As she left, I added, "He's really okay, Agent Thyme. He had a rough morning. It's not his fault." It was mine, but there was only so much info I was willing to volunteer.

"Don't worry about it; his rep precedes him. So does yours." That was never good news. "And quit with the 'Agent Thyme' stuff already. I'm Emma Jan and I collect unusual deaths."

I blinked. "Yeah, uh, nice to meet you. I'm Cadence Jones and I'm a little freaked out by what you just said."

She laughed. She had a wonderful laugh, deep and rich, like good coffee. I think. I didn't like good coffee. Specifically, I didn't like hot coffee . . . but I would admit to a hard-core Frappuccino addiction.

Anyway. I didn't like hot coffee. It made me

(*geese daddy don't throw that don't throw that at them*)

nervous, people could

(*too hot burns it burns*)

get hurt.

"Sounds like I'm gonna fit right in around here."

Whenever anyone said that, it usually meant there was no way they were going to fit in. But I hung onto my smile. "That's great." She seemed friendly and genuine. And that accent! I could listen all day, if she said things that weren't about unusual deaths. "Welcome to BOFFO."

"Thanks. Want to hear my top three most unusual deaths?"

Gross. "No thank you."

"Aw, come on," she wheedled. "It's wild, I promise."

"I'm sure it is. Why would you collect them otherwise?" Gross. "No thank you."

"Just one unusual death?"

"Not even the beginning part of one." Yeesh. It was a stupid question, given BOFFO's employment roster, but was she nuts? Who . . . who'd want to. . . ? Gross.

"Are you suuuuure?"

"Gross. I mean, yes, I'm sure. Thanks anyway, though," I added. "It was, um, nice of you to want to share." Gross.

"Fine, fine." She sighed. "Could you show me around? And I'd love to hit a vending machine. My greatest fear is waking up with a skinny butt like yours. My butt needs constant tending with potato chips and pie. And I've got to pee. I don't think you'd like it if I went right here."

"Nobody would, I'm pretty sure." I had no comment on her butt. I had no comment on anything. She was sort of a weirdo. Not that I enjoy judging or anything. "Okay. Here comes the government-sanctioned tour. Keep your arms and legs inside the vehicle at all times. First stop, the ladies' room."

She trotted after me (she was really short) and as little as I wanted to talk to her, I was glad I had to give the tour. I was in no rush to pick up the June Boy Jobs folder.

Agent Thyme wasn't just a random transfer. She was supposed to help us catch the JBJ killer. And I prayed she'd be able to tip the balance in our favor, because so far we had diddly-iddly. Just a score of dead teenage boys. And paperwork.

chapter sixteen

I saw the JBJ's handiwork for the first time on the Fourth of July. And I think if I'd seen his handiwork on, say, Labor Day, or on an ordinary Tuesday, it wouldn't have bothered me so much. It wouldn't have been so hard to get those poor dead kids out of my head.

But July 4th? It wasn't just an excuse to get off work and blow stuff up . . . it was a family holiday. Whoever heard of a Fourth of July barbecue . . . where everyone was a stranger?

No, the Fourth was about grilling hot dogs and teasing your dad because it took him forever to get the grill lit. It was about setting a picnic table with red, white, and blue paper plates, and loading the plates with Grandma's homemade potato salad. It was lugging blankets and coolers over to the town golf course, setting up your family and friend's little stretch of blanket territory and waiting, cans of pop and beer for everyone, for it to get dark enough for the fireworks. And afterward everyone went home dirty and full and tired, but everybody slept well because they were full of hot dogs and tired, and mosquito-bit to beat the band.

(I, um, sort of researched that whole bit. But I didn't just read books; I interviewed people. All that, the stuff I just listed, that was all Fourth of July 101. But I think it's fair to point out that, not having a family to grow up with, I probably romanticized family holidays. Which makes me a romantic, but not necessarily incorrect.)

On a day I should have been wolfing down hot dogs and worrying Adrienne would pop up when the fireworks came out—not to mention making out with my new boyfriend and trying my hand at making potato salad—I was instead standing over the dead body of a fourteen-year-old boy. And my pastry-chef boyfriend had alternately sulked and worried when I wouldn't bring him.

Patrick Flannery had a view of me I loved (I think): he thought I was awesome yet vulnerable, yet awesome. We'd been going out for a few months and he took turns bragging to people about me and worrying about me.

"I'll make you coconut custard," he wheedled as I methodically dug out my ID and found my gun (Adrienne had used it last to express her displeasure over the new paint job in my living room). "With homemade whipped cream."

"Back off, Baker Boy, I've got work to do. Come on, if I was a guy friend of yours, would you really want to tag along to a murder?"

"Sure."

"Gross. I mean, 'bye."

Patrick was stupidly handsome whether he was kissing or pouting or busily whipping up crepes with flour on his hands and nose. At least he didn't know it. He was also my best friend's brother. And the only man I'd ever met who wanted to date Adrienne, Shiro, *and* me. My therapist was endlessly interested in the whole weird thing. Possibly more than I was.

Sometimes I was thrilled to have such an understanding guy in my life. Someone I could come home to now and again, someone

I could tell about my odd, odd days. I knew, even if I didn't quite understand, that mine was an unusual life. That most people do not and cannot live like this. Patrick was my shot at normality. So, yes, absolutely, sometimes I was beyond thrilled he was in my life.

And sometimes I was jealous, and didn't want to share him. Even with Shiro and Adrienne. Maybe especially with them.

As if a murder scene on the glorious Fourth wasn't bad enough . . . wow. I'm complaining a little too much. I mean, sure, my Fourth had been derailed, but then, so had the victim's. I should be counting my blessings.

Still, I couldn't shake that first impression. Murder was dreadful in all its facets; I would never argue otherwise. But there was something particularly awful about knowing that every single Fourth of July holiday, from now until they died, would be ruined for every single member of this kid's family.

Poor kid didn't look more than twelve, which I knew wasn't right. We later confirmed he was fourteen. They were all fourteen. They'd all been killed with the same signature weapon.

And we had no idea who or why or when.

And the file just kept getting thicker and thicker.

I remembered I could smell BBQs all over the neighborhood; could still smell them, even inside the house. It was a smell I would forever after associate with the JBJ killer.

It wasn't like I hadn't seen brutality before; I'd witnessed worse before I was five, for jeeper's sake. But something about the boys, their childhood only a couple of years behind them but adulthood still a couple of years ahead . . . the sunny gorgeous days when they were found . . . the ones who weren't found on or near July 4th were still found on gorgeous sunny days. Murder was dreadful in February and October and March and July, but there was always something about a gorgeous, cloudless sunny day. You *expected* bad things to happen in the middle of a blizzard. You *expected* bad things to happen when it was cloudy and had been raining for three days.

Their extreme youth was no fun, either . . . it made me feel worse to see them like that. It made the loss of their potential all the more sad and senseless and In Your Face. Give me a wife-beating mouth breather whose body was found in the middle of a hailstorm at midnight.

Anyway, it would have been a memorable unpleasant day anyway, *and* I had to meet up with the FBI guys who'd been told (told, mind you, not asked) they would now have to play nice with BOFFO. Past experience had taught me this would be trouble. Divisions tended to be territorial.

Which is why Special Agent Greer greeted me with, "Are you kidding me with this shit, or what?"

"It's nice to meet you, too." I was busily pulling on booties and gloves. "I'm Cadence Jones."

"And I'm pretty damned annoyed they're calling you weirdos in."

I just looked at him. I hated confrontations. Why couldn't everybody just be nice all the time? I sort of hoped Shiro would come out and smack him around. Okay, not really. Wait. Yes, really.

"Why are you staring at me?"

"Uh . . . sorry." Stupid Shiro, who wouldn't show up on command. "Listen, you get that it's not my fault, right?" I heard my tone: anxious. Trying to soothe. Pathetic. *Shiro! Come out already! This guy can probably smell my wanting-to-please, like a dog smells fear, or Snausages.* "I mean, it wasn't my decision or anything? You get that?"

"BOFFO? Friggin' false flag ops? They're handing this unbelievably tragic mess over to the nuthouse inmates?"

Was he asking me or telling me? "Um. Yes?" That seemed safe enough.

Shiro? Hellooooo? Anybody home?

Darnitall! Therapy was starting to work a little too well. We had been focused, of course, on fewer blackouts, and fewer kidnappings of my body by my sisters. But according to my doctors and, more important, Michaela (who had no investment in stroking me), I *made* Shiro and Adrienne to help me in stressful situations. I made them when I was little, when I watched my father run over a Canada goose with a riding lawn mower and then get murdered by my mother. So where the gosh-heck-fiddly-darn were they?

"This really hurts." Greer was still bitching. I reminded myself that I could be in a worse situation: I could be standing over that poor boy's body. I could *be* that boy. *Count your blessings, count your blessings.* So I just stood there. "First off, you guys are more like some sick urban legend than an actual department, okay? Most of the Bureau thinks you don't exist. You're the Area 51 of the FBI."

Good.

"But to find out you do exist . . . and to find out you're all . . ."

"Heavily medicated?" I suggested. "Emotionally disturbed?"

"No. *I'm* heavily medicated and emotionally disturbed; I'm in the middle of my third divorce. You guys are all certified crazies."

"That's true," I admitted. "We are." And we had the charts to back it up.

But Greer wasn't interested in a conversation; he wanted a rant. So he groaned and moaned and made yanking motions in his hair—which would explain his monk's fringe—and shook his head and rolled his eyes. I expected him to burst into flames at any moment, and/or collapse into a seizure.

And his suit was dreadful. Shiny at the elbows. Frayed at the cuffs. His paunch was emphasized by the coffee stain between his third and fourth buttons. I might be crazy, but I'd been able to drink without spilling since I was four.

"It's unbelievable! Crazy people wearing sidearms?" He scraped at his shirt with a fingernail. "It's like a bad joke."

"Or a genius idea," I suggested. "Set a thief to catch a thief, and all that."

"No, it's a joke. Did Congress approve this? Where's your budget coming from? Are you telling me somebody looked at the proposal for BOFFO and said, 'Yup, sounds like a plan, here's a check and don't worry, we'll keep 'em coming year after year, let's be careful out there'? I don't believe it!"

I blinked. He didn't? That was strange. How was this a puzzle? "It's the government."

A short pause. "Okay, well. That actually makes sense." A fellow government employee, and thus tortured by the same payroll/health benefits/administration personnel, he had to admit the truth, even if he didn't like it. "But, come on. You've got kleptomaniacs pilfering at crime scenes—"

"He eventually bags anything he can't help grabbing."

"—agents who are convinced their reflections are out to get them—"

"How do you know they aren't?"

"—agoraphobes who *live* in their offices—"

"Yeah, but think of all the money's she's saving on commuting costs. And rent."

"—claustrophobes in tents on the roof of your office building—"

"It's cheap 24/7 security."

"—a phallically obsessed department head—"

I didn't really have an argument for that one.

"—and agents who . . . well . . ." He gestured vaguely at me.

"Who have Multiple Personality Disorder, now more commonly known as Dissociative Personality Disorder," I supplied helpfully. "Sybil Syndrome. Please don't ever call it that."

"Yeah, that. And don't even get me started on Pinkman."

"Nobody wants you to get started on anyone." *Especially* Pinkman. I paused. "Since you know about us anyway, I figure there's no harm in explaining."

"Oh, goody."

"What civilians and the occasional fed don't understand is, I'm effective *because of* my psychological quirks. Though 'quirks' may not be the strongest word, to be fair.

"A sociopath thinks nothing of bending a few rules to get his man. And a kleptomaniac knows how to take things away from a bad guy right under his nose. A histrionic can turn in an Oscar-worthy performance in any undercover situation. Like that."

"Mmmm, sure. *Just* like that. Uh-huh."

"So, are we at all helpful?"

"You're being rhetorical, I guess."

I answered myself. "Sure we are. Are we a pain in the tuchus? Yes. Worth the hassle to get the job done? Well. We have an eight-figure budget that sails through congressional budget justification every single year. What does that tell you?"

"That I should have voted for the other guy."

I giggled. "Do you have anything else to get off your chest?"

He gave me an odd look. "What are you, my therapist?"

"No. Just someone who wants to catch this guy. Like you."

"Catch him." He nodded slowly. "Yeah, well, I don't want to catch him. I want to hang him by his testicles until they fall off."

"It's good you've got goals." In this instance, he had my sister's goals.

He smiled, and it completely changed his face. He instantly looked younger and much less testy. He almost looked friendly and everything. It was like a magic trick! A really good one with lots of mirrors and a pretty girl in an indecently short sequined costume. I wondered why he didn't smile more.

"Do you feel better now?"

He thought about it. "Yeah. I kinda do. Sorry. Thanks. Uh, I know you're just following orders."

"That's true," I teased. "I am."

"I hate today. I'm supposed to be at my daughter's baseball game right now."

I nodded. "Fourth of July stuff."

"Yeah! I'm the Number One Guy on the Grill." That's just how he said it, too. You could hear all the capital letters. "I got all this hamburger meat at a huge discount—my cousin works for Lorentz Meats."

"Oh, yum," I replied, impressed.

He nodded. "I know! And about fifty kinds of brats, and now my wife's gonna cook and she'd burn water. You should have heard all the bitching when my pager went off. And not just from me. My wife was pretty mad, too. Instead I gotta—"

"I'm sorry you had to leave your family on a family holiday."

"You, too."

I didn't volunteer anything, and when I didn't say anything he sighed, then opened the front door for me. "Come on. Kid's in the basement."

Thus making the basement the place I didn't want to go. But I had work to do. We all did, thanks to JBJ.

chapter seventeen

Too soon, I was looking at another dead body. Caucasian teenage male. COD: severe head trauma. Dressed in a striped shirt and jeans, clothing that wasn't his.

For whatever reason, the killer snatched them in June, beat them to death, then dressed them in clothes he or she or they brought with them. Clothes we hadn't been able to trace, other than the fact that you could buy them at any Target or Walmart. Cheap, and cheaply made. Forgettable.

Like any puzzle, the entire thing seemed mysterious and unsolvable. And like any puzzle, once we solved it things we didn't catch would seem obvious and even, sometimes, logical.

This boy was the seventh. Which, if anyone asked me (but no one did), was seven too many. The FBI was called in when an ambitious data tech put together the pattern. And so here we were.

chapter eighteen

Did she just call me an ambitious data tech? For heaven's sake. I, Shiro Jones, was a field agent, as Cadence was. There was no need to throw around inaccurate job titles simply because I enjoyed crunching data in what little spare time I had.

No one was more surprised than I to see a pattern where before, we had only seen what Michaela liked to call "the random."

Once, when we were much younger, not even seven, Cadence and I took turns working on a 500-piece jigsaw puzzle. It was all black except for a tangerine in the center. It took us over a year.

When I was running the body I would work on it, and when Cadence was in the driver's seat she did. I will not go into what Adrienne would do to it, but needless to say we had to start over many times. Neither of us would quit. Neither of us would let Adrienne's temper tantrums stop us from finishing.

Even now, I have no idea what triggered that stubbornness. It was one of the rare times Cadence and I were in complete accord. One of the rare times we did not feel like we were fighting each other for the same body.

It pains me to admit this, but if Adrienne had not kept forcing me to examine and re-examine the puzzle, if I had not had to start and stop and start again over and over, I am not sure I would have seen the JBJ pattern.

And then, one day, just as I deduced where everything fit around the tangerine years ago, I saw a pattern in what I had assumed was the random.

I disliked assumptions, but occasionally indulged. And the reason I had assumed it was part of the random is because, though it is an ugly truth, teenagers are murdered every month in this country. In every country, actually, with the exception of Antarctica. This is what a toxic species we are . . . wherever we settle, we hurt and kill each other.

Sometimes there is no way to make sense of all the numbers. And sometimes, after you look at it long enough, after you start and stop and start again, there is a way.

I took the data straight to Michaela, as was department policy. Different states (thus, we had federal jurisdiction), different days in June, *every* June for every victim.

What the data did not show was what we badly needed to find out: how JBJ was choosing them. What seemed like chance to us was, of course, anything but chance to him/her/them.

Other than the fact that they were dead by the same person/persons, the boys had nothing in common. Different backgrounds, religion, upbringing. Different hair color, build, eye color. Some were one of many siblings, some were only children. Some were raised by loving parents, but two had been in the foster care system. Some came from poverty, some had eight-figure trust funds.

And now I knew something I had not known two hours ago: Dr. Gallo's nephew had been the seventh, and last, victim. It made the timeline just about perfect—enough time had passed to give notice to an employer, pack away belongings, apartment-hunt, and move across the country.

But knowing that did not bring us any closer to a true suspect. The whole thing was baffling. And maddening. To think a random wretch was out there killing children like a farmer picking chickens out of his personal coop. Oh, I had *so* many questions for JBJ. And I expected to get the opportunity to ask them.

I *would* solve it.

chapter nineteen

"Hey! Space case! Time to go to work."

I blinked. I had been thinking—no, *Shiro* had been thinking about the yummy Dr. Gallo. It spoke well of his devotion to family to have picked up his life and moved everything to come at his sister's call. "George, I'm right here. No need to scream."

"You've been staring at that file for the last ten minutes. With that really dumb look on your face that you know I hate."

"Which one?" George would just have to be more specific. He didn't like all sorts of things about me. Which was okay, because the feeling was more than mutual. "The dumb look when I'm hungry, or the dumb look when I'm concentrating, or the dumb look when I'm trying to think how to tell you that you complain about my dumb looks too much, or—?"

"Aw, shit, never mind. Are we going? Let's go. Yeah? Cadence?" George shook his keys at me. "Want to go for a ride, girl? Huh? Wanna go in the car? Huh?"

"Wow," Emma Jan said, staring at George. Or at his tie, which was chicken feet with a purple background. "You're really unpleasant."

"Thanks," he said, pleased. "You're probably a bitch or something, too. I don't know you that well, but I'm sure you've got qualities I'll hate. Really! You just have to give it time. Or me time."

"Thank . . . you?"

"Don't try to make sense of it," I advised her. "You never will and sometimes it'll even give you a headache."

"No, it just gives *you* a headache, Cadence," he snapped, and I could see he was still mega-ticked about yesterday's ER/handcuff/gurney adventures. Normally he didn't hold grudges so long. It was one of the few reasons our partnership worked. "Then goddamned Adrienne pops out and smacks the shit out of me, and then *I* get a headache."

"Riiiight." Emma Jan nodded. "I *heard* about you." She looked at me with bright dark eyes, like a sparrow. A sparrow with a .45 single-action riding on her left hip. "Uh, is there anything I should try to avoid doing or saying so I don't have to deal with the crazy one?"

I just looked at her. *This* weirdo wanted to know how to avoid *my* craziness?

Meanwhile, George was happily in mid-rant. "Are you fucking kidding? Like there's a list? You think if we knew *that* we'd provoke her, *ever*?"

"You used to like Adrienne," I pointed out mildly. In fact, I always thought it was odd (and proof of *his* craziness) that he loved playing *Halo* with her. And she occasionally cooked him omelets. Some were even glass-free.

"I still do, when she's not using my head for a soccer ball. I had to get a crown fixed last time!" He hooked his finger and stuck it in his mouth, pulling his right cheek back. "Ee? At un air."

"Please stop showing me your teeth." Gross. And his health benefits were excellent; I don't know what he was complaining (so much) about. About the only government agency that had better bennies was the NYPD. "And we can go in just another minute. I'm expecting—"

"Hey, gorgeous!"

The three of us looked; I could already feel the smile blooming on my face, chasing away my yucky mood. Patrick Flannery had come to pay me a visit. And . . . yes! He was carrying a cake box!

He practically galloped up to me; I was always surprised at how quickly he could move for such a big man . . . six foot three, two-twenty, and none of it was fat. Amazing, given what he ate. The man practically drank cake batter.

"Great." George threw his hands in the air. "It's goddamned Little Debbie."

"Shush," I said, and then the breath whooshed out of my lungs as Patrick hugged me so hard he pulled me off my feet. Gaaaah! "Agh, stop, you're gonna crack my short ribs."

"Oh, please." He set me down, smiling. Like a love-struck idiot, I grinned back. The force of his extreme good looks was more intense than the hug. He had dark red hair, like cherry Coke with real cherry juice, and chocolate truffle–colored eyes. (That was a lot of food imagery . . . I shouldn't have skipped breakfast.)

Despite the December weather, he was dressed in khaki knee-length shorts (his favorite brand—he had at least six pairs) and a denim shirt with the sleeves rolled back, showing the dark reddish hair shading his heavily muscled forearms. (You wouldn't believe what an intense upper-body workout baking for a living was.) He wore shorts all year around. I thought it was impractical (Minnesota winters!) but who was I to judge someone else's strange habits?

I knew he'd looked at me carefully as he approached: he needed to figure out which one of us was driving the body. He'd gotten really good at reading our expressions and body language. He was better at it after three months than some co-workers I'd known for years.

He didn't run up and hug me without a careful look anymore.

"Hey, Cadence. We on for tonight?" he asked, handing me the box. I didn't have to look to know he'd made me a coconut cream pie. I had become very popular at work once I started bringing his home-baked treats to the office.

Coconut cream was a safe enough choice: it was my favorite, Shiro didn't hate it (her fave was baby turtle bread from Kyoto), and Adrienne wouldn't eat it as her favorite dessert was sirloin steak, but she *did* like to channel her inner Three Stooges and *throw* coconut pie. So it was all good. I guess.

I was so busy remembering how hard it had been to get coconut pie out of my washing machine that I realized I hadn't answered him. "Should be," I sort-of promised. "I'm sorry we haven't had a lot of time together lately." I was, too. Except when I wasn't.

He reached out, put his finger under my chin, and gently tipped my head up. "You're worth waiting for. All of you."

I started to melt. I could actually feel the muscles in my legs go all rubbery. I guess clichés became clichés for a reason, because melting was the perfect word to describe me. I was becoming a *beurre blanc*! No, wait, that had vinegar in it . . . *beurre noisette*? Drat it to dratdom; Shiro was the one who was fluent in French. I'd taken Spanish.

Regardless, soon I'd just be a puddle in an empty shirt, jacket, and slacks. They'd only be able to identify the puddle that was me by my federal ID. (Ooooh, I love accidental rhyming!) Meanwhile, best of all, he was still there. He was still touching me. Even better, *I* was still there. "Patrick, you're the best."

He leaned closer. "That's true. God, you look gorgeous today. Every day."

"You always say that."

"It's always true." His mouth was very close now, and I was glad. The whole world had sort of tipped away from us. It was scary and exhilarating at once.

"Gimmee!" George "I will always kill the mood" Pinkman said, then snatched the box out of my hands. "Awww, Little Debbie, you shouldn't have."

"Tell me," he replied grimly, giving my partner a level stare. "Despisement" would not be too strong a word to describe how he felt about George. Nor would "loathe," "detest," and (not "or") "abhor." George could usually charm females (and female sociopaths could almost always charm males), but could almost never fool a man. He sure hadn't fooled Patrick, who followed up his glare with: "Shouldn't you be stomping puppies or whatever it is you do when you're not torturing my girlfriend?"

George laughed. "Oh, Little Debbie, you're so cute! You have *no* idea what torture is."

"Hi," Emma Jan said, sticking out her hand. I was startled; I'd forgotten she was there, but now was glad. The atmosphere had gone from loving to murderous in about half a second. "I'm Emma Jan and I collect unusual deaths."

There was a short silence while Patrick digested that, followed by, "Nice to meet you?" he guessed.

"New girl," George said by needless explanation.

"Patrick Flannery." He shook her hand. Since he knew about BOFFO, I could tell he was trying to guess what her superpower was. (That was how Michaela occasionally referred to our, um, special psychotically-based talents.) He wasn't rude enough to ask, at least not where she would hear him. "You sound just like Paula Deen."

"So I hear."

"I hope you like it here. But I'll get out of your way. I'm sure you've got evil to crush and stuff." He turned to me. "Tonight?"

"Yep."

He bent and brushed a kiss on my cheek. In that moment, all thoughts of the good Dr. Gallo fled my overtaxed brain.

(*I wonder how Dr. Gallo kisses?*)

Now where in heckfire did *that* come from? I must be sleep-deprived. It was the only explanation.

Patrick smoothed my bangs away from my eyes, then tenderly whispered, "Don't let your asshole partner have even one crumb."

"Aw. That was so sweet."

"'Bye!" George was clutching the cake box like a mama cat hung on to one of her kittens. You could practically hear him hissing *my own, myyyyyy precious.* "No, really. *'Bye*! Hope you don't fall down the stairs and land on your face, or accidentally get your shirt caught in a tractor engine and spend the next year growing back all the skin on your chest."

Patrick headed toward the elevators, muttering. I caught "asshole" and "shithead" and something that sounded like "mucker." Oh. Wait. It wasn't "mucker."

"How long have you two been partners?" Emma Jan asked. I understood her surprise. There was a bet going around the office about when one of us would snap and beat the other to death. If I killed George in September of next year, I'd win almost eight hundred bucks. And if he had killed me last month . . . well, let's just say he wouldn't have had to borrow lunch money twice last week.

"An eternity," he sighed, opening the box. "Ohhhh, baby! Where you been all my life?" He heaved the pie plate out of the box. The coconut custard was piled high with fluffy meringue, and had been sprinkled with toasted coconut. The shortbread crust looked like tender, buttery perfection. "Now I remember why you keep Little Debbie around in the first place—besides, I can assume, his big dick."

"He bakes?" Emma Jan guessed while I felt my face go red to my eyebrows.

"You must be a trained investigator for the federal government," I teased. Patrick was actually the head of a baking empire, his pies and cakes sold in supermarkets across the country. George's nasty "Little Debbie" nickname was vintage Pinkman: it was meanly funny, with more than a smidgen of accuracy.

"Cancel my lunch plans, I'm eating your pie. Oh, awesome. I can't believe I got to say that to your face after all this time."

"I've got three words for you, George," I said sweetly.

"Merry Christmas, baby?" he guessed, sticking a finger into the delicate meringue and scooping some up for a taste. "I want you? What a stud? Please bang me? Little Debbie blows?"

"Splenda Sugar Blend."

"What? Fuck!" He shook his finger like it had burst into flames and he was trying to wave it out. "Get it off, get it *off,* get it off off *off*!" Then he thrust the pie at me and sprinted toward the men's room.

After a long, thoughtful moment, Emma Jan said, "It's really weird around here. Are there forks?"

chapter twenty

After George had finished sterilizing his hand (I'd never seen someone go through two bottles of Purell in less than three minutes) and screaming curses at me, Emma Jan, the absent Patrick, the pie, Johnson & Johnson (the company that made Splenda), the absent Patrick, Shiro, Adrienne, the absent Patrick, coconut, meringue, and Splenda, we were able to hit the road.

While we headed to the suspect *du jour*'s house, I took another look at his file.

Joseph Behrman was a long shot, but he had known the latest JBJ victim, had a criminal record including assaults on teenage boys, and was vague about his whereabouts the night of the murder.

George drove. Emma Jan huddled in the backseat, averting her eyes from the rearview mirror. I pretended she wasn't doing that, kept my mouth shut, and re-read his file.

Sentence: Ten years, criminal assault
Inmate name: Joseph Aaron Behrman
Sex: Male

DOB: 12/20/1975
Ethnicity: White
Identifying marks: Swastika, left bicep. 88, right bicep. 88, left shoulder blade.
Custody status: Parolee
Releasing facility: Stillwater Penitentiary
Date received: August 17, 2001
Date paroled: January 5, 2008
Crime, Description: Criminal assault. Tampering with a witness. Burglary in the first degree.
Minimum sentence: 6 years
Maximum sentence: 6 years

He looked good on paper (actually like a routine scumsucker), but I had my doubts. He was a little old to have nothing but agg assault and the like on the books, and I didn't think he'd began secretly killing teenagers practically the day he was paroled.

He also wasn't exceptionally bright; testing had revealed an IQ of 109. Not that serial killers had to have good IQs like, say, Bundy. But it sure helped.

Behrman was also a misandrist, and he *had* hurt boys in his past. So we'd go talk to him, more to eliminate him than anything else. It was also a good way to see Emma Jan in action when (probably) our lives weren't at stake.

I was glad for the chance; she made me nervous. And I was worried about the rearview mirror. George wasn't. He was always up for excitement.

"Aw," George said as we swung into the small trailer park. We had just pulled off Highway 149 outside West St. Paul, after passing a few strip malls. George had cruelly refused to stop for a Frappuccino, so we were actually a couple of minutes early.

There was not a heron in sight in the Heron Estates. Only a small, slumped group of mobile homes, no more than two dozen, in various shades of blue and white, green and white, and yellow and white.

Typical of every trailer park I had ever seen, some of the residents appeared to be indifferent slobs who forgot they parked their cars on the lawn. These same people painted their homes about every forty years, and mowed their sad, straggly grass every ten. The gravel roads and general lack of vegetation always made it look like it'd be ninety degrees outside, even in December. You could pretty much smell the despair, and hear the soundtrack from the movie *Bastard Out of Carolina.*

The other group took meticulous, almost fanatical care of their property. They painted every other year; they grew tons of flowers. They mowed obsessively. Their homes looked like mini-estates, and all the stranger because usually the one across the gravel drive looked condemned.

Behrman lived in one of the former, a faded yellow mobile home with tired white trimming. The dirty snow surrounding the walk was stained with the comings and goings of a small, depressed dog. We could see where the chain had been anchored through the snow and into the ground.

The chain led to a miniature black Lab, or an enormous dachshund. She twitched her eyebrows at us, rose from the nest she'd hollowed out in the snow, and approached, wagging her tail. She was thin, and cautiously friendly. There was a small round blob of white fur on top of her skull; the rest of her was black.

"Huh," George said aloud. "A neglected dog on a chain outside a shithole. What are the odds?"

Emma Jan didn't say anything. She just reached into her bowling ball–sized purse and pulled out a muffin. The muffin wasn't wrapped, and it hadn't broken in her purse. This was miraculous, given that she had a brush, a wallet, Chapstick (blech! couldn't stand the taste . . . like eating a candle), a spare clip, Kleenex, sunglasses, and airplane peanuts. And that was what I just *glimpsed* when she'd opened it earlier.

She broke the muffin (blueberry) into pieces and offered them to the dog. It must have been hungry, but at first was too scared to come closer. But then it did, gently taking the muffin chunks while also flinching away like it was all a big, mean trick. Like the pain was coming . . . the dog just didn't know when.

I could relate. I bet Emma Jan could, too.

Her lips were pressed together so tightly they almost disappeared, and she finally said something I didn't think was bizarre: "Some people don't deserve a dog."

"You probably should have asked the owner," I said, hating my inner (and outer) Goody Two-shoes, but compelled to blather about rules anyway. "It's, uh, not cool to just walk up and do that."

"Unusual death number forty-seven: Prince Popiel, Polans tribe. Ninth century. Eaten alive by mice. That'd be okay for the guy in there," she told the dog, letting it lick the crumbs off her glove. "That'd be okay for the guy who thinks it's fine to treat you like this."

Her Southern accent got thicker when she was angry, I was alarmed to notice. Oh, dear. We did *not* need another rabid PETA member . . . the last one had been reassigned after a month in the field. He'd started shooting at cars that ran over squirrels.

It's not that I didn't feel bad for the dog. It's that there were rules.

"Let's get this show on the road," George said with jarring cheer, trotting up the short sidewalk without even glancing at the dog. "Ladies first. Then Emma Jam."

"Emma *Jan*."

"Like it matters. Then you, Cadence. Come on, *ándale* already."

He banged on the front door. "FBI! Secret Santa! FTD delivery! Avon calling Joseph Behrman, *come on down*!"

"Don't have ta yell," Mr. Behrman said, pulling open the front door. He looked like his intake photo: heavy, short, with shoulder-length dark blond hair. He was in a T-shirt and jeans; bare feet. He smelled like Marlboros and gravy. "Don't worry about the dawg." Really! He said it just like that: dawg. You could hear the W. "She won't hurtcha."

"Don't worry, we're federally sworn upholders of the law and are prepared to shoot her at any moment," George promised. "Your PO let you know we were coming?"

Behrman sighed. Marlboros, gravy, and grape bubblegum; I stood corrected. "Yep. Talkin' to the wrong guy but come in anyway."

He stepped aside for George. George stepped aside for Emma Jan, who had given the dog a final pat and then joined us on the sagging porch. And that's when the poop slammed into the rotary blades.

chapter twenty-one

When I thought about it later, I realized I should have been tipped off at once. When I thought of George, "helpful" wasn't the first word that came to mind. How many times in my life would I have to relearn the same damn lesson? Puppies caught on quicker than I—

chapter twenty-two

I had no time to listen to more of Cadence's woe-is-me catechism; New Girl was, as George would put it, "losing her shit." I found that phrase revolting to contemplate yet had to acknowledge how apt it was.

The entire west wall of Behrman's living room was a mirror. Tacky and smeared, and I had no idea when it had last been cleaned, but a mirror. And it was the first thing Agent Thyme saw when she walked past him into the room. Which would have been no problem at all, except Agent Thyme suffered from Mirrored-self Misidentification.

"Watch out!" Agent Thyme's terrified shriek seemed as though it would shatter the mirror—which, depending on how large the shards, would have solved the problem, or exacerbated it. Her normally pleasing alto was climbing into a deafening upper register. "She's going to try to kill you!"

Then she launched herself at the west wall.

I managed to get between her and the mirror, but she had gotten up such momentum my back slammed against the mirror. "Stop it," I managed, trying not to wheeze. When Cadence got the body back, she would wonder why her kidneys were throbbing. And possibly why she was urinating blood. I would have to leave her a note . . .

Agent Thyme was a blur of clawing fingers and kicking feet. In the extremity of her terror, she'd forgotten even the simplest takedown moves. Not that they would have worked on a mirror. I think.

I was good, but I had my hands full. I was constrained as I could not kill or seriously injure her. She was constrained by nothing, since in her mind she was saving us from the evil double who lived in the mirror. Thus, every few seconds a fist would get past me and clip me on the ear, or my shins would take another knock. Was the woman wearing steel-tipped yet sensible flats?

Behrman was staring at us, openmouthed. My partner turned to him and said, "This is a thousand times more awesome than I ever could have hoped."

"Agent Thyme, stop it—ouch—right now. Ouch! You are on the—argh!—list of people—ow—I do not want to hurt. Ow, you pointy-toed shrew! You are *not* on the—stop it!—list of people I *will* not hurt."

"You have to let me kill her," she panted. She seemed to suddenly remember she was armed, because her hand was a blur as it slapped her hip. Except it slapped my hand, which I'd just managed to slap over her gun. "She'll kill us all if you don't let me kill her."

"Enough." I let go of her with the hand not restraining the gun, took the punch to the face (oh, to be an octopus right now), and gripped her jugular until her eyes rolled up and she plopped to the floor.

I stepped away from her, breathing hard. She did not look it at all, but was stronger and faster than I had anticipated. She had put up an excellent fight.

The clapping caught my attention. George and Behrman were applauding and (this was the sick/annoying thing) doing so with genuine approval.

"Wonderful, Shiro," George said. "Really. Just great."

"That was awesome," Behrman added. "What just happened?"

George grinned. "My girl-on-girl desires were almost satisfied and everything. Whew—is anyone besides me feeling flushed? I can't thank you enough."

I rubbed my lower back. "Prepare for a Splenda enema, pig."

chapter twenty-three

Much later, after the fight and interrogating Behrman to be sure he was not the one we sought (though it would have been a pleasure to arrest him for any crime), I cornered George in the men's room back at the office.

"Finally, you appreciate the awesomeness of my dick," he said, urinating proudly. "So, did you just want to do it right here, or should we get a motel room? Or should we stay here? It's pretty gross in here, I dunno . . ."

"Stop it."

"In my mind," he said, twirling a finger near his left ear, "we do it in the mail room right next to the big copy machine, the one that starts to shake after it's been running for an hour . . ."

"Do not point that thing at me," I ordered. "And if you do not stop, they will write *books* about what I do to your body before I let you die."

George shrugged. "You followed me into a *bathroom,* Shiro. What did you think I was going to do?"

He had stymied me, the rat bastard, but I would never let him know it. "Behave, for ten seconds. Now. Since Agent Thyme is, ah, being debriefed by our lovely-and-efficient supervisor, I have an opportunity to ask you to explain."

"Explain. . . ?" Zip. Flush. Stretch. Yawn. "What'm I supposed to explain?"

"Do *not* pretend to be an idiot."

"Who's pretending?" he asked with honest bewilderment.

"Are you claiming zero knowledge of Behrman's living arrangements? Knowing BOFFO's, uh, occasional idiosyncrasies . . ."

"Occasional idiosyncrasies!" he said, delighted. "That's excellent, Shiro. I'm putting that one on my Facebook page."

"You will not. Are you telling me there was not anything to indicate the presence of a gigantic mirror when we least needed it?"

"Sure there was." George shrugged. "Got a description of his whole living situation from his parole officer." I nodded; that was standard. Parolees had to prove they had a home and a job, and were not murdering anyone in their spare time, or committing mail fraud. "Wanted to see what would happen."

"What?" Why did I not foresee this?

"She's the New Girl, I've never worked with her, she might have to save my gorgeous ass someday, I've never seen mirrored-self misidentification before, I wanted to see her in the field—are you getting all this? I wanted to see what would happen. Did you get how she pretty much cowered in the car on the way over? Wouldn't look in the rearview? Didn't you wonder what would have happened if she had?"

"No," I said, "because I read her file. It would have been something to be devoutly avoided. Not wondered about."

"Not for me. I wanted to see what would happen." He shrugged again. "So I did. Worked great. Besides, I knew you'd save the day."

"Would you like to see what will happen *now*?"

"Not really."

Though I was tempted to shove his sinuses into his brain, I restrained myself. Why hadn't *I* checked out the same paperwork he did? Too busy looking at the big picture for JBJ instead of the individual pieces of paper. In hindsight, it was all quite clear. The trouble was, it should have been clear before it even happened. I was smarter than this. Cadence was even smarter than this. My shame was deep.

chapter twenty-four

After he washed, I followed him back to our desks. Thyme was still in Michaela's office, and though I did not envy her (having sat in that chair myself many times) I made a mental note to put in a positive word.

Thyme had a silly problem but I admired her in spite of it. She had truly thought an evil doppelgänger was hiding in the mirror to kill her and anyone with her. So she had acted at once . . . to help us. Many wouldn't. My sister wouldn't. (My *other* sister would have tried to liberate the Mirror People.)

Now here she came, head down, watching the carpet all the way up to our desk. "I'm so sorry," she told the carpet.

"Why, what'd you do to it?" George anxiously scanned the carpet. "Is there Splenda on it? If you put fuckin' Splenda on this shitty government carpet, I will *not* be responsible for wherever I end up dumping your body."

"Take a tranquilizer, George. Agent Thyme is apologizing to us."

"More to *you*." Thyme looked up. Her dark eyes were red-rimmed, her cheeks puffy. She'd been terrified, then humiliated. I had no idea if telling her we saw that sort of thing all the time with newbies would comfort her, or upset her further. There was always an adjustment period—except when there was not, and the newbie ended up being institutionalized or, worse, fired. George had not been my first BOFFO partner. "I can't apologize enough."

"That's true," George said. "You can't. I'm still traumatized by the whole thing." He let out a fake sob. "Oh, Agent Thyme. Hold me."

"Are you *trying* to goad me into beating you to death? Shush your flapping tongue." I turned to Thyme. "No harm done. We have seen worse." Much, much worse. Of course, we had also seen better. Much, much better.

She sniffed and smiled. "Ohhhh boy, I like you, Shiro. It's . . . it's still Shiro, right?"

"Of course it is. Can't you tell by her grim, humorless manner and the way she pretends she's not dead inside?"

"I dislike you," I told him, "so much."

Thyme sniffed again, then scrubbed her face with the backs of her hands. The act was reminiscent of what a child would do, and it did something odd to the middle of my chest. Uncharacteristically, I wanted to hug her and explain that it would be all right. Which was illogical, and possibly untrue.

"D'you want to hear my top three unusual deaths?"

"Of course I do."

"Aw, come on, I've had a hard day—wait. What?"

"I want to hear about them. And I will bet I can guess at least one of them." I was thinking in particular of Martin I of Aragon, who literally laughed himself to death; Eleazar Maccabeus, who jabbed a spear into an elephant's belly and was crushed to death when it died on top of him; David Douglas, who fell into a pit (along with a bull!), then was crushed and gored to death; and Sigurd the Mighty, who beheaded an enemy, strapped the severed head to his saddle, then later died of an infection caught when the dead man's teeth scraped his leg. (My favorite. Ah, irony, you are a cruel mistress.)

"You really want to hear?" She seemed delighted and suspicious at once.

"I really want to hear."

Thyme abruptly sat down, as if she were afraid she'd lose her feet if she had not. This was alarming and interesting. "What?"

"I'm sorry. It's been a long day with a lot of surprises and I just . . . no one ever wants to hear about them."

"Cops and FBI agents do not want to hear about unusual deaths?" Odd. Why *wouldn't* they?

"They always say they can top me and when they can't, they get mad." She sighed. "So nobody asks anymore."

"That's terrible." I was moved to rare sympathy. "Some people are just rude."

"Okay, well, since we're talking I'd have to say my favorite is prob'ly Dan Andersson—the Swedish writer? He died of cyanide poisoning. The hotel staff forgot to air out his room after spraying hydrogen cyanide for bugs."

"Yes, that follows." No mint on the pillow for him. "Though if you want to talk about writers and their odd demises, don't omit Tennessee Williams."

"Are you going to listen, or just try to one-up me?" she asked irritably. I noticed her accent thickened in proportion to her mood. "That man was a disaster area . . . choking on an eyedrop bottle cap was just the coup de grace."

"Not a big *Streetcar* fan, hmmm?"

"He'd unscrew the top of the bottle, stick it in his mouth, then put his eyedrops in. They think his gag reflex was reduced because of all the booze and pills, so he choked to death on the stupid thing. My gosh, a writer abusing drugs and alcohol—*what* are the odds?"

"So it isn't just the manner in which they died? We have to discuss personal lives and hobbies, too?"

She threw up her hands. "Oh, come on!" Long gone was the fiery hysteric intent on saving me from the Thyme in the mirror. And the weepy apologizer had also disappeared. "Since when is abusing booze and drugs a hobby? Now listen up: number two on my list. Lucius Fabius Clio. Choked to death on a single hair in his milk."

"Good one." Unusual *and* repulsive. "Keep going."

"Francois Vatel."

"No."

"Killed himself when he was unable to provide King Louis XIV with enough seafood to serve his guests."

"*No.* That was never proven."

"There are firsthand accounts! People who *saw* what happened."

"Yes, and as agents tirelessly fighting crime we have never come across an unreliable witness."

"It *happened.* You—"

"If your list is part myth and part fact, we should just—"

"Sorry to break up the hugely geeky argument, you huge geeks, but I've had enough of you two for one day." George was checking his phone and grabbing for his suit jacket. "Later, bitches."

Meanwhile, Thyme had not backed off so much as one inch. "There were several sources for— You know what? You want to get some dinner and talk about it?"

"I would. Now, if you want to talk about *factual* unusual deaths, I could mention Jim Creighton."

"Ruptured his bladder swinging too hard at a baseball. Sure, but then you've gotta think about Tycho Brahe, who had to hold it so long—because it would have been really bad manners to leave the party and pee—*his* bladder ruptured."

"Another myth!" I took Cadence's suit jacket off the back of my chair (why she thought she could pull off a butterscotch-colored pantsuit I did not know) and shrugged into it. "Are these unusual deaths or unusual myths?"

"How are you not getting that these deaths have been corroborated?"

"So has everything in the *National Enquirer,* and they are constantly incorrect. They are famous for it. If you were to suggest Humayun, however, I would agree his death was unusual *and* factual."

Thyme grabbed her enormous purse and trotted after me. "Oh, what bullshit! He died in a stairwell, Shiro, a *stairwell*! He heard the call to prayer, and since it was his habit to kneel when he heard it, he fell down the stairs. How is a lonely, slightly hilarious death in a stairwell more unusual than someone dying because they never got to pee?"

"All right, do not get shrill. Jeff Dailey?"

"Nuh-uh. Teenagers die all the time—look at our June Boys Jobs! Dailey died playing video games, which is more lame than unusual."

"Nineteen-year-olds do not drop dead of a heart attack after marathon video-game sessions," I protested. "They drink enormous quantities of Red Bull and ingest copious amounts of saturated fat and then try to have sex. How can you— All right. All right." I tried to calm myself. This was a fascinating conversation. This was a wonderful conversation! "You cannot question Basil Brown's fitness for your list."

"Drank himself to death with orange juice."

"Carrot juice," I corrected.

"Wanna bet?"

"Yes. Bring much cash."

She did. And I won some of it. Then she won some of it back.

I could not remember the last time I had enjoyed an evening more, though I would not deny Agent Thyme brought out an enormous competitive streak in me. By evening's end, I was laughing almost as often as I was restraining the impulse to boot her in the ankle. It made me wonder: Is this how normal people get to feel, all the time?

chapter twenty-five

I opened my eyes and was thrilled to find myself in my apartment, in Shiro's gray kimono pajamas, in my very own bed. *This bed is juuuuust right!*

It was dark out and I looked at my bedside clock: 2:37 A.M.

It felt like a gift. And an even bigger gift as I carefully glanced around. No strangers in here with me. Nothing appeared to be trashed and/or set on fire. I wasn't in a holding cell. I wasn't bleeding. I wasn't even hungry, though the last meal I could remember was a hastily bolted breakfast sixteen hours ago.

No, not hungry at all . . . pretty full, in fact.

I got out of bed, stepped into my sock monkey slippers, and went into the kitchen. Shiro had left files, extensive notes, and a memo addressed to me (and CC'd to Michaela, George, and Emma Jan Thyme) on the table.

I went to my bathroom and looked in the mirror. The skin around my left eye was slightly swollen. And I'd bet my yearly therapy bill that the explanation was sitting on my kitchen table. I always got all the gory details of Shiro's assault shenanigans; if

I occasionally woke up with a black eye or a cast, she at least kept me in the loop. Puffy skin around one eye hardly rated as an injury.

Ah, the old saying: a day without a trip to the ER is a day without sunshine. Ha!

Okay.

Okay, then. Shiro had been driving our body for several hours. It could have been so much worse. (It *had* been so much worse.)

Curious, I checked the fridge. I usually did that when I knew I should be hungry but was really, really full instead. There was a sizable doggy bag on the first shelf. The Oceanaire Seafood Room. Only the best place in the Twin Cities to get fresh seafood. Jeepers Louise, we couldn't afford that on our salary! Ah . . . but I knew who could.

Shiro had sure been busy, which I expected. But what was this? Everything was expected, except the trip to a wonderful expensive restaurant. She must have gone with someone; she'd never go alone. In fact, most of her meals were at sushi bars or bolted over our kitchen sink.

Okay! Shiro had kept my date with Patrick. I would rather have gone myself, but if I couldn't, I hoped Shiro had had a good time driving my body. Sometimes I hated having to share it. But sometimes, I was glad when another piece of me could have a little nondestructive fun.

Bemused, I went back to bed.

chapter twenty-six

In the morning I sat down in a Perkins to have breakfast with my best friend, Cathie Flannery. She'd gotten there first, which was unusual. What she was doing wasn't.

"Agh, what are you doing? Stop it." I flopped down into the bench across from her. "Leave that stuff alone."

"Back off, triple threat." Cathie suffered from OCD, among other things. In the five minutes or so before I'd arrived, she had alphabetized everything on the table, then laid it all in a straight line (still alphabetized, remember). F is for fork. S is for salt; it's also for Splenda, which was right next to it. And, at the end of the line, W is for water glass.

"Give me that. I was thirsty all the way over." I liberated the water glass from the line of OCD tyranny and gulped noisily. Shiro must have had a lot of plum wine last night—I'd woken up wanting to drink the world.

My friend had bright red hair and freckles (not a huge shock for someone named Flannery), was teeny—she barely came up to my chin—and whip slender. And she had the vitality of a dozen people.

This is a terrible thing to say about a best friend, but I sometimes found hanging around with her to be exhausting. I'm not even going to say how Shiro felt about it.

We'd met, years ago, at the MIMH (Minneapolis Institute of Mental Health). She was there because she was a disturbingly enthusiastic cutter. Her folks thought it was a suicide attempt. Unfortunately, they were old school: ignore anything that could lead to years of therapy. Don't talk about it. And get rid of the problem. And deny, deny, deny.

So they'd institutionalized her. And when we got to talking after a T-group session, we found we were really interested in what the other went through. She was amazed that I lived at MIMH. And more so when I told her I'd been conceived there, too. And I was amazed that "normal" parents could do that to their own child.

Anyway, we'd liked each other straightaway. Neither of us was in any position to judge the other, so the only other options were to ignore each other, be friends, or be enemies. We liked the middle choice, and went with it.

Now, years later, I was dating her brother and she was the only family I could remember. Given what my mom did to my dad

(look out look out look out look out PLEASE DADDY LOOK OUT)

that was a sizable blessing.

I greeted the waitress, who looked at the odd table arrangement but had no comment (one of the many reasons we liked it here) and ordered the usual: pancakes with extra butter and extra syrup.

"Vomit vomit vomit," Cathie commented.

"Do I critique your meals?"

"All the time. So, hey. Listen." She rested her elbows on the table and rested her chin in her hands. "Why'd you stand my brother up?"

That was a strange question, and it must have shown on my face because she added, "I don't mean just you. I meant all of you. None of you showed up."

"Wait. Patrick wasn't with my body last night?"

"It really skeeves me out when you put it that way." She shuddered. "And no. He called last night to see if you were at my place, but no soap."

"Oh, fudge nuts! Gah, I can't believe it!" I ran my hands through my hair. "Oh, boy, that's—wait. Shiro went out to dinner. I assumed with him. But then who was she hanging around with all night?"

"What, like *I* know?" She pulled out some of the Handi Wipes she always had in her purse, picked up the salt shaker, and thoroughly wiped it down. Then the pepper shaker. "Did you have to go nab a serial killer or something?"

"I wish." Oh boy, that would have been soooo great. "Huh. That's . . . okay, but there was a doggy bag. I doubt they'd hand those out at a crime scene." (And gross! Imagine if they did.)

"Those poor kids. How many murders have—you know what? Don't even tell me; it'll wreck my whole morning. And isn't that weird? All those dead boys scattered like dice all over the country . . . How has it been kept out of the national news?"

"I have no idea. That's Michaela's job." And she was really, really good at it. It helped that nearly every reporter she ever met was terrified of her. "Mine is to catch that rotten fish-smelling bum."

"When? *When* are you going to learn how to swear properly?"

"That *was* proper," I protested. I could be a badass when I wanted. Well. A bad butt.

"Proper?" A voice from behind us. I turned and looked. "Must be Cadence, talking about proper." Yes! Patrick.

I patted the seat beside me and couldn't resist: "I know we've talked about this before, but you numskulls really need to not wear shorts in December." Cathie had that in common with him! I figured they had hardy knees immune to frostbite. Was it an Irish thing?

"Please. It's almost thirty degrees out there. Tank-top weather." Patrick slid in next to me. "So where were all of you last night?"

"I'm really sorry. I assumed Shiro had been out with you, y'know, because of the leftovers from the restaurant, so I didn't even bother to call. Girlfriend-wise, I suck."

"Girlfriend-wise, not hardly. So Shiro ate out? In the middle of a big case like yours?"

"She was with someone, I just have no idea who. Like I said, I assumed it was you."

"And I assumed you were arresting a scumbag, hence your lack of presence on our date. Look how wrong we both were. What a tragedy."

" 'Lack of presence'?" Cathie asked, red eyebrows arching. "Who talks like you do? I mean, without medication."

If you looked at Cathie and Patrick side by side, you never would have thought they were siblings. Okay, she had coppery hair and his was a much darker, deeper red, but in all other ways they were dissimilar. He was tall; she was teeny. He was muscular, she was slender. He was a baker/entrepreneur, she was an artist.

There was also a ten-year age gap. Cathie hadn't seen much of her big brother growing up. They didn't know each other at all, even after all this time.

He'd flattered me by insinuating he was moving back to Minnesota to pursue a relationship with me/us, but I'd known that was only part of the reason. (No, Shiro didn't have to tell me; I figured it out on my own.) He wanted to get to know his sister better. Their parents were in a nursing home, their brains slowly disintegrating from Alzheimer's. Patrick and Cathie only had each other.

I could relate.

"This is none of my business," Cathie began. That was her code for "I absolutely think it's my business and you're going to sit there and listen." "But what if Shiro was out on a date?"

"But she's dating Patrick. All three of us are. We're exclusive and everything."

"And what a wild rumpus it is," he said, switching F for fork with S for sugar. "Ha! Now your orderly little world is in chaos—ow!" He rubbed his chest where the salt shaker had smacked into it. "Okay, okay. It's too early for projectiles."

"Cadence is bisexual," Cathie said, as if I hadn't known.

"Ergo she's slutty? Boo! Leave the stereotypes at home."

"Ergo she might start seeing someone."

"We've had this discussion before," I said, uneasy. And we had. Although my relationship with Patrick was my longest so far (lame, lame), I'd dated in the past. Shiro had, too. (Adrienne didn't date . . . exactly.)

"Yeah, but you weren't dating my brother before. Like your weird situation isn't weird enough? You've got to worry about Shiro seeing someone on the side?"

"I think you miiiiiight be jumping to conclusions."

"But she's so cute when she's all protective," Patrick said, leaning over to drop a kiss in my hair. "Cathie, it's okay. Let up. If I'm not upset, you shouldn't be, either."

"That's another thing. Why aren't you upset?"

"Whoa. Are you really asking him that?" Because it was none of her business, which I'd never dare say. "Are we having an argument? I hate arguments. And is it you and I who are arguing, or you and Patrick? Because it's not me and Patrick."

"I can't help it if I'm cracking under the pressure," she mumbled, and didn't say a word while the waitress set down our meals, then brought refills. Only when we had relative privacy did she speak again. "The dating, the house hunting. The Patrick. The new shrink. I don't do well with change."

"Who does?" Patrick and I were holding hands under the table. He studied Cathie's face, concerned. "Honey, what's the matter?"

"Nothing."

"Come on." His voice was gentle, coaxing. Almost paternal, which, given their age difference, made sense. He sure looked after her better than their father had.

"Why does something have to be the matter for me to be looking out for you? Both of you—which is as difficult as you can imagine."

How about, Because you're meddling and nagging, which isn't exactly your MO? I'd never say it out loud. "This isn't your usual . . . um, this isn't like you."

"It is, too!"

"Nope." Patrick shook his head.

"Fine, fine, *fine*." Cathie abruptly gave in. "The nursing home called. Dad's been asking and asking for us. And they think . . . I guess there might not be a lot of time."

"So," he said quietly, "we'll go see him."

"I don't *want* to see him, that's the whole problem. He locked me away when I was a kid who needed his help, and our mother helped him yank me out of all your lives." She slammed her hands, palms down, on the table. "He can rot in there for all I care."

"If that was really true, you wouldn't be upset." I reached across the B is for butter pats and took her hand. "If you don't see him, you might be sorry later."

"What do you know about it?"

"Hey!" Patrick warned sharply.

"No, it's a fair point. I can't look to my own family to know what you're going through, but you don't really think I've never run across a victim or suspect estranged from their family? You don't think I've seen what a lack of closure can do to the rest of a person's life?" *I can't believe he's dead. I can't believe we fought like that. I can't believe the last thing I said to her was something mean. I can't believe she died without knowing how much I loved her. I can't believe we had that stupid fight. I can't believe I can't believe I can't believe I can't believe . . .*

"I'm not going." I had no idea if she was talking to us, or herself.

"Don't blame them for everything." Patrick was speaking in such a low voice I had to strain to hear him. He was staring at the tabletop. "I let it happ—"

"Shut *up* with that shit, Patrick, we've been *over* this."

He shook his head, but didn't speak further. Something was going on, and I had no idea what it was. Worse, thoughts of the June Boys Jobs killer were starting to crowd out thoughts of my boyfriend and best friend. I really needed to get back to work.

Cathie cleared her throat. "The thing is, we're not done. I mean, I am, but Patrick, I asked you to breakfast to tell you he's calling for you, too. It wouldn't have been right to not tell you that."

I squeezed her hand. "You're a grown woman; you don't have to visit anyone you don't want to. I'm just asking that you think about it."

She grinned and I saw a spark of her usual vitality, something that was missing from this sad and angry woman. "Well, I'm not *gonna* think, so there. Here. Give me that."

It took her an entire pack of Handi Wipes to get the syrup bottle clean to her satisfaction. But when she was finished Patrick and I both agreed that she'd done a fantastic job. I think she even believed us.

I made an effort to push work out of my head, and so the rest of our breakfast was as affable as it could be with me preoccupied with chasing a serial killer, Cathie cracking, Patrick being stood up (and house hunting), and Shiro dating (maybe).

That was good enough for me. I'd take affable over argumentative every time.

chapter twenty-seven

Patrick staggered back as I rained kisses on his upturned face. "Oh boy. Oh boy," he said, hanging on to me. "There goes my center of gravity."

"I wanted to make it up to you."

We had just walked out of the restaurant. Cathie wanted to stay and clean the ketchup bottles (the ones across from our booth were pretty bad).

Once we had a bit of privacy, I'd sort of leapt on him, crossing my ankles behind his back as he held on to my butt for dear life. "Couldn't let you get back in your car without making it up to you."

"You couldn't just text me?" He leaned against his hybrid and kissed me back, hard. "Never mind. This was a good plan."

Passing cars honked cheerfully at us; I probably hadn't thought it through. PDA in a restaurant parking lot during the breakfast rush . . . well, it was his fault, drat everything. He was too handsome and smelled too good and liked me too much. All his fault. I was the blameless victim who was sort of assaulting him in a restaurant parking lot.

Just being this close to him was enough to make me want a

whole lot more than kissing. But I was still saving myself. Maybe for Patrick. Of the three of us sisters, I was the only virgin left. At my age! Yes, that wasn't *too* weird.

His mouth tasted like syrup (he'd hogged half of my breakfast) and beneath that, his own smell, his clean cottony scent that made me think of clothes drying on a line under a spring sun.

I ran my fingers through his thick, dark red hair, then cupped his face in my hands, our mouths pressing so hard together it was like we were trying to sear each other. I could feel his grip on my butt tighten as his arousal, like mine, ran higher and higher.

With deep regret, I broke the kiss. We both panted at each other for a few more seconds, and then I said, "I have to go fight crime, now."

"Awwwww." He gently set me back down on my feet. "Have I told you you're the best kisser I've ever met?"

"How many have you 'met'? And yes." I smiled. "About a hundred times."

He grinned back and kissed me again, smack on the cheek. "Cadence, you are ridiculous good fun. You sure I can't talk you into taking the day? We'd go anywhere you want, for as long as you want."

I shook my head. Tempting, but . . . the autopsy photos would haunt me. Their school pictures would, too. "Maybe later. Maybe, if we catch him."

"You will."

I shrugged. Patrick reached out and cupped my cheek. "Cadence. Listen. *You will.*"

"Okay." *Please God, let him be right.* "I'd better go."

"Be careful."

"Always," I told him, which he must have known was a rather large lie.

chapter twenty-eight

UNCLASSIFIED
FOR OFFICIAL USE ONLY

To: Cadence Jones
CC: George Pinkman, Emma Jan Thyme, Michaela Taro
Date: December 9, 2012
RE: Joseph Behrman

Due to unforeseen circumstances, we did not get a chance to do a full interview with Joseph Behrman (see attached: BOFFO UNCLASSIFIED Internal Memorandum, Joseph Behrman's coram nobis). As referenced in the attached paperwork, BOFFO will return Tuesday, 10:00 A.M., to finish the interview.

I found a major discrepancy in the alibi he offered during the brief time we were there (see attached: Minneapolis/St. Paul *Star Tribune*, Lifestyle Section, Movie Reviews/Start Times).

The fact that he lied suggests one of two things: 1) he is the killer, or knows who the killer is; 2) he is not the killer but was somewhere he does not want law enforcement to know about.

The latter is not uncommon with parolees who may be skirting the rules. It is unlikely Behrman forgot we can revoke his parole and return him to Stillwater for reimprisonment should he violate any condition of said parole (see attached: Behrman Community Service Plan, Behrman sentencing paperwork, Case number 320441-B).

I suggest we hit him hard with the lie. Depending on what the lie is, we may want to consider seeking a sneak-and-peek warrant for Behrman's trailer.

Thank you for your attention to this matter.

SJ/sj

"Why did you just read that to us?" George asked. He and I were at our desks, and Emma Jan had pulled a chair over to sit beside us. We had only been in the office half an hour and we were already sick of each other. That was always a good way to tell when we were getting fried on a case. "We all have copies. We've all read the damned thing. I hate when you read me stuff I already read. Stop reading stuff to us!"

"I just wanted to make sure we're all on the—"

"We're all on the *same* page because we all got the *same* memo. And tell Shiro to stop CC'ing the fucking world with these things. I'm surprised the janitor didn't get a copy."

"Don't talk about janitors," I said sharply. "Um, custodial engineers."

Emma Jan's eyes widened. "Oh, shit! The ThreeFer Killer! One of them worked here."

"Cadence is right," George said, and I nearly reeled back and fell out of my chair. "Let's not talk about it." He rubbed his eyes. "It's too early for this shit."

"It's past ten in the morning."

"Don't remind me."

I wasn't surprised George didn't want to discuss it. We'd had an awful time tracking down the ThreeFer Killer, because it wasn't one killer; it was three. Murderous triplets, not two words that usually go together. One of them, I was sorry to see then and sorry to say now, worked here, right here at BOFFO, as a custodial engineer.

He's dead now. So's his sister. The third one, the remaining triplet . . . well. The third one wasn't. Probably.

Anyway, one of their many atrocities was kidnapping George, trussing him up like a roast ready for the slow cooker, and bundling him into a closet for hours and hours and hours and hours.

Even now, months later, I wasn't sure if George had gotten mega-pissed because of the trussing/stuffing thing, or because the ThreeFer Killers had framed him, or because he deliberately pooped in his pants to provide us with a clue to his whereabouts, and no one noticed. (We can be a pretty self-absorbed bunch. Also, there were all sorts of weird smells on the floor, all the time, so what was one more?)

"What's this she's talking about?" Emma Jan asked, tapping the memo. She was dressed in a bark-colored jacket and pants, with a crimson blouse and, of course, her gigantic purse was at her side. If I'd tried to pull off those colors I would have looked like a bleeding tree. She looked like the suit had been designed for her, and only her. "This *Star Tribune* thing?"

"Yeah, while you bimbos were taking your sweet time getting here—thanks for nothing by the way . . ."

"You beat us by not quite three minutes," I said.

"Shut up. What, d'you keep a stopwatch on your person at all times?"

"Well, if you must know, after you kept making the same comments about you always being super-early and me always being super-late, I—"

"Shut up! Anyway, I pulled the data she was talking about. Behrman told Shiro and me he'd been to the movie theater in Apple Valley—that great big place by Target and Best Buy?"

I nodded. It was big and shiny clean, and they sold frozen Coke slushies, which I just loved. (If I couldn't have a Frappuccino, an ice-cold Coke would do, and a *frozen* Coke would be even better.)

They had a big gorgeous lobby with lots of tables and chairs spread around, so you could relax and socialize before or after the movie, and there was a Red Robin across the street. It was a good place to meet up with friends, see a flick, grab a burger, go back into the theater for frozen Coke number four . . . like that.

There was also a sizable video arcade if your kids wanted to kill time before the movie. Or if, um, you really, really liked playing *Magicka* even though you were in your twenties and childless, and had an alternate personality who felt as strongly about *God of War*, and another one who felt like that about *Rage*.

Best of all, the theater had lots of screens—so there was almost always a movie playing that was worth seeing—and ran lots of previews. I loved previews. If they had a two-hour movie that was just previews, I'd go. Twice.

"Right." George carefully dug through a pile of folders—stacked higher than his head when he was seated—until he found the autopsy paperwork.

Here's a sad thing I wish I never had to know: there are doctors who specialize in pathology; for whatever reason they are more comfortable having dead patients instead of live ones. And within that group they specialize further. There are coroners who specialize in performing autopsies on children.

So that's what they do. They cut up dead kids. All day long.

See what I mean? Don't you wish you could un-know that?

"Okay." George was flipping through the report. "The coroner was able to put the TOD somewhere between six P.M. and ten, right? And this fucko, he's not keeping them alive for long—the histochemistry proves that."

"Yeah, but—" Emma Jan began.

George was too intent on making his point, and cut her off (she should get used to that right away). "Yeah, this fucko is beating them to death but he's not taking, say, three days to do it, right? They're not walled up somewhere getting poked and paper-cut and stuffed with, I dunno, suet and cranberries, right?"

"Uh . . ."

I was right there with Emma Jan. Did George think teenage boys should be on the lookout for suet salesmen? Or cranberry bogs? And if so, shouldn't we get BOLO paperwork started? What *was* suet, any—

"What's suet?"

I flashed her a grateful look.

"Duh, you need it to make mincemeat pie. It's fat. S'matter with you?"

Emma glanced at me and I could, for those few seconds, read her mind: *What's the matter with* me?

"Can you two focus, please, pretty please? Forget about the fucking suet. Who cares about the fucking suet? Why are we talking about suet?"

Well. Now that he'd brought it up, *I* cared. How often could you fight crime and discuss the merits of suet in the same morning? I loved my job. Except when I hated my job.

"My point is, if Behrman can't tell us he was home jerking off to a rerun of *Sons of Anarchy*, then—"

I couldn't help it. I knew he hated interruptions when he was on a roll, but I had to know. "Why would he be masturbating to . . ."

I trailed off as George gaped at me. His expression was wondering, yet filled with contempt for whatever poor idiot loser didn't know all about *Sons of Malarky*, or whatever the thing was called.

I don't mean to sound like a snob, but I didn't watch much television. Why would I? Why would I get hooked on a show when any second one of my sisters can show up, kidnap my body, and get me tossed into a holding cell? There's not a big enough DVR in the world to make that fret disappear.

"Are you fucking kidding me, Cadence? Who *wouldn't* he jerk off to? Have you seen the show?"

"Uh—"

"Yeah, don't fucking tell me, you don't have time to watch much TV, spare me. I've got three words: Katey Fucking Sagal, okay? Here's three more: Kim Fucking Coates."

"I'm sure Kim is very pretty, but maybe we should get back to—"

"Kim's not pretty, Kim's a guy, you TV-free dumbshit."

"Wait. Are you bi, then?" Emma Jan asked. Then, to me: "Is he gay? I didn't think he was. I don't care," she was quick to assure us, "it's just that I'm finding this kind of confusing."

I shook my head. "Oh, George isn't gay. I don't think. I'm probably the wrong person to ask. I don't think he's entirely straight, though, either."

"If you two harpies don't stop talking about me like I'm not sitting here hearing every harpy word from your harpy beaks . . ."

"Is anyone truly entirely straight, though?"

"Good point," I admitted. "In George's case, most of us here think he's that thing where he's sexually attracted to anything."

"What, anything?"

"Anything."

"I mean it, harpies! You're inches away from my permanent shit list!"

I shrugged. "Men. Women. Large domesticated farm animals. Ice cubes. It's . . . it's something like ambisexual. Wait. I know this. Intersexual?"

Don't you hate it when you can practically *feel* the word in your brain, but can't think what it is? I knew this, too . . . I'd just read it, or Shiro read it . . . Argh! It was right on the tip—

chapter twenty-nine

Pansexual.

chapter thirty

"Ah-haaaaa!" I screamed into Emma Jan's shocked face. "I *did* know! Pansexual. I knew that. I knew I knew that. It's pansexual; the word is pansexual."

It was odd, though. The thing that had just happened. When Shiro came out, she usually stayed for a bit. But not this time.

This time she remembered a word I couldn't, a word I didn't know because *she* was the one who read the government study. So she surfaced long enough to give me the word, then sank back into my subconscious or psyche or what-have-you, leaving me in control of the body so we could finish the briefing.

It was helpful. The thing my sister did for me helped matters, it improved my quality of life. Not in an obvious way, like a physical fight where she saved me from being mutilated in a dozen horrible ways. This was subtle, it was something that hardly ever happened. It was something I . . . liked?

My doctor was pushing for reintegration, but all three of us were resistant. They didn't want to disappear, and I didn't want to kill them. My doctor kept telling me/us it wouldn't be like that, that I'd/we'd all live on through the new personality, the fourth, the one who was whole, the one no one had seen for decades. The person I had been until the day my mother killed my father.

Maybe . . . maybe it would be like that. Helpful and not bewildering and scary. Maybe being one instead of three really was the best thing for all of us.

I didn't know. I didn't. And because I was a coward, I didn't want to find out.

"If you two are done playing Guess What George Is, can we please pretty please get back to the string of vicious murders we've decided, for funsies, should stop? Cripes, I thought *I* was self-involved."

He had a point. When a sociopath is knocking you for being too self-involved, it was time to reexamine your life.

When we had no comment, he added, "Yes? Everybody back on board? Peachy. *Anyway.*" He glared at both of us, obviously silently daring we, the TV-less dumbshits, to interrupt once more. "Anyway. My point is, if Behrman can't account for his whereabouts that evening, he's cooked, right? So he tells us he's at the movies to see . . . what the fuck was it?"

"*Fast and Furious VI: Even Faster,*" Emma Jan read, checking her own paperwork.

"God, God, God." He shook his head and smoothed his tie (a run-over poodle with a black background). "Don't even get me started on goddamned movie franchises. *Fast and Furious* did so well, there's an *F&F* Six? A *six*? When they only made one *Independence Day*? Jesus. Unbelievable. The things you find out about when you can't get your hands on a bomb.

"Anyway, the theater this movie was playing in, the one Behrman says he saw? They had a major projection malfunction during the last matinee that day. They couldn't fix it, so they refunded everyone in the theater their money—which morons who'd go see that piece of shit did *not* deserve—and they didn't even sell tickets to the show Behrman says he went to. He should have told his story that way, but he didn't. He didn't because he wasn't even there. Get it?"

"I get that he picked the wrong alibi, and has bad taste in movies, but—"

"Think about it. It's nothing the movie theater would have, say, told a reporter. They focused on fixing it and getting back to charging admission for their shitty movie. So yeah, Behrman picked the wrong alibi, but even better, he has no idea that we know what a fucking liar he is. *That's* our angle. That's what we hit him with."

"Nice," I said, and I meant it. Shiro had been getting A's on her homework since before we were in training bras. Trust her to root this out and serve it up, practically on a dessert plate. And George had that tally-ho-the-fox look in his eyes. "Oh, wow, that's very, very nice."

"So!" Emma Jan was on her feet. "Let's go see him. And on the way, do you want to hear about Saint Antipas, who was roasted to death in—"

"No thanks."

chapter thirty-one

"I don't want to criticize," I began.

"Don't listen to her," George told Emma Jan. "It's a trick. Whenever she says she doesn't want to criticize, or make waves, or question judgment, she starts with *that*."

"Thanks for the warning."

"It's just . . . you know that saying about the definition of insanity is doing the same thing over and over but expecting a different result?"

"Know it? It's the damn motto for BOFFO. People have cross-stitched it on samplers."

"I'm bringing it up because we're on our way back to Heron Estates. And we're going into the same trailer. The one with the gigantic mirror. And Emma Jan is with us."

"Thanks for the update," he said, and Emma Jan laughed from the backseat.

"So I'm clearly the only one worried."

"It's okay, Cadence. The truce is on."

"Truce?" I propped my arm on the headrest so I could turn around and make eye contact while I fretted. "What truce?"

"Between me. And her. The woman in the mirror."

"And. . . ?"

"So I won't engage this time. It's the solution my doctor came up with after years of trying other stuff. I'll try not to look. And if I do look, I won't engage. We had a hypnosis session first thing this morning; it should hold."

Hmmm. Hypnosis. As a subject of that same therapy, I had great respect for it. Hypnosis had been the only way I unlocked memories I'd repressed for decades. It made sense that it could help someone with their delusion.

"It doesn't matter anyway."

"No?" I asked.

"After all," she said bitterly, looking out the window (I wasn't sure why; the only thing to see was Highway 35), "it's not like I'll never see her again."

I didn't say anything. More miraculous, neither did George. I won't deny I thought the whole Mirrored-self Misidentification thing to be pretty weird. But a delusion was a delusion was a delusion. There were BOFFO employees who thought aliens were beaming commands through the internet. And ones who thought the late bin Laden had been the reincarnation of porn industry actor John Holmes. Was that any nuttier?

I decided this was a good time to bring up someone who'd been on my mind, strictly in a professional capacity, so I told them about Dr. Gallo.

"No shit," George said, eyes widening and then narrowing with interest. "Here to help out the family? Huh."

"I know what 'huh' means."

"Enlighten the gal in the backseat, then," the gal in the backseat called.

"He's wondering—and now he's got me wondering—if Dr.

Gallo might make a good suspect." And I had to admit, on short acquaintance the good doctor gave off that vibe. Not the murder vibe, the I-can-handle-anything-even-felony-assault vibe. "I'll go back and talk to him, officially this time." I was thrilled at the thought. Because it would help the investigation. Not because I wondered what his long black hair felt like. Or how he smiled when he was truly happy.

"But what about the blackout?"

"It's for the media, not family members," I pointed out. "He's too good a resource to waste by keeping him in the dark about what I'm doing. It's worth the risk."

She shrugged. "It's your risk."

It certainly is my risk, missy, and I'll thank you to let me be the one to worry about it.

We pulled into the trailer court, and thank goodness. Not one of us had said a word the rest of the way, and the time draaaaaagged. Long silences were something that I, as George Pinkman's partner, wasn't at all used to.

chapter thirty-two

Joseph Behrman opened the door and didn't look at all happy to see us. This cheered me up; guilty people usually weren't happy to see us, either.

"I thought you were gonna call before you came. Like you did last time."

"Yep, well, that's the thing about the FBI, sometimes we can be rude like that." George was leaning on the house, well back from the door. "You gonna let us in, or are we gonna have this chat on your sidewalk?"

Behrman pointed. Ick. His nails were filthy. "And *she's* back."

Emma Jan shrugged and smiled. "Sorry. A minor overreaction."

"Overreaction," he repeated, dumbfounded. "That's what you'd call that?"

"It's not *my* fault the woman living in your mirror wants to kill me. Where's your dog?"

"Inside," he said shortly, then stepped back to let us in.

It made me wonder, would Emma Jan think the dog's reflection was the pet of the woman who lived in the mirror? Or did the delusion only affect her reflection? I tried to imagine poor Emma Jan in a fun-house mirror . . . terrifying. No wonder George was smiling; he loved any kind of excitement or trouble. Exciting trouble was his favorite.

"You're in deep shit, Sylvester," he said cheerfully. It was a line from Stephen King's *The Stand* he liked to trot out when busting someone's story. "Oh, now, you've got company. Who's this?"

There was another man in the living room, slowly climbing to his feet. He looked like a truck driver who'd played lots of football: big, thick shoulders and arms, sturdy legs, a small-ish beer belly that would probably give him trouble as he got older and didn't decrease his beer consumption. Black hair pulled back into a ponytail, blue eyes. A face that was more strong than handsome . . . broad forehead, big nose, big chin. Not handsome, but far from unattractive.

He greeted us with, "Got a warrant?"

"Ooooh, rookie mistake. You hate to see it," George said, miming sorrow as only a dedicated sociopath could. "We don't need one to chat. Besides, your boyfriend let us in."

"We're not faggots," Behrman snapped. Then, pointing to Emma Jan: "We gonna have trouble with her again?"

"What 'we'? My partner fixed everything while you hid behind the couch."

"That's a fuckin' lie!"

"Oh, there's no shame in it," Emma Jan piped up. "The whole thing was scary and dangerous and surreal."

Yes: those three words summed up my life.

"We didn't get your name, big guy," George said.

"Philip Loun."

"L-O-O-N?"

"No, like 'loud' without the D. After you've added an N. Me and Behrman go to the same AA meetings."

"You do know that lying to cops isn't one of the twelve steps, right?"

"Nobody's lying." Behrman reluctantly shut the door and went to sit in the chair opposite Loun.

"Wrong yet again, Mr. Behrman. *You* were lying. Which sucks for you, because now we're at least ten times more interested in you than we were yesterday."

"What the hell are you talking about?"

"The movie, Mr. Behrman. The one you didn't go to."

"Don't look at the mirror," I whispered to Emma Jan, who'd been staring, wide-eyed, at the living room.

"I don't know where I *can* look."

I understood, sure. A small Confederate flag had been tacked up over the television. And posters were all over exhorting how swell the Third Reich was.

There were also quite a few old mug shots that had been printed out, framed, and hung for some reason. All the subjects, except for one, were black males . . . the stereotypical Bad Guy pic showing a brooding African American male with features exaggerated to make him look meaner, wearing the hey-look-at-me-in-standard-prison-issue striped shirt.

The exception was a white female, wearing a long dark skirt and nice blouse, buttoned to her chin. She looked like she'd come straight from Central Casting for Stereotypical School Marm.

I wasn't close enough to read any of the names, but the pictures were old, early-to-mid twentieth century old.

Finally, Behrman's big gurgling aquarium—it was half as long as the entire living room wall—was so green, I could barely make out the fish that were in it . . . and they didn't look like fish. Turtles? Body parts?

"You can see 'em when they swim close to the glass," Behrman offered.

"Hey, don't worry about a thing, Officer," Loun told Emma Jan. "You've got nothing to worry about from The Good Citizens."

"It's 'agent,' actually. And I don't?"

I wanted to ask, but had low interest in displaying my ignorance. Fortunately, George knew I was clueless, and could never resist a chance to show off. "*The Good Citizen* was a monthly 'yay, facism!' rag that quit printing around 1933."

"Well, there was other stuff going in on 1933," Emma Jan offered. "Their to-do lists probably got hard to manage after a while. 'Hmm, shall we stop earning money to pay the mortgage, or should we stop our malicious hate-mongering which we're hoping will spread to the next generation?' You see how it is."

"We took that name for our militia," Loun confirmed.

Outstanding. Serial murder and white supremacists. It was shaping into a lovely week.

"You said I shouldn't worry, but now I'm extremely worried," Emma Jan said. "You recall Waco, right? Didn't work out so good for you guys. Right?"

"The Good Citizens follow the teachings of Edith Overman. We're all about women's equality."

"All women?" she asked. "Or just white women?"

Both men shrugged.

"I see. Can't win them all, I suppose."

"Edith Overman?" I asked. Because of two bad things, I had to ask. Bad thing one, Edith Overman was obviously a mover and shaker in the booming business of bigotry and racism and I should've known who she was. Bad thing two, there are so *many* of them, so many zealots and racists and warlords-in-training, no matter how much I read I can *never* keep up with them. And they always found someone—or someone found them. For every JFK, there was an Adolf Hitler. For every Gandhi, there was a Jim Jones.

"Bad boys. Very bad boys." George shook his finger in mock-scold. I think it was mock-scold. "You left a few things out. You're also all about anti-Semitism, racism, anti-Catholicism, and anti-immigrant.

"Here's the hilarious part, guys: Overman hated immigrants, and yet she was *not* Native American." He swung on Emma Jan, throwing up his hands in mock-despair. Or real despair. "This, *this* is why I can't ever get on board with these dumb shits. Can you imagine going through your whole life teaching your kids and your neighbors how to hate immigrants while being so dumb you don't know you were descended from illegal immigrants?"

"That's the only thing holding you back from the Bigotry Bandwagon?" I asked, and Emma Jan laughed.

"It's not our fault if the Indians couldn't hold on to their country," Behrman said. Instead of sounding defensive or mad, he sounded proud. "That's how we justified throwing England out of our business during the Revolutionary War, and nobody's running around saying we committed genocide all over the most powerful country in the world at that time. We claimed our territory and we defended it. 'Zactly the same thing."

"Hmmmm." George was trying to pace. Tough work in this tiny living room. "Let's see. Let's take a look at that. Patriots chafing under a tyrant's rule rising up to take control of their destiny. And then there's deciding that blacks and Jews are inferior and they should all be dropped into the deep end of the ocean. Oh, sure. Exactly the same thing. The whole thing just smacks of patriotism. Yep."

I watched carefully, but he was under control (for now). George had a thing about skinheads and gay bashers. No one knew why.

"So, do you want your friend to hear why your alibi sucked? Or should he leave?"

"You don't tell anyone to leave in my own house," Behrman warned.

"Trailer."

"What?"

"Your own trailer. We don't tell anyone to leave in your own trailer . . . yeah, you're right. Doesn't have the right ring to it. House it is."

Behrman glared. "Anything you say to me you can say in front of Loun."

"Oh, goody. Mr. Behrman, the movie theater you claimed as your alibi didn't show that matinee . . . they had technical difficulties. That whole theater was shut down for the rest of the day." George shook his head, then wagged his finger in front of him like a spinster scolding a school boy. "You've been baaaad."

"Maybe I told you the wrong movie. Maybe I meant—"

"That's a terrible idea, changing your story like that. It's making all the red flags in my brain pop."

"Oh, that's bad," I said to the men. "You don't want to pop his flags."

Loun and Behrman exchanged glances. "Maybe I should call a lawyer."

"Awesome, Mr. Behrman! You've got no idea, man. That makes our day. Yaaaaay!"

"He's right," I said while George literally jumped up and down, clapping his hands together and yelling "yay, yay, yaaaay!" He looked and sounded like a demented cheerleader. One that would stick a knife in your ribs if his team lost. "It does."

"Innocent people never want to talk to a lawyer. Yaaaaay!"

Emma Jan and I looked at each other and shrugged. We knew it was true. It had happened again and again in our careers.

Loun sighed and looked greatly put-upon. "Just tell 'em, Behrman. The Good Citizens weren't doing anything against the law. We have the right to lawful assembly."

Oh, fudge cakes. He was about to confess, but not to the JBJ murders. He was about to tell us he'd been at a white supremacist meeting. It explained his lie while being boring and sad at the same time.

"I had a meeting with my white brothers. Morale's been low. We needed to be reminded not just howwcome we were there that night, but howwcome The Good Citizens got started in the first place. So we got together to talk about it, brother-to-brother."

"Sounds cozy," Emma Jan commented.

"And there are at least twenty people who can testify to that."

George sighed. "That's nice."

He was sort of right. It was nice in that we'd never seriously considered Behrman a suspect, and it was good to get that confirmed. Still, it left us with zero leads.

"You, you're the worst kind of race traitor," Behrman told George.

"Reeeeeeally?"

"They can't help being lazy," he added, pointing to Emma Jan. "But you. You're not just a race traitor, you work for the government. There's not a man around, I don't care if he's a killer or a thief, none of them's lower than you."

"But I want to be with you!" George wiped away an imaginary tear. "And here I thought we were gonna be best friends and spend the day giving each other blow jobs."

Gross! And Behrman looked like he was thinking the same thing, if the revulsion-induced twitching was any indication.

"You should be ashamed," Loun said.

"Should be, but aren't. Shame? Me? Ha! I *never* feel shame. For anything. Ask them . . ." Pointing at me. ". . . if you don't believe me. And while we're discussing shame, you skinhead troglodytes, you mentally deficient dumbasses—"

"Hey!" Both men pointed at their heads, and Loun added, "Do we look like skinheads to you?"

"You look like assholes to me."

"Easy," I muttered, in a voice low enough so only George could hear. "Don't lose it. Their time will come."

"Goddamned right about that, Cadence." He turned back to the skinheads-who-weren't-skinheads. "We'll need allll those names to check your alibi."

"I was there," Loun said. "I can tell you right now, Brother Behrman was there, too. You don't need to know anybody else."

"Gosh, thanks, that's super-helpful, Mr. Loun, and yet I don't feel like taking the word of someone dumb enough to make character assumptions based on skin color."

"I'm not running down *your* beliefs," Loun replied with what I was annoyed to see was touching dignity. I liked my racist fartfaces incoherent and rage-ey. "I'd like the same courtesy from you."

"A million-zillion pardons. Names. *Now.*"

Loun shot Behrman a black look, and the other man shrugged and shook his head. The situation they now faced was what he'd hoped to avoid with his lie: federal agents bugging his "brothers."

So, we'd check the names and make sure Behrman was in no position to kill our last victim and then . . . and then it was back to the drawing board.

We could hear muffled whining from the other end of the trailer.

"Is that your dog?" Emma Jan asked. "I wondered why she wasn't outside."

"She's sick. Vet said she has to stay inside for a couple days. Shut up back there!"

More whining.

"Shee-it. Be right back." Behrman stomped through the living room and kitchen. "Shut up, Dawg!"

Loun rolled his eyes. "I don't know why that man even has a dog. They're not too fond of each other."

Golly, who'da thought?

"We can—" I began, only to be interrupted by a thump, and then a loud, agonized yelp.

"Oh, man, he stomped that poor dog again." Loun shook his head. "Toldja. I think Behrman's more of a cat person. Did you know Hitler tested a cyanide pill on a dog before he decided to take one himself?"

He must have seen something on my face he didn't like at all, because he took a big step backward and added, "Are you okay? You don't look too good."

chapter thirty-three

doggy!

Doggy doggy who's got the doggy?

Stomp he likes to stomp he likes to see if he likes it see if he can make a noise like the dog see if he

is a dog he IS a dog he IS

does emma jan have a muffin for me this time the dog the doggie got the muffin

oh does that hurt does that feel like somebody stomped on your foot hard enough to break a couple of bones too bad so sad oh now who's howling

Ha! Ha ha, Behrman, ha, the doggie has her day every doggie has her day

Ha! His head hurts

like a bus

The wheels on the bus

The wheels

Doggie you come with me doggie don't be don't be don't be scared

Don't! See?

I only hurt the ones I hate.

chapter thirty-four

I stretched, glad I'd splurged on the electric blanket. Forty-nine ninety-nine at Target, and worth every penny. It kept my side of the bed nice and . . .

Um.

I didn't *have* an electric blanket. At the time I'd thought fifty bucks was way too much to spend, so I never got the thing. So why was I. . . ?

I opened my eyes. Curled up next to me was Behrman's dog, Dawg.

Oh phooey fudge cakes on a toilet!

"What are *you* doing here?" I asked Dawg, horrified. She was alive, right? I hadn't actually killed a dog and then stuck it in my bed, like the horse head from *The Godfather,* had I? Gross. Also very, very disturbing.

Dawg yawned but stayed pressed to my side. Gah, she needed a bath. Several, in fact.

"Better question," I muttered aloud. "What am *I* doing here?" The last thing I remembered was hearing the dog crying in the back of the trailer, being angry and sad that someone could stomp his dog and not be ashamed to do worse.

I groped for my cell, which had been left on the end table beside my bed, along with my car keys and two Chicken McNugget cartons, both empty except for crumbs. (I hate Chicken McNuggets.) I pulled up my texts and, yep, there were a couple of new ones.

A. kidnapped the dog. E.J. and I finished Behrman interview; alibi checks out. Does your building even take dogs?

No.

Met A., which was weird. I think she likes dogs more than me. Also, B. and L. are in the hospital recovering from concussions. A. grabbed them both by the back of their necks and drove them, headfirst, into a wall. Hard. Don't sweat it; they're so humiliated by being taken down by a fed they don't want to bring charges. Does your building even take dogs?

No!

And then a text from Michaela in her typical terse style:

Get back to the office ASAP.

"Oh, great," I groaned. Dawg wasn't especially concerned; she just snuggled deeper into my side. "Oh, that's just flippin' pancake great. And what am I supposed to do with you?" Take her to the pound? Do they even have a dog pound around here? And what if they wanted to execute her right away? Would they do it immediately, or give her, say, a three-day grace period?

Why did I not know these things? Oh, right . . . I was raised in a hospital full of crazy people. No dogs allowed. And occasionally, no sanity.

"The day has barely started and it can't get any—" There was a firm knock on my door. "Drat shoot darnit!" What fresh heck was this?

I got up and Dawg jumped down right behind me. She followed me to the door. I peeked through the peep hole and was relieved to see it was . . . "Patrick!"

He stood in my doorway, khaki shorts (idiot . . . he couldn't hold off frostbite forever) and a long-sleeved navy blue T-shirt. Bare feet (madness) and thick clunky sandals.

"So it's true," he said, grinning as he looked past me. "You got a dog."

"I *didn't*." He stepped inside and I shut the door. "Adrienne kidnapped her."

He squatted and put out a hand, but she whimpered and shied away. "It's okay," I told her. To Patrick: "Her owner was pretty abusive and his friend didn't much care. I don't think she likes adult males."

"Who'd want to abuse a cutie like you?" he asked, inching forward. She submitted, trembling, and he gently stroked her silky black ears. "Tell me Adrienne did something memorably awful to him."

"To them."

"Oh?"

"Concussion."

"Excellent."

"I can't take her back to her owner—"

"You're her owner now."

"No, I'm *not*."

"Does your building even allow dogs?"

"No! It doesn't!"

"I'm standing right here, babe, you don't have to shriek. Guess you'd better move."

"Well, *great*. Sure, that's what I'll do. I'll indulge Adrienne's latest tantrum and uproot my entire life."

"What's the dog's name?"

"Dawg."

"Oh."

I ran my fingers through my hair and paced, channeling George. "Do you believe this? I can't believe this. She's never kidnapped someone's pet before. Other *people*, sure, and she's occasionally rescued abused kids after beating the bananas out of their abusers, but never a pet. And now I have to deal with it! She's so thoughtless and destructive and completely self-absorbed. Why are you here?"

Patrick had been nodding sympathetically, so I think my abrupt question took him by surprise. "Uh . . . Adrienne called me. She said you needed a babysitter. I thought she meant *you* needed a babysitter. Or that she did. But I guess she meant Dawg does."

I stared at him. Which got me nothing but a return stare. "She . . . called you?"

"Yeah."

"To watch Dawg."

"Yeah."

I sighed. He put a hand on my shoulder, gently turned me, then started rubbing my shoulders. The muscles were so tight I could hear him grunt as he tried to loosen them. A chiropractor could make a fortune off me.

I closed my eyes and leaned back into his touch. "It occurs to me," I said without opening them, "that I've done nothing but whine since you came over. Sorry."

He laughed, then bent and kissed the back of my neck, then laughed again when I shivered. "You're entitled, hon. If I had to put up with a tenth of the crap you do . . . I can't even imagine it."

"I'm really, really lucky you're here. Not just here in my apartment cleaning up another of Adrienne's messes. Here in my life. Our lives," I corrected myself.

"When are you going to get it through your head?" Patrick turned me around, then bent and kissed me softly on the mouth. "I'm the lucky one."

I stretched up and kissed him back. So he kissed me back more. Naturally, I reciprocated. Before I knew it we were both shirtless. "Aw, nuts," I managed, clutching two handfuls of his hair. "Michaela."

"Ooooh, here comes the dirty talk." He'd been planting kisses along the left side of my neck, and his words were muffled. "Now call me Big Jim."

"I have to go." I managed to extricate myself. "Agh! Sorry. My boss really wants me to get back as soon as I can."

"Kiss me quick!"

I did. Then I put my shirt back on. "I have no dog food and no idea what you should do if she needs to go outside."

"We'll muddle through." This time, when he knelt by Dawg, she sat still for it. "She's nice, huh? I'd think most dogs jerked out of their homes and kidnapped by a nutjob—sorry, honey, but there it is—would be a little more freaked out."

"Even my sterile, non-dog-proofed apartment is an improvement, believe me." I guess it makes me a bad person; I wasn't mad about Adrienne concussing those two men. Just about how Dawg would inconvenience me.

With that selfish thought, I finished getting ready for work and headed out the door.

chapter thirty-five

"Look who's back!" Emma Jan paused. "Um . . . it's Cadence or Shiro, right?"

"Cadence," George said without looking up from his computer. "Note how she's disheveled and out of breath after busting ass to get in here. Also note the large Frappuccino she didn't have time to stop for but did anyway. Shiro'd never do any of that stuff."

"Oh. Okay." She cleared her throat. "Um, Shiro and I are supposed to go to the range after work today. That woman . . . that woman actually thinks she can outshoot me with a Beretta! Me! I was field stripping semiautos before I was in training bras."

"Calm down, it's—"

"I'm going to prove her wrong many, many times tonight. I'm bound to get at least half of my paycheck back," she added, grumbling. "My pride, and my last twenty bucks before payday, are riding on this. It's got to happen! Did you . . . I mean, is that okay?"

"You made a date with Shiro?" Could Emma Jan be Shiro's mystery date from the other night?

Emma Jan blinked. "Not a date, exactly. A competition. Did you not hear all that ranting I just did?"

Sorry, Emma Jan, but I was the partner of George Pinkman. Ranting was about as unusual as George snorting Splenda.

I tossed my bag on my desk and shrugged out of my Man Coat. (Yes, okay, I bought it in the men's section at Target. It was an unattractive brown, and too big, and it also kept me warmer than any Woman Coat I'd ever bought.) "Shiro can't just . . . just make appointments with *my* body."

"She did, though," George said, still not looking up.

"You stay out of this. Please." Emma Jan was dressed in yet another suit that looked gorgeous on her (brick red, with a matching jacket and a tan blouse) that would have been a disaster on me. "Listen, if Adrienne scared you or hurt you, I'm really—"

"Oh, no! It was fine. I mean, it was weird and cool, but also fine. You just sort of . . . okay, your eyes sort of rolled up and then you were *leaping* at Behrman, and then his friend made the mistake of trying to help him, and then the dog got out—you know what? It doesn't matter. Did Michaela tell you? They aren't pressing charges."

"The one piece of good news I've had in the last two days." I sighed, moved my bag, and slumped into my chair. "Bet you had no idea what you were signing on for when you got your transfer, huh?"

"I like it here," she said cheerfully. "It's always interesting."

Yes, that was one word for it.

"When do you think Adrienne might show up again?"

That brought George's head up. "Proof you're the New Girl. Nobody ever looks forward to seeing Adrienne. Except me, sometimes, and I'm . . ." He shrugged. He didn't need to finish. *I'm a sociopath. I feel nothing, but live for pleasure. People are objects. I am the center of the universe. And the center of the universe really hates skinheads, for reasons I will never discuss. There is no room for skinheads in* my *universe.*

Sometimes George reminded me of that funny guy from *Braveheart,* the one they all thought was crazy and who claimed Ireland was "his" island. "My island. Yup." "I'm the most wanted man on my island, except I'm not on my island, of course." "It's mine!" Like that.

"I'm looking forward to seeing Shiro later." Emma Jan was still talking, which, if I didn't think she was such a weirdo, normally wouldn't bother me. "Not that I don't like spending time with you," she added hastily, seeing my expression, "but Shiro and I had *such* a fun dinner. What with all the competitive betting and shouting. And tonight's the range! Sorry about the upcoming overused word, but I'm psyched. I'm . . . I'm so psyched it's awesome. It's totally, totally . . . give me some more eighties slang."

I rolled my eyes. "Emma Jan . . ."

"I'm new; I don't really know anybody up here. We couldn't believe it . . . we thought we'd been only talking for about half an hour, but it was past eleven! Did you try the leftovers? She said she was bringing home the doggie bag for you."

So she *was* Shiro's mystery date!

Ah. A glamorous evening out for Shiro, dog-rescuing antics for Adrienne, and I had meetings. And, probably, dog poop to clean up. Of the three of us, I was the one who'd clearly lost a bet with God. And he was a vindictive entity if there ever was one.

"Just don't be upset if she can't make it to the . . . where'd you say you were going?"

"The gun range."

"Right, for your little contest." Hmph. A perfect date for Shiro, unless she stumbled across a combat dojo and took on all comers. She was scary-accurate with a gun. With anything.

Michaela stalked past us carrying a stack of files and gripping the handle of a cleaver in the other, so much so that I could see how white her knuckles were. *Wüsthof,* I thought. *Maybe Shun.* She was a huge knife snob. She was into knives the way some people were into antiques, or breathing.

"Cadence, go talk to Gallo and then get back as quick as you can. When you're back, meet me in my other office. JBJ briefing. Go," she ordered, and I heard and obeyed.

It . . . it was wrong that I was so interesting in seeing Dr. Gallo again, wasn't it?

It's for the job, dummy, I reassured myself. And I was sprinting through the building toward the parking garage for the job. Yep.

Sure.

chapter thirty-six

"Official capacity?"

"Yes, well . . . I couldn't really get into it at the time." I was once again hooked up to another machine designed to deprive me of my bodily fluids. I reasoned that I might as well donate while I was here, and let Shiro whine about it as much as she liked. They were *my* platelets, drat it all. "Stuff about the case . . . we're keeping the media out of it as much as we can . . . and confidentiality issues . . ."

"Not much confidentially anymore," Dr. Gallo said sorrowfully. He was dressed yet again in scrubs that were so soft they were almost tattered. When he frowned, as he was now, the planes of his face really stood out. Was there an American Indian somewhere in the family woodpile? He was lean, but not geek-skinny. I'd never seen cheekbones you could cut yourself on, on a *guy*. And I had the feeling the small laugh lines near his eyes were stress lines, or grief lines. It made me want to fix him a meal and offer him a shoulder to cry on. Or a mouth to— Whoa. Whoa! I was happily involved with Little De—uh, Patrick. I *had* a boyfriend.

Was that it? Was I so unused to having a serious relationship that I was compelled to smash it once I'd had it? Or was I so sure

I'd be dumped any second I was always on the prowl for a new guy? Shiro would say it was pathetic, that both reasons were pathetic, and she'd be right.

"Pathetic!" I said aloud, apropos to nothing, and bless his heart, Dr. Gallo didn't so much as raise his black eyebrows.

The donating area was almost deserted except for another patient across the room, donating whole blood and chatting with her nurse. She'd been tucked in with a couple of Red Cross blankets. Oooh, lucky girl, I could feel 'em now. They kept them in a special dryer, so the blankets were always piping warm and snuggly. Donating blood was the closest I ever got to being tucked in by a mom.

Ohhhhh, boy. I just heard that. I mean, *really* heard that. Behold, my sinister motive for selflessly donating blood all these years: because I missed my mommy! As Adrienne would say, "The wheels on the bus go boo fucking hoo." Then she'd find a bus. Then she'd blow it up. Then I'd get sued by the bus company. Round and round, my big flabby tuchus.

I'd trailed after the doc and gotten settled for yet another donation . . . but I wasn't taking any warm blankets *this* time, thank you very much! They weren't going to trick me with their fake mothering and soft snuggly blankets and warm chocolate chip cookies that they pretended were homemade but which anyone dating a baker knew were *store bought*. Fascists.

Dr. Gallo and I had relative privacy—as much as anyone could have, I s'pose—so while I donated and fumed, I also bugged the poor guy.

"Here comes a dim one," I said in an apologetic tone, "but how's your family taking it?"

"They've turned into total fucking basket cases, that's how." His black eyes were narrow slits of dark fury. You know how some people are like oatmeal? They take a long time to boil over but when they do, it's a big old mess? Dr. Gallo was the opposite of that. On short acquaintance, he seemed like one of those people who always had a reservoir of rage to draw on. I grew up with one; I know of what I speak. "They've lost it in pretty much every way possible: emotionally, financially, religiously . . . their world turned to shit in half a second. Their world turned to shit when they were looking away—just for a few hours. They took their eyes off their boy for a few hours. And why not? He was fourteen, not two. And now they have to live with that. They also have to live with my nephew's death." He blinked, and seemed to really see me for the first time. "I don't usually drop the F-bomb with patients."

"I'm an FBI agent."

"Good."

"I'm so s—"

Dr. Gallo stepped on my platitude. "They're taking pills to wake up and more pills to go down. They're drinking to forget and forgetting to drink. They are, to sum up, as dead as my poor nephew . . . they just don't have the sense to find a goddamned cemetery plot to nap in for the rest of their miserable fucking lives."

I couldn't think of a thing except, "I'm so sorry."

"Me, too. Sorry about the language, again. None of this is your fault. I'm . . . I'm kind of relieved to hear you guys are still working the case."

I hid my smile. Dr. Gallo had watched too many episodes of *Law & Order.* Nobody in the biz said "working the case." We also didn't talk about "collaring perps," or "taking the death penalty off the table."

"Of course we are! Shame on you for thinking otherwise, Dr. Gallo. We are working the heck out of your nephew's case. We are working that case morning, noon, and night. Dr. Gallo, believe me—"

"Max."

"Ah . . . yes. Max." Mmmmm . . . Max! Mad Max? Maximum damage? (I should have definitely been paying more attention to this interview.) I won't deny it; I really liked his name. Max Gallo! He sounded like a cartoon superhero. Or a real-life underwear model. "We want this guy, Dr. G— Max. We want him so bad—we want him *so* bad." Just the thought of what Shiro daily fantasized about doing to JBK once we got him was enough to make me run for a toilet, both hands clapped over my mouth. "We want him almost as badly as you do."

He nodded and sat on the bed across from me. "So what can I tell you?"

Little enough, as it turned out. His nephew, Chris Glazier, had been alone in the house. His sister and brother-in-law had found their son's body when they returned from a fishing trip. They were now thoroughly addicted to Ambien, the sleeping pill, which seemed like a thoroughly sensible response.

Their son had been beaten to death. They wished it had been them. They went over everything in their minds again and again and again. They've thought up a dozen different scenarios where their son wasn't murdered. They've come up with a hundred revenge fantasies about their son's killer. They wished it had been them, oh God, they wished it had been them.

Dear God: You're fired. Sincerely, the Glaziers.

The usual, in other words. His family was going through the usual. It was almost textbook, and who wanted to hear that about their grieving process? *So sorry, and did you know what you're feeling is so common it's been documented all over the world?*

"You said you were glad to hear we were still working the case. Does that mean you were going to try and do some detective work yourself?"

"It meant I was going to try and find the guy and then shoot him in the fucking face," Dr. Gallo replied crisply.

He looked capable of it. Of that, and more. His fists were clenched and the veins in his arms stood out like garter snakes. His eyes were gleaming with . . . with terrible, wonderful things. Yes indeed, "capable" was putting it mildly. And why was that turning me on? There was no room for horniness in an FBI interrogation. Or while I was donating platelets.

Still: the question. Why *was* that turning me on? Because I was still a virgin, so all sorts of odd conversations turned me on? Because I couldn't picture safe, sane Patrick doing such a thing? Sick, sick, sick!

"Sorry again about the language."

"Don't be sorry. *You* don't have anything to apologize for, unless it's loving your family and wanting to take away their pain. And we're on it, Dr. Gallo, my partner and I are on it until JBK is dead, or in custody, or dead."

"Good. Because so am I." He stuck out his hand. We shook. I could feel his strength of purpose; I could feel his anger—it practically slammed up into my arm from his. I wasn't quite sure what we were shaking on, but it seemed the thing to do. And I could always be counted on for stepping up and taking care of the right thing. You know, when I was in the driver's seat.

And I was a bad enough person to be glad Dr. Gallo's thoughts were only of his slain nephew, and not of my chart and (on paper, at least) spotty medical history. I'd dodged crucial questions . . . again.

Sick, sick, sick!

Beyond the usual, even.

chapter thirty-seven

I had nothing to show for my meeting with Dr. Gallo except inappropriate tingling. Which I was going to try to keep out of my report. Meanwhile, I'd raced back to BOFFO just in time for Michaela to spot me (uncanny how she always showed up wherever we were . . . she must have cameras stashed everywhere, including our molars), stick one of her Wüstofs back in its sheath on her hip (which did not and never would go with her very pretty suit), and bark, "My other office. JBJ briefing. Five minutes."

"Always a pleasure, Michaela!" I called after her, panting only a little. At least I wasn't late for the briefing. That was something, right?

"Gulp."

I turned to Emma Jan, who'd been standing by our desks for who knew how long. "Did you just say 'gulp'? Instead of actually gulping? Why would you do that?" Unspoken: *You are very weird, and I'm just not warming up to you. Also, Shiro only likes you because you can give her a challenge. Also: I'm just not warming up to you.*

"What the hell was *that* all about?" Emma Jan was staring after our boss with a combination of wariness and interest. "Does she just . . . just walk around up here carrying huge knives?"

"No," I said, stung into defending Michaela. "Sometimes she carries paring knives."

"And you don't find that extremely weird?"

"Look where you are, Emma Jan," I said patiently. I watched her glance around the large cubicle-filled room. A room that looked like any office in any city, except . . .

Brian was acting out his last T-group session, which appeared to have gotten violent, due to the stabbing motions he was making, and the *Psycho* squeal: "Ree-ree-ree! Ree-ree-ree! So then she said, 'Stop bleeding all over my linen placemats!' And I said, 'You're the one who hit me in the first place,' and she said—"

Sara was working on her laptop from underneath her desk. She occasionally thought the fluorescent lighting was shooting rays into her brain.

Don't judge: sometimes I wondered about that, too, with all the weird things that happened at work. She offered to make me a tinfoil hat, but Shiro and Adrienne would never have let me live it down. I won't deny being tempted, though . . . nope. Never knock the healing power of shiny hats.

Karen was handing out paperwork, resplendent in her flannel pajamas (pink background, with poodles).

And let's not forget George's tie *du jour*: a tasteful piece with broken-winged birds against a lime green background.

Taken separately, maybe not so unusual (okay, except for Sara), but as a whole . . . yeah.

"Why would Michaela bring a knife to a meeting?"

"Depends on the meeting. I know she's been working on the budget with a bunch of the suits."

"Why would Michaela bring a knife to a budget meeting?" Emma Jan was like a dog with a bone. Let it go, woman! Don't question; it takes longer.

"Why *wouldn't* she bring a knife to a budget meeting?"

Emma Jan giggled.

"Hi, Emma Jan. Hi, Cadence. How's it going?"

Pam Weinberg, my boss's administrative assistant, was handing out the mail. That wasn't her usual job; someone must have called in sick, or been carted off for a Thorazine injection.

"Good, Pam. How's by you?"

"SSDD." She handed out a small pile of mail. Emma Jan was trying, and failing, not to stare. I knew what the problem was. So did Pam.

"You're wondering how old I am," she said, handing Emma Jan some memos.

"Well . . . it's just . . . you look . . ."

"Seventeen."

Her eyes widened. "Our boss's right-hand woman isn't a legal adult? How does *that* work? Aren't there child labor laws in this state? Did you come as an intern and they just never let you leave?"

"Long story, and I come off really emancipated in it. You know about the briefing in . . ." She glanced at the clock on the wall in front of us. ". . . three minutes?"

"Yeah, thanks, Pam."

We watched her walk off. I understood Emma Jan's confusion. In a building filled with mysterious government operatives, Eyes Only/Classified documents, and doctor/patient privilege, the biggest puzzle was how seventeen-year-old Pam Weinberg not only worked sixty hours a week, but no one ever heard a peep from family members or the foster care system (most of us didn't even know if she had family or not, though, of course, Michaela did). I didn't know if it was a good thing that no one seemed to notice she was missing, or a bad thing.

I didn't even want to *think* about the circumstances that landed her in the middle of the FBI's very own cuckoo's nest.

Pam knew everything, too. It was uncanny and scary. She always knew who was in, who was sick, who was faking sick, who was foaming at the mouth, who was late, who was early, who was behind on their payroll sheets, who blew off their weekly shrink session, and who had moved into the waiting room and secretly brushed their teeth in Michaela's private bathroom.

I only had to live there for a few days, so don't judge. It was Adrienne's fault, anyway.

So anyway, Pam almost never left the office. Which suited her fine . . . and us, too. She also typed 140 wpm, never had to be told something twice, kept Michaela's staggering schedule updated, knew who'd been naughty and who'd been nice, and only needed about four hours of sleep a night (I was soooo jealous of that one). In other words, she was the perfect palace guard. The fact that she wasn't yet a legal adult was the least important thing about her.

"Just think, in a couple of months this will all seem totally normal to you."

Emma Jan didn't look especially soothed. "Then God help me."

"God's out sick."

I looked down at my mail. Memo, memo, sale at Staples (why was I on their mailing list at all?), and a plain white #10 business envelope. It had a number three where the return address should have been. And it was addressed to me.

And Shiro.

And Adrienne.

chapter thirty-eight

Cadence had, quite rightly, left this mess for me.

Could it be a hoax? Or was it a missive, doubtless stuffed with anthrax, from the remaining members of the ThreeFer triplets? Since they had nearly killed us, I did not blame Cadence for fleeing the premises.

"George," I said.

"Busy," he replied. "I gotta bid on this or eBay's gonna let somebody else have it."

I did not want to know what had George so enchanted he'd barely spoken. "George!"

"Whaaaat?" He looked up and saw I was pulling on a pair of evidence-handling gloves (we kept several pairs in our desks). "Wow. That's never a good sign with you, Shiro. Unless you're up for some really sick sexual shenanigans. Or, wait. Is that dumb dog Adrienne kidnapped on her way? If that animal drops *one load* near my workspace, I'll—"

"Take a look," I invited, snapping first the right, then the left glove in place.

He ambled around to my desk and looked down at the envelope.

"Baaaad shit," was his very accurate comment. "You think it's from them?"

"Them" being Tracy Carr and Jeremy Scherzo, two-thirds of the ThreeFer Killer, triplet serial killers who had used the Cities as their own private killing pen. Opus, the third one, had been fatally shot by Michaela. They left their slow-witted brother to certain death while they fled to save their unworthy hides. They were quite high on the FBI's Most Wanted list—spots one and two, respectively.

And on my list, too.

I spent too much of my time irritated with Adrienne and Cadence, there was no doubt.

But I would *never* abandon them.

That made me think of Dr. Gallo, oddly. I knew what he had told Cadence. I could understand the rage he was keeping locked down. I will not deny it made me even more curious. There was something compelling about the new physician in town; he seemed to walk around with his own internal temperature gauge always on simmer and, now and again, on boil. Ummm. It might be something to see if he truly let go, if he . . .

For shame. Thinking about a man when I had work to do. So: enough with the distracted musings about Dr. Max Gallo. Back to business.

Great name. Max Gallo. Like something out of an Ian Fleming novel.

I picked up the letter, felt it carefully—no watch battery lumps, no gritty powder—and then noticed Agent Thyme for the first time. "Good morning." It *was* morning, correct? "Nice to see you again."

"Whoa," George said. To Thyme: "She never does small talk."

"You owe me money."

"See?" he cried triumphantly, pointing at me.

Emma Jan glared. "Best two out of three, you said. We can settle it at the range, you said."

"And we will." I felt the envelope around the edges. Still good. "We absolutely will. And you will owe me still more money. Fret not. I take personal checks."

"Cadence thought the killers sent that letter?" Emma Jan was looking from me to George to me, not nearly as interested in her debts as in our mail. "So she . . . disappeared?"

"But luckily, Shiro is here to save the day." He could not finish the sentence without rolling his eyes.

"But how'd you know it was Shiro?"

"Shiro stands tall and her babbling tends to be more clipped. And she doesn't use near as many contractions. Cadence slouches, like she's trying to hide in her own skin. Which I guess she does."

"That was almost profound," I said. It was precisely times like these that made it impossible to simply dismiss George as a sociopath. I would almost prefer it if he was an ass 100 percent of the time.

"Don't tell anyone."

"You're not opening that," Thyme protested, seeing me prepare to do so.

"The probability of it being safe for me to handle is quite high. It is too small and thin for any kind of charge. No C-4 sheet. And every piece of mail that comes into this building is routinely scanned. You may also recall that the post office irradiates all mail addressed to government offices, and has since the anthrax scare.

"Finally, these people are smart. They will have left no DNA or prints. They would not make the mistake of licking the envelope flap or mailing it from a city they were anywhere near. They're likely using a mail service. We won't find anything, and what they've written for us could be of critical import."

"In other words," George said with a grin, "she knows she's not supposed to, but she's gonna anyway." His green eyes sparkled. George loved trouble, especially when someone else was going to get into it. "Here we go, ladies! Yee-haw!"

"Well put."

"Can I have your gun after Michaela fires you?"

"Be quiet." I carefully slit the envelope and pulled out a single sheet of paper.

Dearest Cadence, Shiro, and Adrienne,

How we have missed you! Life is simply not the same. We apologize for having to leave the party so soon this past summer; terribly rude.

You may recall that through your actions, you created a vacancy in our family. After giving it some thought, we have decided you are responsible for filling it. Any one of you will do. Or all of you! My. Wouldn't that be an embarrassment of riches?

We are thrilled to see you working the June Boys Jobs; you do have experience in these matters . . . need we remind you just what kind? But we disapprove of JBK's agenda; our murders were puzzle pieces you eventually put together. JBK's murders are simply fuel for a blood-hungry malcontent.

We want only your happiness, ladies, and thus would like you to keep in mind that the trite clichés about the racial demographics of serial killers are not always cold truth.

If you don't believe us, then look at the three of us! Oh. Excuse us. The two of us.

Stay in touch, won't you, dears?
Because we intend to.

With all our love and respect,

Two of the ThreeFer

chapter thirty-nine

"We have a break, I think." Agent Thyme, George, and I had reported to her other office for the JBJ briefing.

"This is her other office?" Agent Thyme seemed bewildered to see we were all assembled in the department kitchen. We were perched on bar stools in front of the sizable granite-covered kitchen island, while on the other side Michaela was chopping a peeled banana.

"Fruit salad," she said, though no one asked. "I see it's Shiro and not Cadence, which can only mean something's happened." She scraped banana bits off her knife and into a large red bowl big enough to hold a chicken. "What break?"

I held up the letter for her to read. No use getting banana smeared on it.

"It doesn't *look* like it's been to the lab and back," was her first comment. I almost smiled. I admired our boss quite a bit; she was the epitome of cool control. Most supervisors would have gone the "Holy shit!" route.

"I felt I should bring it to you immediately."

It didn't work; she arched a silver brow at me as I carefully put the letter down on a clean stretch of counter. "Indeed. After you opened it and read it."

"Well. Yes."

Michaela glanced at the letter again, then went to the large stainless-steel fridge and withdrew two zucchinis. She rinsed them in the large industrial sink (also stainless steel), then began slicing them. She was not a timid slicer: *Thwack! Thwack! Thwackthwackthwack!* "It has the ring of authenticity."

"I thought so, too."

"A pity they're still fixated on you, but not entirely unexpected." *Thwackthwackthwack!*

"No." Goodness. For Michaela, that was warm concern. Wait until I thoroughly defeated Agent Thyme at the range, I thought. Michaela would enjoy my triumph.

For a moment, I was deeply confused. Why . . . why had I thought that? Why did I want to prove something to Michaela? And at the new agent's expense?

Ye gods. Cadence couldn't stop mooning over the darkly irked Dr. Gallo (he was, I grant you, rather moon-able), and I was plotting to bring our boss a tale of victory, like a cat takes a dead rat to her owners. One would think Michaela was some sort of—ha, ha—mother figure to me. Ha ha!

I probably needed more sleep.

"But why didn't they send you something, too, Michaela?"

We were still getting used to having Agent Thyme in our midst, so for a few seconds nobody realized what a relevant question it was, or that she had even spoken. Usually, when a new employee had their first meeting in Michaela's other office, they needed several minutes to take in the large, gleaming, restaurant-size (and quality) kitchen.

Thyme caught on fast. It appeared that if reflective surfaces were not involved, she was on her game.

"Sorry, what?" Michaela asked. "I didn't catch that."

I looked at Agent Thyme. Her eyes were so wide they showed whites all around, like a horse about to flee fire. Tremendous fear, then. Or tremendous excitement. Given our line of work, I was betting on the latter.

"I mean . . ." She coughed, realizing she had the full attention of all three of us. "Michaela shot their brother. They're down to two because of you." Pointing to Michaela. "Not you." Pointing to me/us. "I read up on the case before my transfer. Which reminds me, I have many, many questions for you guys."

"Later."

"Yeah, I agree, Shiro. Just so you know, 'later' doesn't mean 'never bring it up again' in my vocab. But like I was saying, why didn't they send something to Michaela, too?"

"Because they don't think they're in love with me," she replied. "Though I doubt such damaged people have any idea what love *is*."

"Awww," George said, smiling. "Who couldn't love you, Boss? Your hair is so silver. And your sneakers are so white!"

She pointed the tip of her very sharp knife at his left eye. "Stow it, Pinkman, or I'll have you shot."

I considered taking offense at her statement about damaged people and love. Everyone in this room was deeply, deeply damaged. But I knew about love. I loved . . .

Patrick? Yes. I . . . think so.

I loved that he loved me. Was that the same thing? I did not know, and was too proud to ask.

Focus, Shiro.

"Even though Michaela performed the coup de grâce, I can assure you the two of the three hold my sisters and me responsible."

"Because they killed all those people, all those sets of three, to get your attention? So you'd stay with them. All of you, I mean."

"Correct." Michaela had dumped the sliced zucchini into a different bowl. "Not that Shiro, Cadence, or Adrienne should blame themselves for the murders, or Opus's death."

"Worry not," I replied. "We don't."

"No, but they should blame themselves for my kidnapping!" George bitched.

"We decline," I said, smiling. "Your own fault for letting psychotics get the drop on you."

"Must have been a Thursday," he mumbled.

"Riiight, I remember reading about that," Thyme said. "They stuck you in a closet, and you shit your pants so you'd be found, only . . ."

"Only I'm surrounded by dumbasses so my brilliant plan didn't work. At all! Those slacks were ruined. My dry cleaner actually cried, you believe that? *Cried.* The man's been cleaning unspeakable stains out of my work clothes for years, but that . . . it broke him, the poor bastard." He checked himself, then added, "How many times did you read that fucking file?"

"Oh, lots. So we think the note is real," Thyme said.

"What 'we,' New Girl?" George was getting whiny again. Not a pleasant harbinger for the rest of the meeting.

"Yes, Agent Thyme, we do. We'll have it analyzed, of course. But I am proceeding under the assumption it's genuine." Michaela pointed her knife at me. "You need some careful habits when you're not here."

"Agreed."

"If it's real, then, how did they know we're working the JBJ killer?" Thyme asked. If they came for us, I hoped it would be while

I was driving the body. Cadence was *not* up to that confrontation. "How could they know that?"

"Well," I said gloomily, "they're brilliant. That's one unfortunate happenstance."

"The three of them were brilliant," Thyme corrected. "And then there were two. When it was all three, it was almost like the triplets had a sort of . . . of . . . hive mind. I know how it sounds," she added hastily, "and of course it's not an actual, y'know, 'hive mind.' But they were pretty formidable *then*. How about now?"

"You saw the note. They know things they have no business knowing." I paused. "George had a good question."

"Goody," he grumped.

"How many times *did* you read that fucking file?"

Thyme laughed. "Lots and lots. My only alternative was the new Stephen King book, and he's been phoning it in since he kicked the coke and the booze."

"Ouch," Michaela said mildly. "We have a book critic."

"So—and tell me if I've got this wrong—Opus was the idiot savant—"

Now Michaela's knife was pointing at Thyme's face. "Savantism. You need to be up on all your politically correct terms for various mental and psychological malfunctions if you want to work here, Thyme."

"Yes, ma'am," she replied in a tone of great respect. Since the tip of the knife was less than two inches from her nose, I was certain she meant it. She need not have worried. Michaela hardly ever cut *people*. "Okay, so . . . Opus was the one who had savantism. He couldn't tell you what he had for breakfast, but he could add a stack of six-digit numbers in his head in all of four seconds." Thyme shook her head. "That's amazing. I need a calculator to add double numbers, for heaven's sake."

"What was it Treffort said? The researcher? 'Their minds were deep, but narrow.'" I must admit, I loved the elegance of that explanation. "Tracy, the middle triplet, has Asperger's syndrome. Same family of disorder."

"Correct." Michaela had pulled a celery bunch (Ugh! As my hero, Newman, would have said on *Seinfeld*, "Vile weed!") from the fridge and was now rinsing it. Soon the thwacks would begin again. "A mild form of autism. But unlike autism, the person in question retains linguistic development."

"They just absolutely suck when it comes to reading social cues," George added. He was steadily munching on the bananas our supervisor had chopped. I thought he was insane to put his hand so close to that knife every time he reached into the bowl, but it was not my concern.

"Oh, 'they' do, do they?"

Munch, munch. "Remember Jamison? Photographic memory, but he had to learn that when someone does this . . ." He showed us a ferocious smile, all teeth and malice and mashed banana. ". . . it means they are happy, it's a smile. And when someone does this . . ." His scowl would have made a pregnant woman miscarry. "It's a frown, it means they're mad or sad or both. He had to be taught stuff that most people suck in with breast milk or formula or whatever-the-hell."

"Thank you so much for Asperger's 101. The third triplet, Jeremy, had a stutter. But there was nothing wrong with his mind."

"Except for the whole serial killing issue," I prompted.

She shrugged. Now she was pulling the stalks of celery apart, the better to slice you with, my dear. "Correct. Yes, losing a third of their little . . . 'hive mind,' did you call it?" At Thyme's nod, she continued. "It's as good a term as any. So they're damaged, certainly. But by no means neutered. They were all brilliant in their own way, and there's still two of them. Jeremy and Tracy . . ." Michaela paused, then started thwacking the celery. "They'll be formidable."

"So maybe they hacked into the JBJ file? Did Opus have clearance?"

"No, he was the janitor. Uh, custodial engineer." I hid a smile; Michaela normally did not make PC slips like that. "He never had clearance."

"Still. They know about it, which is a good trick given how the press has stayed out of it, more or less. And even if it had been in the press, how could they know Shiro would be working it?"

"That," Michaela said, "is a wonderful question. One I shall ponder for some time, you can be sure of that."

I thought about it. It seemed to me there was a pretty logical explanation . . . I could almost feel it. It was on the tip of my brain.

"I need to think about this," I told them, and left.

chapter forty

I blinked and saw I was in Michaela's other office and, judging from the mounds of chopped fruit and vegetables, had been there about twenty minutes.

"Okay. What'd I miss?"

"Nothing." George's voice was muffled; he appeared to be devouring slices of banana as fast as Michaela had chopped them. Gross. "A big fat pile of nothing, that's what you missed."

"May I see the note?" I knew, *knew* Shiro would have opened it. What FBI procedure? Yeah, right. For someone who insists everyone should obey rules, she flouted them an awful lot.

"You won't liiiiiiike it," George warned with a mouthful of mush.

"I didn't like it before the envelope was opened." I read it—I was still wearing Shiro's evidence gloves—then carefully put it back down. Even with gloves, my fingers felt dirty after handling it. Greasy, even. You could pretty much feel the insanity crawling off the page. "Gross. And how do they know we're working JBJ?"

"That's what we're trying to figure out. It's why you're . . . back? Is that the right word, Cadence?" Emma Jan peered at me. "You're back?"

"I'm back. And not liking it much, either." I didn't like Emma Jan's too-interested expression. I wondered if she looked at Shiro like that . . . like she was an interesting and slightly yucky lab experiment. "Great, they're still fixated on us."

"You cannot be that surprised," Michaela said mildly. She was chopping celery . . . yum! Nothing better than ants on a log . . . celery sticks smeared with peanut butter and then sprinkled with raisins. Mmmm . . . ants on a log . . . when *was* lunch, anyway? Had I skipped it? Had I been someone else?

"Surprised, no. But I had hopes that they'd turn themselves in or whatever."

George laughed at me.

"Fine, call me naive."

"Naive! Naive!"

I glared, for all the good it would do, which was none. "A girl can dream." I, for example, dreamed of the day George would become a *real* boy. Oh, Blue Fairy, why have you forsaken BOFFO?

"Shiro and I had a bet . . . she calculated there was a better than forty percent chance they'd kill themselves."

I didn't say anything. I was too grossed out. Shiro had bet. . . ? Had hoped, even? Ugh! Never. I'd never wish suicide on anyone. I didn't like the remaining two of the trinity, but I didn't wish *that* on anybody.

And it doesn't have a dang thing to do with my mother.

It didn't!

"Assuming Tracy and Jeremy know their stuff, did they actually give us a worthwhile clue?" I asked.

"Clue? Clue!" George hooted. "Oh my God, nobody says 'clue' anymore! Where's your Sherlock hat and meerschaum pipe, Sherlock? Clue. Jesus."

Emma Jan picked up the hateful, hateful letter and read aloud: " 'We are thrilled to see you working the June Boys Jobs; you do have experience in these matters . . . need we remind you just what kind?' "

"Why," George demanded, "are you reading that to us?"

She ignored him and continued (she was definitely a fast learner . . . too bad I just couldn't warm up to her):

" 'But we disapprove of JBK's agenda; our murders were puzzle pieces you eventually put together. JBK's murders are simply fuel for a blood-hungry malcontent.' "

"Seriously. We all read this note, more than once, mere minutes ago."

" 'We want only your happiness, ladies, and thus would like you to keep in mind that the trite clichés about the racial demographics of serial killers are not always cold truth.' "

"Stop it!" he screamed. *Huge* pet peeve of his. He went to too many conferences and lectures where the only instructing was the teacher reading aloud the handouts he'd just given anyone. That sort of thing left George in a foul mood for days. "Will you *stop reading that*?"

" 'If you don't believe us, then look at the three of us! Oh. Excuse us. The two of us.' "

"Don't read the rest," I begged. Like I needed to hear it out loud in addition to it being burned into my brain. "What's your point?"

Emma Jan looked up. " 'Trite clichés.' What's that mean? And it's in the same sentence as 'racial demographics.' Y'know, in addition to me being a proud Black gal with the stereotypical awesome ass, I'm also under psychiatric care, which counts as a disability. I'm a two-fer for the FBI. It's why I'm even in this room right now."

"Your point?" Michaela was steadily whittling her way through all the celery.

"My point is, racial demographics are all over the place. Including figuring out who serial killers are. Trite clichés . . ."

"Aren't they all by definition trite?" George had finally tired of banana munching, and had his elbows on the counter, with his chin propped in his hands.

"Well. The trite clichés about serial killers are . . . I'm sure we can all rattle them off. First off, by definition a serial killer is defined by having killed three or more people."

I nodded. "Sure. Down to the basics, then. Uh . . . they usually kill for psychological gratification—"

"Not all the time," George interrupted.

"Yeah, I know. Thus the word 'usually.'" But he was right, that was a slippery one and didn't know if it would count as a trite cliché. Plenty of serial killers did away with strangers and loved ones for money. Plenty of serial killers killed to protect themselves, or a secret they didn't want to get out. "You're thinking John List?"

List was a so-charming fellow who murdered his wife, his mom, and all three of his kids. The rock-solid reason? He didn't want them to find out he'd lost his job. In his mind, there were two choices: come clean, or kill everyone.

Even after years of seeing this and finding this and hearing about this and reading about this and talking about this and thinking about this, I was always, *always* mystified by it. I literally couldn't hurt a fly (it's no more trouble to shoo them out a window than swat them). But these guys . . . they weren't human. They just *looked* human.

"I was thinking of Diane Downs. Remember? Shot all three of her kids because her boyfriend, who was married, didn't want to be a dad. Slut! Anyway, the middle kid died, the youngest and oldest survived."

"Bushy-haired stranger," Emma Jan offered.

"Yeah, she claimed a bushy-haired stranger did it." George rolled his eyes. "I guess she thought the one-armed man theory was played."

"But she only killed one person, not three. How about the Philadelphia Poison Ring?"

Michaela nodded. "Excellent example. One hundred fourteen poison-murders. All for profit." Back she went to the fridge. Out came English cucumbers, the really long skinny ones.

"Okay, so, back to trite clichés. Serial killers tend to have trouble holding jobs."

We nodded. Michaela chopped.

"The MacDonald triad," I suggested. "That's pretty classic. Maybe even trite?" Sociopaths were commonly believed to have indulged in three particular behaviors as kids: they liked to torture animals, they liked to set fires, and they wet their beds for years, long past the age of five (I had no idea if they liked it or not).

Suddenly, the three of us were very careful not to make eye contract with George.

"I can read all of your minds, you worthless jerks," he sighed. "Hey, the dog attacked *me*, okay?"

"*All* the dogs?" Michaela asked slyly. Which was great, because she was the only person (except maybe for Shiro) who could have gotten away with that. I knew George really, really wanted to say or do something to her. I also knew he didn't dare.

"Background of abuse as children," Emma Jan said. "And that sure seemed to be the case for the ThreeFer Killers."

"How many times did you read that fucking—never mind, I

don't care. And I think you're right. Big clue number one being, there isn't a single family member still alive who could give us any good background stuff on those three freaks." George was clearly relieved to be away from the bed-wetting chat. "Remember that picture you talked about?"

Unfortunately, yes. It was when we thought Tracy was a victim instead of one of the killers. She'd shown me a picture of herself with her two brothers, a simple four-by-six-inch snapshot, nothing out of the ordinary, nothing especially special, good, fine, terrific.

That picture *still* gave me the creeps, and I'd never been able to put my finger on why. I think . . . I think it was the house. It wasn't behind the triplets as background so much as it lurked behind them. The triplets had all looked too pale and too thin; I'd wondered at the time if it had been some sort of hereditary vitamin deficiency. Knowing what (little) we know now, I had revised my thinking.

I think they had a vitamin deficiency, sure. Because among other abuses, their family didn't feed them.

"Bullied as children. That's a good one." George looked down at the counter. "Believe me. That's a really good one."

Darn it to heck! It was so annoying when George showed the abused, scrawny, lonesome little boy he'd once been, as opposed to the well-muscled, black-belted psycho he was now.

"With Opus as an id—as someone with savantism, and another brother who stuttered, and the sister with Asperger's . . . oh, yeah. They were bullied all right. Count on it."

"None of this is helping us with JBK," Michaela pointed out. She had finished the cukes, gone to the bread drawer, and hauled out three French baguettes, each one over two feet long. "Though I won't deny it has been one of the more interesting chats I've had this week."

"They tend to be men. White men."

"Hey!" George said to Emma Jan in a tone of pure outrage. "We can't help it if we like running the world."

"Except you don't anymore," I said. "I'm guessing you didn't vote for Obama?"

"Let's not get into *that* again," Michaela said firmly, sawing at the first loaf with a big shiny bread knife (the other one was now in the sink, where she would later wash it lovingly by hand). Ah! It was her newest toy, her pride and joy, the Shun classic nine-inch bread knife.

"They tend to kill in their own racial group: white guys kill white guys or white women. Ted Bundy, Dahmer, Robert Hansen . . . white guys killing white guys and gals. And Anthony Sowell, Lonnie Franklin—"

"The Grim Sleeper!" George chortled. "Don'cha love it?"

"Yeah, it's swell." After giving George an odd look (no worries; he was used to it) Emma Jan continued. "And Wayne Williams . . . black guys who killed black."

"So?"

"So, we're assuming JBK is a white guy, based on racial demographics and trite clichés. What if JBK isn't a white guy? Maybe that's what two of the ThreeFer was trying to tell us?"

Michaela's eyebrows arched, disappearing beneath her silver bangs. "Hmmmm." She sawed more bread. "Hmmm."

George had straightened up. "Now *that's* interesting. JBK's killing white teenage boys. Maybe we should be looking into black guys. Or gals, as New Girl puts it."

If it was true, our investigation would have to go in an all-new direction. Since we didn't have bubkes going on the old direction, I was all for it.

I wasn't sure what I thought about Tracy and Jeremy helping us, though. How embarrassing!

Then I remembered BOFFO's motto: Set a thief to catch a thief, set a psycho to catch a psycho. Who'd know more about a psycho than two other psychos?

Sometimes I hated my job.

chapter forty-one

So back to the drawing board we went. Yippee. But this time we spread the net a little wider than white males.

In fact, we followed TwoFer's advice and looked only at African Americans, male and female. This was not racial profiling! And even if it was, I'm going to take more classes!

Ahem. Anyway. The new software system, HOAP—Homicide Apprehension and Prevention—started munching through the data, and I wasn't the only one in the office giving in to the urge to cross their fingers.

HOAP was brand-new—in fact, it was *brand* brand-new. BOFFO was testing it; I didn't even know if Michaela's bosses knew about it yet.

HOAP was designed by Paul Torn, one of BOFFO's own. Nobody knew how he did it. Nobody knew why he did it. Nobody knew why it worked—or, at this early stage, if it reliably worked. In Paul's case, we let him have his head and stayed out of his way as much as possible.

Michaela had had a few big-time numbers-and-software geniuses look over his . . . algorithms? Is that what they were? Math and science were not my thing at all. Now, if you wanted something cross-stitched onto a hand towel, I was your girl.

Anyway, she showed the geniuses whatever they were, and let me tell you, those big-brained boys and girls would have had better luck trying to translate Klingon. Every one of them left the building with massive tension headaches. (Hmm. Maybe the fluorescent lighting *was* shooting rays into our brains to control us.)

"Oh, boy," George said. He, Emma Jan, and I were back in our corner of the office, our desks and chairs clustered together, the better to solve crime with, my dear. "Here comes Rainman."

"Stop that!" I hissed. Like most of his insults, "Rainman" was cruel and accurate.

"I don't know I don't know I don't know." Paul Torn, BOFFO's resident mad scientist, was pacing back and forth. We could only see him when he paced back out of the kitchen. Back, forth, back, forth. "I don't know I don't know the numbers are the wrong color is anyone else tasting blue right now?"

"Paul?"

"Oh, how are you, Cadence?" Paul brightened and hurried over. He was snapping his fingers in a complex and always-changing rhythm. His nail-bitten fingers were a blur. "Are you tasting blue?"

"No, Paul. I'm not a synesthete like you." Nobody was like Paul.

"Excuse me? Synesthete?" Emma Jan asked.

"What's this, Emma Jan?" George asked. "A BOFFO file you *haven't* memorized?"

"Shush!" I turned to Emma Jan. "People with synesthesia see numbers as colors."

"Not just colors not just colors not not not," Paul said.

"We'd have Paul here explain it to you," George said, "but it would take him about a week a week a week and a half and several tranquilizers."

My foot shot out, quite on its own, and nailed George on one of his tender shins. I had no idea I was going to do it until it was done. I was wearing flats. Flats with wonderfully pointy toes. Oh, Payless Shoes, you never, ever let me down.

"Aaaggghhh." Eyes rolling in agony, he bent and clutched his no-doubt-throbbing shin. "Oh, you hateful cow! They're gonna find pieces of you all along the bottom of the Mississippi."

I ignored his threat *du jour.* "They also feel numbers. To Paul, numbers have shapes and textures. He can do math at a level most people can't, because he perceives numbers in an entirely new—"

"And weird," George groaned, still rubbing his shin.

"—way," I finished. I looked up at him. And up. Paul could have easily played basketball. He was tall and skinny, with a wiry musculature that had taken more than one thug by surprise. With his dark skin, dark eyes, and old-fashioned horn-rimmed glasses, he looked like a nerd out of the 1950s, one who wasn't allowed to use the bathrooms for white people.

Because of how he looked, a certain, um, element, just couldn't resist trying to push him around. Because of what he was, he was used to it, and could handle himself with very little trouble. Paul had greatly enjoyed his self-defense lessons, claiming defensive strikes smelled like red.

Then he'd help himself to the now-unconscious thug's wallet and be enchanted by his driver's license ID number. Or, I guess, all the colors of the driver's license ID number that only he could see.

"Anyway, Paul invented HOAP. The software is pulling anything resembling *anything* for the JBJ killings, and we're having it only run African American suspects. The advantage is, the system will know which departments to query, even if it's looking for data from before their system went electronic. It's better at spotting patterns than a human could be, so it sees holes and knows where to look for the glue. Before, we'd get hung up if the info we needed predated the use of computers, but HOAP was designed specifically to get around that. We hope."

"Like VI-CAP?" Emma Jan asked.

"Better, I think. VI-CAP only knows what you tell it. HOAP can actually draw conclusions and think up probabilities."

"Great." George was deep in sulk mode by now. "Didn't we have this scene in all four *Terminator* movies? Pretty soon Paul's personal SKYNET is gonna wake up and nuke us all."

"Not without the codes and I wouldn't I wouldn't I wouldn't give HOAP those codes."

I froze. George froze. Emma Jan just looked amazed. "Uh, I was kind of kidding about the SKYNET thing," he said after a shocked moment, "but are you telling me it's an actual possibility?"

I was shaking my head and rummaging through my purse for gum, or Oreos, when I felt a paper cut and yanked my hand away with a startled hiss. I reached back in, carefully, and took out a Post-it note I had never seen before.

C-

I will need to discuss his nephew's murder with Dr. Gallo.

-S

Hmmm. Well, we were in a bit of a holding pattern just now, waiting for data. I suppose there was no time

chapter forty-two

like the present.

I zipped Cadence's purse shut and stood. Lounging around like iguanas sunning themselves on rocks was not productive. Speaking with Dr. Gallo, however, could be quite productive. I wondered how he would look at this time of the day. If he shaved daily or endured stubble. He was so darkly striking, he could pull off either look if he—

Darkly striking?

I need a nap. Possibly several.

Or perhaps, I merely need to have sex. Hmm. It *had* been a while. Unfortunately, this was no time to address the problem, so I resolved to put up with the inappropriate hormonal surges. Surges, I realized with no small relief, that had nothing to do with Max Gallo and everything to do with the fact that I hadn't had sex in . . . what year was it?

I left, ignoring George's and Agent Thyme's questions. Although George shrieking, "You don't fool me! That stick-in-the-ass stride is pure Shiro! You aren't Cadence!" almost made me smile.

* * *

I marched into the torture chamber staffed by Red Cross employees, looking for Dr. Gallo. A male nurse I did not know accosted me at the entrance.

"Adrienne, you bad girl, you know you can't donate again for a few more days. So, what? Slumming?"

I eyed the hirsute nurse, wondering if all that body hair kept him warm in winter. "I am not." No, I was not Adrienne, though I knew why I could not say so. And no. I was not . . . slumming. Still, it was galling to be called by the name of another. And no, I was not here for another depletion of my precious bodily fluids. How difficult could it be to synthesize blood? We could synthesize almost everything else. "Away from me, fiend. But first, tell me where Dr. Gallo is."

"You again." I turned and saw my desired prey. He had just popped out of his office and was shrugging into a beat-up motorcycle jacket and carrying an equally beat-up black motorcycle helmet in one hand. The jacket looked as though Gallo had worn it to a war. Possibly more than one. "Back to product-test the latest batch of oatmeal cookies?"

I shuddered. "Not even if you stuck a gun in my ear." I did not say that lightly. I had actually had a gun stuck in my ear. Ah, sweet Pampered Chef party memories . . . "If you attempt to foist a cookie on me I cannot guarantee your safety."

He threw back his head and laughed. He had a wonderful laugh, deep and contagious. I had to struggle not to giggle along with him like a ninny.

"I am here on official business, if I may have some of your time."

He studied me for a few seconds. "About my nephew."

I noticed it had not been a question. In fact, Dr. Gallo had not yet bothered me with a single unnecessary query. It was a rare and wonderful trait in a human being. I could see why Cadence liked him. Though that ninny was already convincing herself that finding someone besides Patrick attractive was the same as cheating. I have never known anyone to be so crippled by their conscience. She punished herself when she *didn't* commit any wrongdoing.

It must be exhausting.

"Yes," I replied. "Your nephew. May I speak with you?" Protocol required "please," "thank you," "sir," "ma'am." But once I had exhausted protocol, I was fine with gutter language and menacing him with a . . . er . . . I looked around. I suppose I could smother him in all those blankets.

"Sure."

Eh? Oh. He had answered me. *Why* was I so distracted? And how could Cadence live like this?

"C'mon, let's take a walk. I was bugging out to grab lunch anyway. Back in a while, gang," he said and tossed a wave in their general direction. They called farewells and waved, too, which I felt was a bit disrespectful given that he was their superior. Gallo did not appear to mind, which I felt was a bad precedent. However, it was not my place to say so, and thus, I did not.

He jerked his head toward the closest exit, and we fell into step together as he headed for what I assumed was the parking lot. His tattered leather went perfectly with his soon-to-be-tattered scrubs. And he needed a haircut; his dark bangs kept flopping into his eyes and he kept them at bay by jerking his head to the side. *Patrick would never let his hair become so unmanageable,* I thought, and then experienced some Cadence-esque panic. Why was I drawing comparisons? And why was I so pleased to be here, alone, with Dr. Gallo? I would not lie to myself and pretend it was for the JBJ case.

"I don't suppose there are any leads."

Relieved we were back to business, I replied, "We are running everything we can. We *will* get this amoral bastard, Dr. Gallo. Of that, you may be certain."

"Hmmm, your eyes went all narrow and squinty when you said that. I'd hate to meet you in a dark alley."

"Yes," I replied. "You would."

He chuckled and held the door for me. At first I thought it was a trick. Then I thought it was chauvinism. By the time I realized it was simple courtesy he had sighed and gone through himself. "I'm making a mental note," he called as I hurried behind him. "No more door holding for you!"

"Would you believe I was deep in thought?"

"Nope." He snickered, fished out a set of jangly keys, and pointed them to the left. I heard a muted beep and we both turned in that direction. "Listen, I've gotta get out of here, and not for a McFlab Deluxe, either. Let's go for a ride."

"A ride?" We had stopped near a sizable black motorcycle that had likely rolled brand-new off the show floor the year I was born. It was immaculately maintained, and seemed to brood while heeled over on its kickstand. It looked like a compact storm cloud on wheels. "Ah . . ."

Hmm. This was not like me. I normally did not eschew new and possibly dangerous situations. Was it that I did not wish to seem less than brave and honorable to Dr. Gallo? A man whom I did not truly know?

Ye gods! I was getting as stupidly maudlin as Cadence! Definitely time to consider a change in medication. "We shall ride *now*," I said, refraining myself from flinging myself onto the seat.

"I'm with you, Adrienne, so calm down." He had bent, and was rummaging, and when he stood he was holding a spare black helmet in my direction. I snatched it away from him and plunked it on my head.

"Very well. We ride now."

"Calm down, Valentino Rossi."

"Who?"

"Your helmet's crooked," he said, like that explained a single thing. He reached up and did something with the straps by my chin. For that long moment we were eye to eye, and why did I feel like it was eye to clitoris? His fingers on the strap, brushing my skin, his dark gaze inches from mine . . . I would think about that endless moment again and again over the next several weeks.

What is wrong with me?

"—fall off otherwise."

"What?" At last, at last he had finished fiddling with my helmet and stepped back and was no longer touching me and I was sad and glad and *what was wrong with me?*

"Are you all right?"

I ignored the question. "So, what is this?" I gestured at his motorcycle. "A Harley-Davidson? A . . . a chopper?" It occurred to me I knew nothing about motorcycles. "A, uh, Triumph?"

"Honda."

"What?"

"It's a Honda. Best in the world, believe it or not." He had pulled on dark gloves and patted the motorcycle with what appeared to be affection. "I got her right before I started med school. Beauty, eh?"

"You sound Canadian when you talk like that," was the only thing I could think of to say. The other thing ("Honda makes motorcycles? How strange. *You* are strange, too, Dr. Gallo, but then, so am I, so you need not fret.") wasn't especially tactful. Or sensible.

"Well," he said, swinging a long leg over the seat, "I *am* Canadian.

Here, hop on. Yeah, right behind—whoa, not so fast, you almost sent us crashing to the tarmac. Usually I like to be going at least fifteen mph before I go crashing to the tarmac . . . There! That's better."

I could hardly see—the helmet radically reduced my peripheral vision. At first I gingerly rested my fingertips on his waist, barely grazing, but Dr. Gallo put a stop to that when he grabbed my wrists and pulled forward, showing me how to wrap my arms around his waist and hold onto my own wrists locked over his flat stomach. Then he did something that made a tremendous noise—annoying helmet! I couldn't see a thing!—and then we

then we

we were

chapter forty-three

Flying!

O we were we were

O we were flying flying and we skimmed
and swooped
and flew

The wheels on the bike
go fly fly fly
fly fly fly
fly fly fly

The wheels on the bike
They make us fly
Dr. Gallo flies!

And it's swoop!
And whoop!
And swoop whoop swoop whoop and here comes

the bridge!

And we're little and speedy and we pass everyone
We pass everyone

The geese are jealous!
The geese want their own motorcycles!

Dr. Gallo can fly
No one told me
Dr. Gallo can fly!

The wheels on the Honda
Help us fly
Help us fly
Help us fly

Dr. Max takes us flying
All across the bridge.

Dr. Max!

Dr. Max can fly!

Dr. Max helps US fly!
Fly fly fly

Don't worry!
We'll find the
(goose)
JBK
JBK
JBK

We will find the JBK
And kill him just for youuuuu!

chapter forty-four

"Want to head back?"

I realized we were several miles from the hospital. Ah! The real Adrienne had joined us, and just as recently, left. Fortunately for the good doctor, he hadn't noticed. I had no idea what Adrienne must have thought of the motorcycle ride, but since she had not appeared to deliberately crash us, she must have liked it.

"Adrienne?" He had turned his head to better hear me. "Ready to go back?"

I smacked him on his left shoulder with the flat of my hand, hard.

"Ow! So, no? Y'know, I respond to verbal cues, too," he grouched. But I knew he was only pretending annoyance. He was pleased that I liked this pastime of his. If only he knew how many of us in here did. Ha! That might be a conversation worth having sometime.

I leaned forward and rested my cheek on his shoulder, and felt the wind whistling past us leaving molecules of good smells, the fresh bread of a Subway shop, the clean snow over a semi-frozen river, a car wash cranking away with soap and wax, The Old Spaghetti Factory, floating all around.

Honda. Best in the world. Yes.

I would not forget.

chapter forty-five

I returned to the BOFFO building with nothing except a newfound love for Honda motorcycles, and pure gratitude that Adrienne hadn't hurt anyone. But nothing that would help us track Dr. Gallo's nephew's killer, JBK. Unfortunately for *that* psychotic wretch, I was now more determined than ever to find him and hurt him. How *dare* that beast cause such pain to a man who knew how to make a pair of scrubs last, and could drive so well in the winter?

This time it . . . well, it really *was* sort of personal. Not that I enjoy sounding like an action hero from an eighties movie.

Ye gods. Before I got any sillier, or more maudlin, or more emotional about a man I *barely knew*

(and we have a boyfriend!)

I realized Cadence was trying to peep through my subconscious. Or was it *her* subconscious? Eh. Either way, I was more than ready to bow out for a bit. I had much to mull over.

Most annoying: I had never discussed Dr. Gallo's nephew. Merely used him for transportation and then let Adrienne kick me out of the body for a bit. I would have considered it a wasted trip, except . . . it did not feel wasted. It felt wonderful.

I made a mental note to make it up to Dr. Gallo. Then I left.

chapter forty-six

Which is why I found myself in an elevator with helmet hair and a weird yearning for a(nother) motorcycle ride. What had I missed?

Too bad for me, I wasn't going to find out anytime soon. Even as I got off the elevator and stepped toward my desk I knew playtime truly was over.

"Pinkman! Jones! Thyme!" Michaela was striding toward us so quickly she hadn't noticed one of her sneakers had come untied. "You've got another one. Get moving, *now*."

"Tell me she's talking about another briefing in her weird kitchen office," Emma Jan begged.

"She's not," I said, now as glum as George.

"JBK's accelerating," George said. "And just think, girls. You didn't think we were gonna have any fun today."

I had to look away from his grin.

Maybe I would have an update for Dr. Gallo after all.

Darn it.

chapter forty-seven

Over bitter (George) and worried (me) and confused (Emma Jan) protests, Paul Torn accompanied us to the crime scene.

"It's all numbers numbers numbers to me right now, I don't know enough for HOAP.1."

"You mean you're already planning the next—"

"It's *not* just numbers numbers numbers," Paul said, sinking lower into the backseat. I was riding shotgun, and so turned around so I could make eye contact. "It's people. Dead people, dead kids. I forget. I forget when I taste red and yellow. They aren't numbers, they're people. I need to see all the permutations because it's people people people!"

"Okay, well, just caaaaaalm down." George was eyeing him via the rearview mirror. "Take a pill, or four, or whatever your dose is."

"I forget, too, sometimes," Emma Jan told him gently. "I get caught up in paperwork and my studies and sometimes it's just . . . numbers. I feel bad after, but sometimes I can't help it."

"Yes! That's right! It's that it isn't people, I have to remember, we *all* have to remember!"

"Well, I'm convinced." George sailed through a red light—there was next to no traffic on 94 this time of the day. "And by convinced, I mean freaked out. Just don't touch anything, okay?"

Paul sniffed. He was either fighting a cold, or . . . "Does anyone else smell yellow?"

George groaned. "You're the only one who thinks you can smell and taste colors, Paul, you slobbering weirdo."

"Hey!" I said sharply.

"Ooooh, Cadence raised her voice and everything. Must be a—what the hell *is* today? Why do I feel like I'm living my life in this stupid POS government car?"

"Because you are?" I suggested. And I knew just how he felt. Sure, entire weeks went by when we merely used the Piece of Stuff car to get from Point A to Point B. Lately, though, it seemed like we were using it to go from Corpse A to Corpse B.

At least George had quit, for which I was equal parts grateful and amazed.

"I'm sensing a long drive," Emma Jan said from the backseat, and never had I heard a more profound truth. "Don't worry, though."

"We aren't," George replied, half listening.

"I still think you guys are pretty interesting."

My partner and I traded glances but said nothing, a rare moment of . . . of . . . what was the word for not wishing the other person was dead?

chapter forty-eight

We stood over the body, the four of us, and even George looked disgusted. He summed up my feelings perfectly when he led with, "What a fucking waste."

Yes. That was exactly right. A waste of a life, a waste of a future. A waste of government resources because we had to catch the jerks. A waste of money . . . our budget had to come from somewhere. All of it: a waste.

The Edina cops had let us in straightaway; they knew what it was the minute they'd broken down the door. They were grim and subdued, and I couldn't blame them.

Edina was one of the tonier suburbs in the Twin Cities; it wasn't uncommon for graduation presents for high school seniors to be new cars or trips to Europe. Edina was clean and beautiful and bustling and full of people who had never worried about where their next paycheck was coming from.

So when an ugly murder—though to be fair, all murders were ugly—when a truly awful murder like this happened within the city limits, there was a lot of the "This Kind of Thing Doesn't

Happen Here" mentality. Even from cops, who of all people should know better.

This house was vintage Edina. Sizable, with a large corner lot, and beautifully maintained. Wood gleamed everywhere—the floors, the built-in bookcases, the staircases, all had the mellow glow of meticulous maintenance.

Aaron Mickelson, fourteen forever, had been stretched out beside the black piano in the parlor/library. He was surrounded by shelves and shelves of books, and had been placed almost exactly between the piano and the fireplace.

"This is bad," Emma Jan said.

"Duh." From George, of course.

"Poor boy poor boy poor boy." Paul was shaking his head. His hands, covered with gloves, were jammed into his pockets wrist-deep. He almost seemed to vibrate. "Poor poor boy; HOAP.1 will help you you you do you guys smell that?"

"I can't smell anything over George's aftershave."

"Hey, back off, New Girl. There are women in this state who would *bathe* in my aftershave."

Emma Jan glanced at me. "I'm pretty sure that's an exaggeration." In fact, George only wore the nauseating Stetson to crime scenes. It was his version of Vicks. A Significant Male Figure in his life (he always phrased it just like that: "Significant Male Figure") had worn it when he was a kid, and it was a scent he cordially despised. Whenever I smelled Stetson I knew corpses were imminent.

Emma Jan snorted. "Bathe. Uh-huh." Then she sobered. "He's accelerating all over the place, boys and girls. Boys being Paul and George, and girls being—"

"We get it get it get it."

"This is *really* bad. What happened to one a year in June? What, it wasn't ambitious enough to get away with twenty-some murders over two decades? Now he's trying for overachiever status?"

"Maybe he thinks we're stupid and can't catch him." George's expression was pretty eloquent: dammit, dammit, dammit! "And guess what? So far, he's right."

"Calm down, George."

"*You* calm down, Cadence."

"Something's not right."

"No shit."

Paul twitched madly in place. "Does anyone else smell black?"

"I smell black," Emma Jan sighed. "Since I got into this damned room I've smelled black. You guys. Tell me we're gonna nail this asshole."

"Worse than Jesus got nailed," George promised. That was him being encouraging, which often came off as blasphemous and gross. "Like I need more weekends like *this*?"

"You guys. Pay attention. Something's not right." I was squatting beside the body, tentative ID: Aaron Mickelson, age fourteen, blond and blue. Strip it all away and we had a boy who hadn't lived to see his senior prom. Or his sophomore year, come to think of it. The only thing ahead of him now was a cemetery plot, and who wants that for a milestone?

We heard a fuss at the back entrance, and I saw a couple of the uniforms running. Suspect? Not likely; the killer was long gone. Some neighbor lookey-loo; my least favorite kind of neighbor. Some people just haaaaad to peek at a nearby dead body. It was behavior I could never understand.

There was a thud we could almost feel, and then here came another cop on the run. Thank goodness for the sizable, clean windows.

"What the fuck?" George whined. "How hard is it for the flatfeet to keep the area clear? Like this job doesn't suck enough."

Wow. That's how I knew the boys, the dead boys, were really getting to my sociopathic partner, a man who cared for nothing beyond his own pleasure (usually). Perhaps it was an issue of convenience—the killer was certainly pressing in on George's play-time. Or perhaps all those fresh-faced dead boys reminded George of another fresh-faced boy. One who lived . . . after a fashion.

"Sorry to bother you, Agents, but we caught this guy—"

"Caught? I disabled your vehicle and led you the wrong way."

"—hanging around—"

"Hanging around?" A deep laugh. "I *led you here*. Maybe you should show me your paperwork before you file that report."

We all stared. It wasn't every day the head of the blood bank made his way onto a crime scene uninvited.

"Him, now, *he* smells like yellow."

"Dr. Gallo!"

"We never did get around to talking about my nephew." His voice was muffled, probably because an officer was leaning on his shoulders.

"So you followed me to a crime scene?"

"Hey, I've got a good staff at the bank. They had everything under control. And Dr. Welch left me with, like, *no* paperwork. Who keeps their charts that up to date? It's not natural."

"Who's this?" George asked. "And should we get a couple more cops to jump on the back of his neck? Because he doesn't seem too inconvenienced by the one on him now. Or the two drawing down on him." He knelt by the wriggling bodies and cupped his hands, as if they couldn't hear him without a fake megaphone. "Hey, mysterious weirdo at the crime scene! If you turn out not to be the killer, we should probably go out. I'm always in the market for a reliable wingman. This is an excellent town for getting laid and then never seeing the woman *du jour* again."

"*De la nuit*," Dr. Gallo corrected from the floor. "And you can be *my* wingman."

"Let him up," I begged. "This is Chris Glazier's uncle."

"Oh," Emma Jan said. Then: "Oh! We're very sorry about your nephew, Dr.—Dr. Gallo, is it?"

George was shaking his head. "Dude, we get it if you feel out of the loop, but there's easier ways to get updated. And less painful ways." George put his hand on the cop's elbow and carefully pulled him off the prone Dr. Gallo.

"Sorry," his partner said. "He had us half convinced he was supposed to be here—"

"Until the *actual* coroner arrived," Dr. Gallo admitted. He was helped to his feet by the cop who had just been kneeling on his shoulder blades. They likely would have been rougher, but now that the trespasser had been revealed to be the family member of a victim, the rules had changed. The cops would be praying to their cop-gods that Dr. Gallo didn't sue the department.

It didn't make what he had done any less wrong, and it didn't mean he might not have questions to answer at a police station in his near future, but for various reasons, PR regrettably being one of them, it changed how we dealt with him.

"Would have worked, too," Dr. Gallo was explaining, sounding absurdly cheerful, "except for the coroner, like I said. Who *left*, by the way."

George rolled his eyes. He didn't say a thing, but I knew what he was thinking. More turf wars downtown. And all because Dr. Zinner lost a bet and no one else on his staff would let him forget it. A coroner would be back, and soon, but not Dr. Zinner.

All George said was, "Long story, but everything's under control."

It wasn't the first time I had admired his ability to tell a flawless, believable lie.

Emma Jan cleared her throat and, now that Dr. Gallo was standing on his own two feet, shook his hand. "Again, I'm very sorry about your nephew. I'm not sure how you knew where we'd be unless you do have guilty knowledge . . ."

She and George looked at me out of the corners of their eyes. I sighed and fessed up. "Clearly, Dr. Gallo followed me back from our meeting this afternoon."

"Clearly," Dr. Gallo agreed. "And it's Max." He made a gesture and, with the automatic deference to a physician shown by most cops at the scene, accepted a pair of gloves from the nearest officer. "Look, you guys have a doc on the scene. I'm licensed and I've been to a million of these. Well." The corners of his mouth turned down. "Not *these*, but you know. You can't tell me you like waiting around for the coroner. So let's go."

I opened my mouth: inappropriate. Against all the rules. He wasn't even the right kind of doctor. Worse, he was a family member. Also—

"Fuck it," George said. (I could have timed it to the second.) I looked at Emma Jan, who shrugged.

"He's here, he wants to. He might see something an emotionally detached doctor won't." *And he's less likely to sue anybody if we let him play in our sandbox.*

Max, I noticed, had busily been snapping on his gloves and not bothering to wait for our permission.

"Rigor mortis is long gone," he said, carefully kneeling by the body. "Kid's been dead for at least twelve hours." He peered at the boy's eyes. They had probably been intense and lovely in life, but now were clouded over. "Chris was found hour eleven. Is that typical of these kids?"

Reluctantly, we nodded. I didn't even want to think of Michaela's reaction when she found out what we had done. What we had allowed the family member of a victim to do. But there was something about Max Gallo. It wasn't just me (or Shiro, or Adrienne). Emma Jan and George felt it, too. That thrumming charisma. The black eyes, so like a shark's. You wanted to please him and were a little afraid of him at the same time. And the silly thing . . . I was *relieved.* Relieved that George and Emma Jan could feel it, too. Relieved that it wasn't just more proof I needed to jettison my virginity ASAP.

"Blunt trauma around the head," Max was muttering. "Probable cause of death. Also like Chris. Parents out of town?"

"Still are, yeah," George replied. "The Edina police are still trying to reach them."

I did *not* want to be around when they got here. To distract myself, I walked around Max and the body. Then stopped. "You guys. This is wrong."

"To put it mildly," Max muttered, gently examining the dead boy's fingers. He beckoned and one of the crime scene officers came over, and obligingly shot several flash pictures of the dead boy's fingers and hands.

"Yeah, Cadence, we covered that; we're all with you on that one. If you think back, we all agreed this sucks *and* blows."

"Look," I insisted. "Jeans, right?"

"Chris had them, too. Was found in them," Max corrected himself. More flashes.

"Right, just like the others. Except these are all beat up. The other boys were found in *new* jeans—remember how they were almost stiff, George? But look."

All four of them—Paul had gotten close, no doubt emboldened by Max—were suddenly crouched beside me. "Those aren't new look at look at look at the holes!"

"Right, Paul. And the striped shirt. It's inside out."

There was a short silence, followed by Emma Jan's puzzled, "What's up with that? And this boy, he's the eighth in seven years. That's *way* off the pattern."

"Somebody getting bored?" Max asked sarcastically. "Ready for you guys to get your thumbs out and catch him? Changing the game so you can?"

We said nothing; we knew why he'd said such a thing. And we knew it wasn't unjustified. I didn't even have to kick George, who just reddened but didn't retort. A miracle for the ages.

"Patterns we can do patterns HOAP can do patterns, you bet!"

"Uh, what?" Max asked, clearly startled by the large bespectacled black man looming over the crime scene and practically vibrating.

"Great, Paul, thanks for the nerd update. And Emma Jan, thanks to you, too, but we can do math all by ourselves," George sniped.

"Shush. Be nice. Let's see if anything else is different." I checked the boy's pockets, being careful of the urine and fecal matter. Pretty much the first thing a dead body does is lose control of its bowels. Death is just . . . awful. In every single way.

"Oh, now look at this." I showed them. "It's not even my birthday."

"A goddamned parking garage ticket?" George breathed. All the color fell out of his face except for two red patches on his cheeks. "You're shitting me!"

"Nuh-uh. This was either an oversight, or the killer did it on purpose." And it wasn't an oversight. Not with JBK.

"Jesus! An actual clue? An honest-to-God clue at the first scene I bust?" Max asked. "Clearly I need to do this. A lot."

"Bite your tongue," Emma Jan muttered, her gaze never leaving the parking ticket.

"Yes! That's right!" Paul was pointing at the body and practically jumping up and down. "The pattern the pattern is there and eight is the wrong color. Eight is wrong; HOAP needs to have that uploaded, eight is the wrong color!"

George rolled his eyes at me. "What are you thinking? Copycat? Max? You must have studied whatever you could of the other scenes. I'm not buying that you just happened to decide to stumble across this scene."

"You're right. And . . . you're right. I think it's laziness, or desperation. Not that he wants to get caught, so much but . . . I *don't* think it's another person. But I'm—" Max paused and spread his hands, still covered with the latex gloves. "This isn't my field. It's *your* call. Adrienne?"

"I . . . don't think so. Remember, we've kept most of this out of the media. The killer got too many things right . . . the boy was beaten to death. The doc—the other doc, *not* you, Max; if you go near this kid's post you'll be in jail eight seconds later—is gonna rule COD severe head trauma. The jeans and shirt are right, just not how the killer showed them to us."

"So?" Emma Jan asked.

"I think he wants to get caught. He wants to stop but can't make himself do it."

"Boy, have *you* been reading too many fairy tales."

"Okay." I met George's eyes. "What's your theory?"

George looked back down at the boy. "Not a copycat," he said after a long pause. "I agree; the fucko got too much right. But I'm thinking he got sloppy, or is having a psychotic break of some kind."

Emma Jan sighed. "Don't tease."

"Psychotic break," Max muttered. "That *would* be nice, if it led directly to suicide, do not pass Go."

"Do you—"

George talked over my interruption, which was fair. "I think he's destabilizing all over the place. Remember how Bundy's last killings were just a fuckin' frenzy? No planning, just whack-whack-and-boom. Because, Cadence, come on. These guys . . . they don't ever stop. You *know* that."

"Careful," Emma Jan said with a smile that wasn't especially friendly. "That sounds like a trite cliché."

We both stared at her.

"That's true," George finally said. "It does. Huh."

"Uh, what?" Max asked. He turned to me. "I thought your name was Adrienne."

"Sorry," George said. "Super-secret FBI stuff. Which reminds me, get lost or you're under arrest. And hey! Call me about the wingman thing."

The police led a confused Dr. Gallo away from the scene. Leaving only the ones who were supposed to be there . . . and we were just as confused, believe me.

chapter forty-nine

Hours later, I was finishing my paperwork. George, who could always get through his faster than I could mine, had left an hour ago. As usual, it was quieter and saner after his departure but, conversely, duller. George was the kind of person who filled a room simply by walking through the door. When he left it could at times seem like an anticlimax.

He'd made a vague threat involving my boyfriend and battery acid (he was probably going to hold a Splenda grudge until the end of time), told an inappropriate dirty joke, and then, in a puff of black smoke (or so it seemed sometimes), was gone.

Max Gallo had been scolded and then ROR, unlikely to ever be brought up on charges provided he kept away from other JBJ crime scenes. ("Unless invited?" I'd asked, only to flinch from the sizzling glare Michaela shot my way. To say she had been displeased would be putting it *very* mildly.)

Paul had wasted no time disappearing into the computer lab; he'd chattered run-on sentence with lots of repeat phrases all the way back to the office. Emma Jan had to keep distracting George from turning around and smacking the poor guy on the drive back. I was a little afraid he'd twitch himself to death. Or get beaten to death. Altogether, a stressful ride back to the office.

George's irritation had eventually changed to mild concern: "I think we broke him."

"Don't talk about it," I had hissed back.

I hated the waiting game when lives were at stake, but it was a fact of life in this business. The FBI computers were now whirring through all the data we'd been able to give it from the latest JBJ crime scene, cross-referencing it with the data from the previous murders. Though we would explore the copycat angle, we were all still pretty certain it was the real deal.

"Still at it?" Emma Jan asked. She leaned back in her chair and stretched. I could hear her back crack. "Ooooh, that was a good one."

"No, I'm finished. And wiped. I gotta get home and take a nineteen-hour nap. Oh, and that dumb Dawg," I groaned, remembering my home situation. Argh. Poor Patrick, trapped with Dawg for hours and hours while I mooned after Max Gallo and peeked at new dead bodies.

"Oh. Um. Shiro and I were supposed to head over to the gun range tonight."

"Oh?" I managed—barely—to keep the irritation out of my voice.

"Yeah. She—you know, we made plans. To go to the range tonight."

Well, too bad, Emma Jan Thyme. Shiro shouldn't have made a commitment if there was a chance she couldn't keep it. Which, FYI, there was. I've neglected my boyfriend long enough, thank you.

I forced a smile. "Here's the way it works, Emma Jan. You can't just decide which one of us you'll see. We're not a doctor's office. You can't make an appointment with the body and just expect the others to

chapter fifty

"Good evening, Agent Thyme."

The corner of her mouth twitched. "Hi, Shiro. Uh. Maybe this isn't such a good idea. Cadence didn't seem at all cool with it."

"Cadence," I said, picking up her jacket and slipping into her boots—she *would* inappropriately disrobe when she became fatigued, "will get over it. Besides, I am far too keyed up with energy to go home. And *I* did not snatch an animal that did not belong to me."

"You're not tired?" She was watching me carefully. "Cadence was pretty tired. She wanted to go home and take a nap. And I think she wanted to check on Patrick."

"Irrelevant. Cadence is not here right now." I shrugged into the coat and found the car keys. "Shall we?"

I took a deep breath. If I had been led here in a blindfold, I would know I was in the indoor range beneath our building. Gunpowder was like perfume to me. And here, *here* was where Agent Thyme would understand I was her superior in *this . . . one . . . way.*

"Agent Thyme, this is Dan Shepard, the high priest of the gun range."

"Meetcha," he mumbled. Dan Shepard was the least threatening-looking person I had ever seen. Short—not much over five feet—and heavy, with wispy blond hair that was slowly jumping ship. His muddy brown eyes swam behind thick lenses.

He was one of the best shots on the planet. Yes. The *planet.* In fact, I strongly suspected he had been a wet boy in his youth, retiring from the rounds of government-sanctioned assassinations to run BOFFO's gun range.

The least interesting thing about Dan was that he suffered from sedatephobia—fear of silence. Something he never had to worry about down here.

He waved a plump hand in my general direction and said, sounding like a distracted mad scientist, which I often thought he was, "You left those hollow points at home, Shiro? Yeah? Do *not* bring that shit into my range again. Use the damn wad cutters like the rest of us. *Capice*?"

"Dan! You wound me," I protested, hoping he wouldn't insist on checking my loads and ammo pouch. "I would never think it after you made your displeasure known."

Emma Jan was smiling. "Do I want to know, honey?"

"No, Agent Thyme. You do not." I was pleased to be called "honey," so long as she understood I would not be easier on her. It was pleasant to have a new friend. If that is what she was. Perhaps she had called me honey to put me off my guard . . .

While I pondered (weak and weary! Shout-out to Edgar Allan Poe; ugh, I said "shout-out" . . .), Dan followed us as we walked the length of the range, staying well outside the red lines. He was wringing his pale, pudgy hands so tightly I wondered if he might accidentally hurt himself. And while he followed us he rattled off all the silly rules he made up after I had begun making use of his gun range.

"No challenging people you don't like to duels. No putting Pinkman's picture downrange and shooting at it. No egging on other agents to shoot at it. No shotguns—"

"Not even twenty gauge?"

"No shotguns!"

"Hmph."

"No armor-piercing rounds, no APLP ammo."

"APLPs," Emma Jan moaned orgasmically. I laughed, I couldn't help it.

"I would *never.*" The second one, that is. Armor-Piercing Limited-Penetration rounds were still wildly illegal, and for good reason. I had been able to get a look at a classified report on the ammo, which had been used three times in the field and caused fatalities all three times. The fact that Agent Thyme knew what they were raised her stock even more. Once I had broken her to my will we could be great friends . . .

But back to the APLPs, and how they were a deep dark secret. Nothing unusual in itself, except the three people involved in APLP fatalities had been shot in the left buttock, the right wrist, and the left thigh.

The man shot in the buttock died instantly, as the bullet shredded everything from his ass to his stomach. The man shot in the right wrist died of shock after seeing his wrist not only disappear but shatter all the way up his forearm. And the man shot in the left thigh also died of shock, as the bullet ripped away nearly all the muscle and shattered the bone.

Our man in the field had noted in his report that it was as if the ammunition had an explosive charge at the tip. Except, of course, it did not. The ammo was so controversial it was verboten pending further tests. The military was currently in the middle of the arduous testing process.

"No eating sushi when you're on the line. In fact, no *chopsticks* on the line; don't think I forgot what happened last time. And no goddamned machine pistols."

"Now you're just trying to hurt me," I chided.

"Are we clear, Shiro?"

"Yes, indeed."

"And you." Emma Jan snapped to attention. "Don't listen to this one. She's pure evil. Follow the range rules and I won't have you killed."

"Yes, sir."

"You say that to all the girls." I was dreamily imagining what it would be like to have access to that sort of ammunition. If there was a God, he would help our military complete the testing as soon as possible. Hmm, but how could I use it while making sure Adrienne never ever got her hands on it?

Sigh. A problem for another day.

"Shiro, you're here." Dan pointed to lane two. "Thyme, is it? Thyme, you're here." He pointed to lane one. It was no coincidence that we were at the other end from where others were practicing. "What'd you bring?"

We unzipped our small duffels and showed him. Emma Jan had brought a Browning 9×19mm Hi-Power and several magazines. She was clearly familiar with it; she took it out of her duffel the way someone would root around in their purse for a piece of gum.

"Huh. Hi-Power." Dan's watery gaze sharpened. "Interesting choice."

"Our Hostage Rescue Team uses it. My last girlfriend got me turned on to these after she'd tried it for a while. I never looked back. D'you want to squeeze off a few?" She extended the unloaded gun to me, butt first with the safety on. She knew her range etiquette. Good. Dan would not have to get the Taser.

I shook my head. "No, thank you. The trigger pull is too stiff for me."

"So get rid of the magazine safety, and get aftermarket trigger springs, the kind with reduced tension."

"What about the bite?"

"What *about* the *bite*?" If she were a rooster, Agent Thyme would be strutting back and forth beside the line, daring me to attack. "That's really the problem for you?"

I narrowed my eyes at her, not entirely unhappy—I liked my quarrels out in the open. *So, this is how it's going to be, hmm, New Girl? Fine. We'll—*

"Shiro, I had no idea you were such a crybaby." Dan was one of the few people on the planet who could get away with saying such a thing to my face. He was nervous and fussy, but I deeply respected his talent and his knowledge. It startled me out of my eyeball-to-eyeball challenge with Thyme. "Waaaaah!" He added to the mockery by rubbing his eyes with his big gnarled fists.

Waaaaah? Really?

I sighed. "Not wanting the web between my thumb and forefinger to get shredded by that damned hammer spur makes me a crybaby? Then crybaby I shall be."

"It's nice to have something to look forward to," Agent Thyme said brightly. "I still think if you gave the Hi-Power a chance you might like it."

"Never. When it comes to firearms, I am obsessively monogamous."

"Not just obsessive?" she teased. My. I *really* liked this woman.

"I prefer this." I pulled my Desert Eagle so she and Dan could take a look.

"Okay, I get it. Because of the gas-operation you can use more powerful cartridges. It's clunky, though." She was looking at it with the critical care of someone who knew her life might depend on her weapons knowledge. "It's better for target practice or silhouette shooting than fieldwork."

I shrugged. I liked what I liked. It was not always logical. If Cadence had been driving, she'd have come up with something pithy like, "Sez you." And Adrienne would have just shot her in the ankle and left.

"All right, I guess that'll do," Dan wheezed. Not for the first time I considered lecturing him on his nutritional habits. "I'm gonna leave you ladies to it. Agent Thyme, standard gun-range rules apply: ear plugs and safety glasses at all times you're on the line. Check out the sheet on maximum caliber size and *don't deviate.* And Shiro, I swear to God . . . you put *one* toe out of line, I'll bounce you for a month."

"I hear and obey, O my Dan."

"It was nice to meet you, Dan, and thank you for the tour. D'you want to hear my top three unusual deaths?"

"Why?" Dan asked, puzzled yet keeping a wary eye on me. "Why would I ever want to know that?"

"Goddammit," she sighed, then slapped in the clip and popped a round into the pipe. "Shiro, have I told you lately how much I loved talking to you about unusual deaths?"

I laughed.

"Now," she said, sighting down the barrel. "Get ready to be made my bitch."

"Those," I warned, "are fighting words. If there will be any bitch making, it shall be I, making *you my*—"

"Shut up and shoot."

So we did.

chapter fifty-one

We had practiced for half an hour when Emma Jan signaled she wanted to talk by popping her clip and pulling the round out of the pipe. Since we were the only two on the line, it was safe to take my earplugs out.

My Desert Eagle clicked empty on my last shot, so I followed her lead. I inhaled again. I truly loved the smell of this wonderful underground room. Better than roses. Better than chocolate.

"You are terrifying," was how she started the conversation. "And you held out on me."

"I doubt it."

"You're hitting the ten every time!"

"I practice a lot."

"For how many years—fifty? Gulp."

"Did you just say 'gulp' out loud to denote—"

"Shiro, no bullshit. You're the best I've ever seen. It's incredible."

"You're very kind, Agent Thyme." Her praise warmed me, and the warmth surprised me. I was not prone to worrying about what others thought, so did not seek their praise.

"However, I'm pretty awesome my own self."

"I noticed." Damn it.

"I could put a few more in the ten if we went head-to-head again. Shiro, I gotta thank you."

"What? Why? What is the matter?"

"Whoa, calm down. I meant it in a nice way. Which I can see is confusing you. Listen, I held back this last half hour. I just wanted to get warm, get to know a new range. You brought everything, and I didn't. You were in it to win it—God, I hate that phrase—and I wasn't. So thanks."

"For . . ." Making you my bitch, as I had predicted I would? Well. I could be magnanimous in victory. "For assisting you to . . . to be better?"

"I should have brought everything." She wasn't smiling. Her dark, beautiful eyes were fixed on mine with no warmth of any kind. What was she seeing, while she said these things to me? "I didn't. You did, and I know better. Next time, I'll remember. I'm grateful, Shiro, for any lesson I don't have to relearn from the inside of a body bag."

I was startled, then pleased. It was a mind-set I could relate to. A mind-set I could have related to when I was five. "You are very kind, Agent Thyme, and do not need my assistance to save your own life."

"Shiro, how many times, hmm? How many? Call me Emma Jan, for Christ's sake."

"This is the first time you have asked me to call you Emma Jan."

"Oh. Well, I've thought it a whole buncha times. Maybe I'm thinking of Cadence."

"Oh, yes, a natural mistake because we look so much alike." Cadence was a big blonde. I was a small Asian American. And Adrienne had deep red hair and a ghastly pale face. "Though I can tell you, Dan prefers Cadence to me on this range." I shrugged. "It's understandable. Everybody likes her."

"Dan seemed a little freaked out by you."

"He can be touchy. You know what's odd?"

"You're asking *me*?" She had begun packing up her duffel, and I followed suit.

"People have told me Dan is laid back and friendly. I never seem to catch that side of him."

"Says the girl who was loading hollow points into her clips."

"Shush."

"Hey, I didn't say anything, did I?"

"No." I almost giggled. We were complicit . . . we were like friends! Friends who shot and shot and then tried, more, to outshoot each other.

I thought about it. "I cannot picture Dan as laid back. I try and try, and fail."

"Nobody's perfect. Uh, listen, Shiro, can I ask you something?"

"You may ask." I did not promise to answer, but hopefully would be able to.

Here it came: What is it like sharing a body with two other people; how old were you when that happened; why do you think you are the way you are; isn't having wacky adventures just all kinds of fun? Tell me secrets I have no use for.

Yes, indeed. For those of us with MPD, the fun never stops.

She took a breath, then plunged in with, "What is the deal with Michaela?"

"What?" I was so surprised, I had trouble believing I had heard her correctly.

"The knives, the chopping, the other office. What the *hell*?"

"Oh. Ah. Well, that . . . I can see how someone new would find it confusing . . ."

"No, Shiro. I find Sudoku confusing. Figuring out Michaela is all the way around the bend from confusing. It's more like she's baffling and I'm confounded."

"Fair enough. I will tell you, but please keep it to yourself." I was not certain why I was going to tell her. Perhaps I thought she had enough of a burden with reflective surfaces without being mystified and even frightened by her new boss. Perhaps . . . I liked her.

Scratch perhaps. I *did* like her.

"Michaela has . . . phallic issues."

Emma Jan snorted. "No shit. Can you get to the part I haven't figured out for myself? For instance, if she spends most of her workday slicing and dicing, when does she find time to do boss stuff?"

"That is a mystery I cannot help you with." The truth. None of us had any idea how she pulled that off. And she adored that we all wondered but could never find out. "But I can give you some background."

"Excellent. My luck to land a crazy boss again."

I laughed. "Did you think the FBI would appoint a supervisor who could not relate to her staff?"

"Ah. Good point."

While I packed my duffel, I told her what she thought she wanted to know.

chapter fifty-two

Michaela was the product of a rape, in itself not necessarily a ticket to the fun house. But she was raised by her rapist, a man who did not discontinue his distasteful habit of forcing women once he was responsible for raising a child on his own.

He had been determined to have a son. And was not the kind to forgive a letdown, any letdown, and was not above punishing the innocent. He never let Michaela forget he was sorry she had been born a girl.

And after he had finally come for her and forced her to be his latest victim, his girl-child castrated him. After his disgusting attack, she had crept up on him with her softball bat and nailed him just behind his right ear.

While he was unconscious she somehow managed to get him duct-taped to a kitchen chair, then spent the entire day castrating *other* things—carrots, pork loin, cucumbers, French bread, celery—so that by the time she got around to gelding her father, he had gone quite mad from stress and terror. His hysterical protests and pleading did not save him from the fate suffered by the celery and loin and bread.

He bled to death waiting for an ambulance she never called.

She had been eleven.

chapter fifty-three

"Aw, God." Emma Jan pinched the bridge of her nose. "That's one of the worst things I've ever heard. And I come from a long and distinguished line of alcoholics."

"I think she has overcome a great deal to get where she is," I said carefully. I did not like Michaela, exactly, but I respected her and, I will admit it, I was a little intimidated by her as well.

Unlike Cadence, I did not believe Michaela hid her affection for us. I believed she did not care about us and was fine with not caring, as long as we were productive. I hoped telling Emma Jan the story was the right thing to do, but there was always a small margin for error.

"I do not like her, you know."

Emma Jan gave me an odd look. "You've said that before. Are you sure?"

"I just wish that *you* could be sure."

"I think you do like her."

"I do not!" I felt my hand tighten on the bulge that was my pistol in my bag, and forced my fingers to loosen. This was no way to nurture a friendship, drawing down on someone not expecting it.

"Not *like* like," she said patiently, unaware she was courting death. "I think you want *her* to like *you*. I think you look up to her and want to please her."

"She is my supervisor." My! That was difficult to force out through teeth that would not unclench.

"Yeah, and maybe a maternal figure?"

"No."

"Yeah, you're right, what do I know?"

"That is correct!"

"Being new and all."

"Exactly! You understand nothing!"

"Chill, Shiro, you're *screaming*."

"I . . . need . . . new ear protection." I shook my head, chasing away fake sound waves. "The shooting match . . ."

"Oh. Well, since I'm up for a rematch to show you how this shit is done, you should get new ones ASAP." Emma Jan sighed and scooped her empties into a section of her bag. "Does anybody here have a happy story? Or at least a sad story with a happy ending?"

I shook off my irritation. Michaela? A maternal figure? To a charging bull, perhaps. "Here, America? Here, planet Earth? Here—"

"Here, BOFFO."

"Ah. No." I gave it more thought. "No. It is a building full of sad stories and massive doses of Halcion."

"And firearms."

I smiled. It felt stiff on my face; then, after a long moment, more natural. "Yes. And firearms."

I thought about asking Emma Jan for her origin story, but pulled back at the last moment. That was my methodology: when I started to pass the barriers people erect around their secrets, I always pulled back.

In many ways, I was as much a coward as Cadence.

"Did I hear you correctly earlier? Your last girlfriend?"

"Hmm?" She was carefully disassembling her weapon. "Oh. Sure. It's no big deal, I'm out and everything."

"Forgive me for such a personal question, but—"

"Yep! I'm a big fat dyke," she said cheerfully.

I snorted. "Is that the acceptable form of address now? I have such trouble keeping apace with political correctness."

"I also go by 'great big lesbian.' "

I thought it over, then went ahead and came out with it: "Is this a date, then?"

She looked up. "Uh, no. Is that a problem?"

"I do not know."

"Who should I ask, then?"

The very question made me laugh. "Sorry, sorry. I'm sexually confused."

"You're telling that to a black lesbo."

"Big deal. You have not cornered the market on sexual oddities. I *have* a boyfriend. He's . . . a wonderful man. He knows about us. All of us. He is . . . perfect for us, I think." I slowed, thinking hard. "But lately, I have someone else on my mind. I don't know why that should be."

"If you did, would it be any easier?"

"I . . . do not know."

"Maybe you just need some time off," she said kindly. "Or to get laid."

"Neither are likely," I said dryly.

"It's funny, I don't usually jump to conclusions. I thought you liked men."

"I do."

"Oh. So you're . . ."

"Flexible."

She laughed. "That's great! Hey, you've just doubled your dating pool."

"And yet, remain remarkably unlaid," I said dryly, and Emma Jan laughed at that for quite a while.

chapter fifty-four

I let myself into my apartment, put my keys back in my coat pocket, then hung up my coat. The apartment was quiet, except for the sinister sound of heavy breathing. Someone was waiting for me. Or someone was having an asthma attack. Now let me think, what did I have nearest to hand. . . ?

Bo shuriken. Crisper.

Chakram. Under sink behind dishwasher soap.

Throwing knife. Inside flour canister.

Beretta 950 Jetfire. Back of silverware drawer. Eight rounds in the mag, nothing in the pipe. Safety on.

Remington SP-10 semiauto shotgun. Pantry behind mop and broom. Legal load: three shells. Actual load: five shells. Fully loaded with buckshot, safety on.

Stun grenades. One behind spice rack. Two in pantry: one in Frosted Flakes, one in Raisin Bran.

Forty-five Colt Magnum. Loaded, not cocked. Back of junk drawer behind Scotch tape and dry erase markers.

Two speedloaders, full. Third drawer down.

Four X-acto knives. Left drawer beside stove under potholders.

It wasn't much, but I would have to make do. I glided into the kitchen, opened the silverware drawer, and pulled the Beretta. I clicked off the safety, then walked back the way I had come, taking a right instead of a left, and then I was in the living room.

Ah. I should have realized. Patrick had fallen asleep on the couch. A small black dog was curled up next to him, also sound asleep.

"Olive!" I said, very surprised. The dog opened her eyes, jumped down, and approached me with her tail wagging. I knelt to pet her. "What in the world . . . oh, no. No, do not tell me."

"Muh . . . Cadence?" Patrick was blinking sleepily at me, and his eyes widened when he saw the handgun. "Hey, Shiro. Guess nobody told you we'd be here."

"Ah . . . no. No one did." Still, I must be tired. I should have remembered. Or assumed. Or at least been ready for anything, instead of ready for nothing.

"Thanks for not shooting first and asking questions later."

"It was just that one time," I protested. "Must you forever hold that over my head?"

"Sure." He grinned, then groaned. "Gah, what time is it?"

"Not quite midnight. Have you been here watching Olive all day?"

"Who the hell is Olive?"

I pointed.

He sat up, yawning, and stretched so thoroughly I could hear things creaking. "I thought her name was Dawg."

"It is *not*. Don't you think the small blob of white hair on her head is the right size and shape for an olive?"

"A white olive?"

"Her name is Olive." I paused and straightened. "I assume Adrienne. . . ?"

"Yup. Then she called me and wanted cream puffs and my

presence in the apartment, in that order. She has some sort of freaky sixth sense . . . How the hell does she always know when I'm making cream puffs?"

I hid a smile. He did it whenever he had not seen Adrienne for more than ninety-six hours. He just was not consciously aware of that fact. He was too close to the pattern to see it. Which made Patrick the one person, other than my psychiatrist, who actively sought contact with Adrienne.

His bravery and devotion to a raging psychotic was almost enough to make me love him unconditionally. Or enough to make me jam him full of tranquilizers until the feeling passed.

"Anyway," he was saying, "I leapt to obey."

I shook my head. Such a glorious, kind, thoughtful idiot. "You are too good, Patrick."

"That's what my other two girlfriends . . . uh . . . never, ever say, come to think of it."

I could not help smiling, both at the small, docile-yet-friendly dog at my feet, and the large man sprawled on the couch.

I might love Patrick. I was certain Cadence did. And I did not know precisely why, for either of us. Adrienne loved his cream puffs, but probably not the man.

Still: Dr. Gallo would simply not leave my brain alone. Why? I had no idea. Was that part of his allure? I was drawn, and did not know why? I hated to think I was so easily bewitched.

"Cadence is not going to like this." And I was not referring to Olive.

"Oh, she sure didn't. At least the hairy thing she woke up next to this time was a dog and not a date."

An excellent point. "We should all give thanks."

He was scrubbing his face with his hands—slow to wake, was Patrick. I envied that.

"Listen, I was able to sneak her out into the trees behind the building—luckily you guys live on the first floor—and she just had one accident in the house. Oh, boy. She was *so* scared of me then. It . . . kind of broke my heart a little.

"I mean, jeez. It's just shit. And not even that much of it—it's not like I'm cleaning up after an elephant. We're talking a hot dog's worth, max. So I didn't praise her, because I don't want her to connect accidents with praise, but I didn't yell or anything, and she still was scared to death of me for a good five minutes."

Curious about this new side of him, I asked, "You know about training dogs?"

"Yeah, when my sister was just a kid, before my parents decided—" He cut himself off, sounding almost . . . angry? Before I could pin that down, he visibly shook himself and said, "You know what? Never mind; it's a story for another time."

"Patrick, what is—"

"Anyway, I didn't yell or anything but it still took me more than ten minutes to coax her out from under the table." He shook his head. "Somebody used to beat the hell out of her for . . . uh . . . everything, I think. Whoa!"

He had jumped to his feet, startling Olive, who ran behind me and peeked at him from behind my legs. "I know that look, Shiro Jones, just stop with the look, okay? Adrienne put her owner—"

"*Former* owner."

"Yeah, anyway, he's in the hospital counting all his broken bones, so don't go all Ninja all over him. Okay?" He was holding up both hands in an attempt to placate what he assumed was my simmering rage. "He's too chickenshit to press charges, but if you show up and start cutting things off the man he might change his mind, so just staaaaay away. Okay?"

Hmph. Through clenched teeth I managed to grind out, "We should make an appointment for her at a veterinary clinic."

"Uh, I'm not trying to step on toes here or anything, so don't beat the shit out of *me*, either . . ."

"Well." I sniffed. "Not tonight." Maybe.

". . . but I had the same thought so I called the clinics in the area, and one of them had a cancellation and I brought Daw—uh, Olive—right over."

I was silent for a moment. We had been casually dating for several weeks, but in truth Cadence saw more of him than Adrienne or I. I was fine with that. I still thought it odd that he was dating all three of us. When I did not find it threatening or comforting.

Patrick was very kind. And quite patient, since none of us had agreed to have intercourse with him yet. But there were times I worried he was the type of man attracted to wounded women. Cadence and Adrienne qualified, to be sure.

And now he had a canine damsel in distress, and had rushed to assist her.

Were we . . . a project to him? Something to be fixed? That was something to ponder later. "That was thoughtful."

"Oh, you should have seen her, she was *so* good. Big waiting room full of cats and dogs, and don't get me started on the kid with the garter snake in the birdcage."

I smiled. "But that sounds like the best part of the story."

"I hate snakes." He patted the sofa. "C'mon, Olive, c'mere!" She trotted across the room and in a flash of skinny black legs had hopped back up on the couch beside him. "She was really scared, I mean, she'd been shaking *so* bad in the waiting room and then on the scale and then on the exam table. But she didn't nip or even growl. The vet fell in love with her, couldn't believe how good-natured she was after all that abuse."

"How many bones, did you say? That her former owner now has to count?" Whatever the answer? Not enough.

"Let it *go*, gorgeous. He was smited big-time by Adrienne. She bashed his head into a wall, for God's sake."

There were times I loved Adrienne and, more important, respected her.

"You sound . . . torn."

"Hey, he was a big-time jerkoff. Who had his *head* bashed into a *wall*. Along with his buddy's head." Patrick, far too good for his own good, shrugged and continued. "Anyway, Olive's malnourished. The vet figured she could have grown a lot bigger—maybe black Lab big—but didn't get enough to eat when she was a puppy or, if she did, it was the wrong stuff to feed a puppy. Actually, she's still a puppy, the vet figures she's about a year and a half old. But she's all done growing, he said. I mean in height. Her legs won't get longer."

"Clever girl," I told her. "You will be easier to accommodate in here if you do not take up as much room as you might have. Well done. And get down." I snapped my fingers and pointed to the carpet. Olive instantly obeyed. "Do not let her on the furniture, Patrick."

"Um, sure. No prob." But his gaze slid away from mine. Lord help the poor man if he had to lie about something serious, because he was terrible at deceit of any kind. "Anyway, he gave her all her shots and told me the best kind of dog food for her and she's also got some puppy vitamins she has to take once a day. I just wrap them in cheese and down they go, slurp! Someone should invent Vitamin Cheese for dogs. And people, come to think of it. And the best news is, when that shithead stomped her, he didn't break anything, she's just gonna be super-sore for a few days."

"Stomped?"

"Whoa!" He bounced up from the sofa and lunged just in time to catch me by the shoulder. Somehow I was already halfway to the door. "Concussion, remember? Humiliated and hospitalized, is that ringing a bell? Head bashed into wall, is *that* ringing a bell?"

It was. It was the bell a boxer heard just before he beat his opponent to death.

And the winner is . . . Shiro!

"Oh, man, I know that look. Quit it, you're making me really fucking nervous. Do *not* go all 'ya feel lucky, punk?'—okay? We've got enough trouble hiding Olive from your neighbors and your landlord."

I thought about it, then relented. Patrick was right, and I did occasionally let cooler heads prevail.

It occurred to me that my boyfriend had asked me to do something against my nature, and I had agreed.

Was this what being in a relationship was? I would have to think about that. And in my mind, I apologized to Adrienne for doubting her methodology. Or her motive.

"I suppose we shall have to move."

He looked relieved that I had discarded my felony assault plan. "Look, the situation's okay for now. C'mon, babe, come back over here and sit down." I followed him, and Olive followed me. He guided me to the couch and then began to walk back and forth in front of me. Olive thought this was a splendid new game and followed him. It looked like he had a small, four-legged black shadow aping his long strides.

"For now, I think you can use the trees behind the building. Nobody ever goes back there because of the fencing."

"And the wood ticks." It was dreadful. If you *glanced* at the small clump of trees you had to start picking the wretched things off.

"Not so much in December, but yeah. And who wants to play in a bunch of dirty snow? I never saw anyone even come near that area all the times we went outside. So I don't think anybody'll notice if we don't push our luck."

"Hear that?" I asked Olive. "Do not push our luck."

"Oh, and see this?" He pointed to the handle of the deck door. There was a small bell on the end of a two-foot-long length of string. "She's gonna associate the bell ringing with taking a dump, and I think it'll help her catch on. That's for right now, but it's not a long-term solution, right?"

"Correct. I am impressed, Patrick. I did not know you knew dogs. And you had no notice. I am—we are grateful."

"Huh? Oh. Yeah, my sister had one when she was little. Before my—it was a long time ago."

He ran his fingers through his thick black-red hair and I realized he was nervous. About what? And for what reason? Odd. I could not recall Patrick being nervous about anything. He was loving and protective and handsome and charming and passionate and handsome and gorgeous and handsome . . . really quite handsome, the man could have modeled suits for Armani.

Hmmm. I was not often so easily distracted by my own train of thought. Now what had I been thinking about?

"You'll be set for a while. Look at this!" He was pointing to a neat pile of canine accessories: a leash, a collar, quite a lot of an expensive dog food (the kind they only sold in veterinary clinics), several toys. As if she knew what I was looking at, Olive went to the pile, extracted some sort of rubber toy shaped like a hamburger, took it in her mouth, and gently bit down.

Squee! Squee!

"If you have your dog on a leash, you can bring them inside PetCo! Now tell me, how cool is that? So I left her in my car, went in and bought a leash, then came back out and put it on her and away we went. That's where I got all this stuff."

Squee!

"That was very kind." I was grinning like a fool at Olive. She just looked *so* cute with her rubber hamburger. "You must let me reimburse—"

He waved that away with the impatience of a millionaire who cared little for green pieces of paper because he knew he had more of them than he would ever spend. "Don't worry about it. Like I said, this'll do for now, but we need a long-term plan."

I raised an eyebrow. "Yes. I suppose 'we' do."

Squee! Olive had trotted over to me, dropped the hamburger on the carpet, then lay down and rested her chin on top of it (*squee!*). Then she closed her eyes and appeared to go to sleep.

If the evening had ended right then, it would have been perfect. Instead, there was a nightmare waiting in the room, and none of us knew it.

Then.

chapter fifty-five

"Okay," he said, preparing to shatter my sense of safety, the poor idiot. "So. I've been thinking about this. You know I close on my house in a few days, right?"

I nodded. We all knew. Patrick had moved back to Minnesota after many years away to reconnect with his sister. Cathie was several years younger; he had been away at college when she was still in elementary school.

What had started as a let's-get-reacquainted-as-siblings visit had turned into roots Patrick wanted to plant in the Twin Cities. Cathie blamed my sisters and me for this, and was not shy about telling us.

For myself, I was not so sure. I think Patrick was looking for what Cadence had sought her entire life: a home. I thought he had decided to settle down for reasons of his own, and they did not all center around the Jones girls.

I had seen the house he had selected. It was . . . dazzling. There was no other word. It had once been a church built in 1910, and had been completely renovated and updated with an eye to being as green as possible. So it had state-of-the art appliances, a heated floor, and had been built to be sustained and sustainable.

If being eco-friendly had not been enough, the church-now-house had been renovated with the very best. Pine floors, red oak floors, rolling doors, a scrim curtain. A sixteen-foot-tall fireplace flanked with slate (and two others, not as impressive but still quite nice). Vaulted ceilings, a kitchen with two islands, a sizable dining room overlooking a lake, two-person spa tub, walk-in shower, walk-in closets, a wet bar, a three-car heated garage, balconies, and decks.

I loved Patrick's house. Or the house that would be his in a few days. I had no idea why he needed so much room, but such things were not my business. His house, his wonderful house . . . even empty, it seemed to be waiting for a family to fill it up and make it cluttered and noisy and dirty and warm. When it came time for that, I knew the house would be ready.

I liked houses. I . . . I had never lived in one. The people I knew who had lived in houses seemed happy. They knew where they belonged. They liked going home to a house. Perhaps someday I could discover how that felt. I considered houses the emotional equivalent of a tornado shelter. I would like to find out for myself . . .

Never mind. It was a stupid thought.

"Right, you've been there, you know what it's like. Shiro, there's tons of room. Right? Tons."

"Yes, that seems how you wanted it." I would not pretend to understand.

"How I—?" He raked his fingers through his dark red hair. "I wanted a lot of room because of you guys. I really . . . it would be great if you wanted to move in with Olive the Dawg. You could stay as long as you wanted. You . . ." His eyes finally met mine. Yes, he was definitely nervous. His hands were fists, and he was unaware. "You could—*we* could all live together."

Live together.

Live together? In that wonderful, wonderful house?

Together?

It was a generous shocking horrifying wonderful terrible offer.

"I—"

"Don't answer right away, okay?" he said hastily. "I know it's a big step. If you're not comfortable—I mean, it doesn't have to be forever."

Ah. So Patrick's plan was to wait until I was used to living in his beautiful beautiful house and then make me leave?

I eyed the side of his throat. One shot with stiffened fingers and he'd flop to the floor and wake up with a ferocious headache. And that was just *one* of the things I could—

"But if it *was* forever . . . Look, I know this is fast."

Did he?

"Just think about it, okay? And if you change your mind, if you don't want it to be forever, you could always move out."

A cold thought from the bottom of my brain: *Max Gallo would not make such a mess of this. He would simply state what he wanted, and then wait for our response.*

"I get that you'll want some time, and like I said, you could always move back here, or someplace that takes dogs."

"Stop saying that."

"Which part?"

Stop trying to make me love you so you can dispose of me as fits your needs. Stop it.

"It's too fast, isn't it?" He shook his head. "I knew I'd screw this up. I've been thinking and thinking and . . . you know what?"

I hardly dared ask.

"Listen, maybe we should just forget I even said anything."

On second thought, letting you live in my house would post great difficulty for me . . . Best if we forget the whole thing.

"I think that is safest."

"Safest?"

"You do not truly know us."

"Shiro—"

"You don't know how ugly we are."

"*Ugly*?" He gaped at me, big eyes getting even bigger in his shock. "Shiro, you and Cadence and Adrienne are the most beautiful women in the world! You're all brilliant and brave and complicated and weird and wonderful and sexy and gorgeous and awesome and terrifying. I feel lucky that I get *all that* in one package, one gloriously smokin' hot package—"

"Inside." There was a roaring in my ears, the way it sounded right before the plane's wheels left the runway. Or crashed right back into it. "You don't know. We are so ugly inside. We can't hide that from you if we live in the same wonderful house. It would be . . . impossible."

Olive had opened her eyes and gotten up to press her body against my legs, whimpering. I could feel her trembling through my slacks.

"You can't see it, Patrick. You can't see our foulness and live. The part of you that thinks you like us would not survive that."

"*Thinks*? Okay. You know what? I shouldn't have sprung this on you. I just . . . it's fast. I know that. But if it's going to upset you, I withdraw the offer, okay?

"Listen, I've done some pretty shitty things in my life, too. Things I don't want you to find out. Things I'm scared shitless you'll find out."

I laughed at him. "You only managed a double for the big

game, not a triple? Your soufflé only won First Place, not Grand First?"

He scowled . . . a first, I thought. "Don't make fun. Just because I don't waltz bad guys into ER wards doesn't mean I haven't had to handle my own shit."

"And I am sure you did so beautifully."

"Are we having a fight? Is this a fight?"

"If you have to ask," I sighed, "most likely it is not." What had I been thinking, toying with this pretty uncomplicated rich boy? I—*we*—needed a grown-up. Someone with a few lines on his face. Someone who knew the world could turn and bite you whenver it liked, with no warning at all.

Max Gallo, I presume?

"Regardless of what *we* decide," he said in a tone I'm sure he meant to be warning but which I found unimpressive, "Olive the Dawg, you can bring her over to my place while you're looking for a pet-friendly apartment. The whole backyard is fenced in, remember? So don't worry about it anymore. I should have kept my mouth shut."

Wrong. That was not your mistake.

I stared at his earnest face and saw, for the first time, the face of the enemy. Olive shivered at my feet while my thoughts raced 'round and 'round like a cheap metal car on a go-cart track.

You should never have made me think there was a place for me in your home. And after you did that? You should not have taken it away. Before you came, I would never have dreamed. Before you came, I would not have dared picture my shattered life in someone else's life. Someone else's house.

You should not have done that, Patrick.

And I will not give you the chance to do it again.

"But about this other thing. I've been meaning to tell you, I've just been too . . ." He stared at his hands, large and strong. ". . . too chickenshit, I guess. I *like* that you guys think of me as a good guy. I'm not, though. A long time ago, when it was never more important to my family to be the good guy, I dropped the ball. And I've been living with that—Shiro?"

I had left. Olive saw; Patrick, too busy bleating at his hands at whatever dreadful thing he thought he did, did not.

chapter fifty-six

Shiro can't come to the phone right now Shiro is crying

Shiro NEVER CRIES Shiro never what did you DO? What did you do with the geese what did you do with the Shiro

Don't! Don't! you are a
BAD Baker Boy you turned

Turned the wheel
The wheels on the bus
The wheels on the bus go
Poor Shi-ro
Poor Shi-ro
Poor Shi-ro

Shiro we should fly
Shiro Dr. Max will teach you to fly

And you won't cry anymore anymore you can't cry and fly

The wheels on the bus go
Poor puppy! Looklook! She's happy she's happy to see me she KNOWS me she knows I'll never I'll
never

let her get hurt
she knows I
she knows me

puppy is George
I will hug her and pet her and call her George

No one gets hurt no one hurts or gets hurt and I promised and George

George loves me and I

love Shiro and she never cries she never and she never hides so why is she doing things why is NEVER not true anymore?

It's YOUR fault, Baker Boy!
Dr. Max would never bake!

You shouldn't have
Baker Boy
But you did
And now I have to now I must now you are dead now you are because I will I will
I will!

I can't.
I can't hurt you, Baker Boy, I can't hurt you
am I broken, too?

You need to go away, Baker Boy! You need to go away before I remember

how to hurt you because I can
You know I can
You know I will

(I won't!)

Am I crying?
Am I crying with Shiro in the dark?

Don't cry don't cry see? I've come
To keep you company

We'll hide
(no not hide we are not hiding we are NOT HIDING)

NOT NOT!

We'll hide here
Until you feel better.

Poor Shiro
Shhhhhhh . . .

chapter fifty-seven

The bell woke me. I was in my own bed and . . . naked? I flipped up the sheets and peeked. Yup. Naked. But no tattoos, no bruises, no casts, no Ace bandages. No body glitter . . . gah, I was so happy when that silly shiny trend died out. No henna . . . but to be fair, the henna designs on my hands those other times were actually pretty cool. They were so intricate and gorgeous, and lasted for days and days. Still, they were *my* hands, darnitall. It would have been nice to have been asked.

No temp tattoos, no treasure map scribbled upside down on my belly so I could read it while looking down at myself (Adrienne's logic can be . . . convoluted). No mysterious Japanese characters on the underside of my arms. No piercings, no sunburn, no frostbite. Annnnnd . . . I felt my face. The mirror was in the bathroom, but it didn't feel like I'd had my face painted.

Nope, I was fine. The tinkling of a bell, *that's* what woke me up. I tossed the covers back, pulled the top quilt off the bed and wrapped it around myself, plucked my cell phone off the bedside table, then followed the tinkle.

Dawg was sitting in front of the sliding door. A bell on a string had been tied to the door handle; it was still swaying. The bell had been hung so it was level with her nose; she poked it again, then heard me and trotted over, wagging her tail.

"Does that . . . you want to go out?" Dawg had a red collar, I saw, and was looking sleeker than usual. No, not sleek . . . clean! She'd been thoroughly washed and brushed, and smelled terrific.

I knelt to pet her and . . . whoa! "What have you been eating?" Her little belly was practically distended, and she was more alert and bright-eyed than I'd ever seen her. Full of dog food and treats, I was betting. For the first time in her life she was getting fed more than what a turd-faced poopie-brain remembered to toss her way.

I popped the lock on the door, then on the screen door, and slid them both open. Then gasped . . . aaggh! Still December. Dawg trotted out, headed straight for a small grove of trees twenty or so feet away, squatted to do her business, then came trotting back. Which was great, because too late, I'd realized I didn't have her on a leash and she might run off without one.

No one ever came back here . . . when there was snow it was unshoveled and depressing. When there was grass, it teemed with wood ticks.

Bemused, I shut and locked the door after Dawg finished and docilely came inside. While she was doing her business I'd taken a quick-and-dirty look around the place. There weren't any clandestine poops, or mysterious wet spots on the carpet.

And Dawg had accumulated a lot of stuff in my absence. There were a couple of dog toys in the living room, a leash hanging up beside the coat closet in the entryway, a food and water dish just inside the kitchen . . . and that was just the stuff I'd spotted in a glance.

"Wow," I told her, stooping to pet her sleek (and clean) head. Dawg nuzzled my palm and then frisked around my bare legs. "You caught on really . . ." Fast. Yeah. She had. But maybe not. How long had I been gone?

I looked at my phone, afraid. One push of a button and I'd know the date and time. And that wasn't all. Shiro had loaded all sorts of helpful apps into the thing (I mostly used it for calls and feeding koi).

If I hit the right buttons, I could also find out where I was in location to BOFFO's office—imagine my surprise once to wake up with the Mississippi River on the wrong side, until the app told me where I was. And that wasn't much of a complication compared to waking up with the *ocean* on the wrong side.

I could also find out what the weather was like (which always seemed like an "oh, duh!" move, but a weather forecast could be surprisingly helpful) and what it would be like for the next few days.

My phone would also assist me in finding the closest drugstore, grocery store, post office, hospital, car rental, airport, gas station, and bar. Or spit out voice memos from Shiro ("Do not be alarmed, but you are in South Vietnam and you have promised to marry the man who is trying to kill you in an honor duel. Also we are low on milk.") or Adrienne ("Duck duck gray duck! Duck duck gray shotgun! Oooooh, the shotgun! Shiny. Where's the milk?").

I could also track flights, Google the Earth with Google Earth, translate languages (my Spanish was workable, my German only fair, my French nonexistent, my Arabic was a joke), and . . . eh?

I squinted and saw a brand-new app; it hadn't been on my phone the last time I looked. It was a white cross against a red background: Dog First Aid. "Wow," I said to Dawg. "Shiro's not taking any chances with you."

All this to say Shiro had gone to a lot of trouble to make our cell phone more than just a phone, stuffing it with apps that would help us when we woke up on a strange continent.

I had been so grateful to her for that. And so angry it needed to be done at all. Cadence Jones: when she's annoyed, she's annoyed. And when she's grateful, she's annoyed.

I should nip this referring to myself in the third person thing in the bud, *now*. And stop asking myself questions when I say, do you know what I mean? *Now*.

I took a breath and pushed the button. December 6th, 9:00 A.M. So, one day. One whole day. Gone.

I trudged back to my bedroom, tossing the blanket on the bed and pulling open drawers so I could get dressed. I don't know why the date bothered me. Sure, I'd lost a day, but there had been times I'd lost days, even weeks. Once I was gone for two months.

Imagine: in my head, it was still hot-dogs-on-the-grill time when I went to bed, but when I woke up it was twenty degrees cooler, the trees were riots of red, orange, and yellow, and everywhere I went there were school buses full of children annoyed summer had gone so quickly. *Oh, children, I can absolutely feel your pain.*

I'd gone to bed wondering if the humidity was ever going to let up—the shortest of shorts still felt like overdressing—and woke up needing a sweatshirt just to walk from my building to my car.

That had been a lot worse. Much, much worse than one lousy day.

Telling myself that wasn't helping. I sighed and renewed my lethargic closet poking. This? I didn't want to wear a skirt to work. This? No, not even a super-cute skirt. Okay, how 'bout this? No, I'd bought the khaki slacks because I'd loved how they looked on the mannequin and refused to admit the slacks made my waist disappear. No matter what top I wore, be it blouse or sweater or crisp T-shirt with blazer, I looked like God had finished my legs and just dumped my head on top of my thighs as an afterthought. The stupid things had been too expensive for me to feel good about packing them off to Goodwill. Of course, I wouldn't wear them, either, so they just sat in my closet.

My phone began playing Napoleon XIV's "They're Coming to Take Me Away, Ha-Haaa!" Adrienne had changed my ringtone again. I made up my mind to suck it up; the last time she'd done it, she'd replaced Paper Lace's "The Night Chicago Died"—the most wonderful romantic scary song ever—with some dreck by Maroon 5. *That's* insanity.

Ah! It was Cathie. She'd cheer me up. She probably had some zany adventure of her own—a painting she couldn't finish so she drenched it in orange juice, maybe, or another gallery owner wanting "this one and this one, and can you do seven more just like that one?"

"Hey, Cath. So you know those khaki pants I—"

"Why is my brother in jail?"

"—hate," I finished, so astonished I almost dropped the phone. "What? Patrick's in jail? *What?*"

"Yes! Jail! And he won't say anything and the cops won't say anything and are you going to fix this or am I going to use your *eyeballs* to hold my *brushes?*"

"Really, the whole thing sounds very bad." My brain kept trying to grasp the concept. And the concept kept refusing to be grasped. Every time I thought I had a handle on it, it just slid away. "Cathie, tell me everything you know."

"He's in jail."

I was hopping through my bedroom—which Dawg thought was a wonderful game—pulling on slacks I hated and trying to hold the phone with my chin and ear. That never worked with these skinny cell phones, but old habits died etcetera.

"How'd you know?"

"Michaela called and told me!"

"What . . . Michaela?" In my horror, I nearly dropped the phone. "My boss, Michaela? That Michaela?"

"Yes! I guess he called her, and asked her to call me to tell me *not* to come—you believe it? She was his one phone call. He could have hired the best lawyer in the tristate area, but he used his call to tell her to tell me *not* to help him."

"But of course you ignored that."

"Duh, Cadence."

Charming. I could almost see Shiro, smiling sardonically. *She frantically calls you for help, and gives you "Duh, Cadence"? So gracious.*

I shoved the thought (almost a vision, I guess you could call it) away.

"But the slippery son of a bitch wouldn't tell me *which* jail," she was saying. "Which in the Cities . . . you know."

I did know. There were a number of counties in the Minneapolis/St. Paul area. The largest was Hennepin, which was home to over a million people. That was *one,* in one city. There were many more just within Minneapolis, never mind St. Paul and the surrounding towns and cities.

I didn't even know where Patrick had been arrested . . . well, when we got right down to it I didn't even know *why* he'd been arrested, or what he'd done, but those were secondary considerations. If he'd been arrested in Burnsville or St. Paul or Minneapolis or Lilydale . . . There were different counties, procedures, and yes, jails, for each. A fed didn't have a lot of pull with the locals. Resentment was too easily stirred up.

"—so I didn't even know where to go, never mind what I could—"

Hop, hop. Make reassuring grunt into phone. Shoo Dawg away

from shoes. Lose balance; crash heavily into carpeted bedroom floor. "Nnnnfff! Ow."

"—could be any one of ten courthouses—Cadence!"

"I'm here, I'm here, did he say anything about an arraignment or . . . come back! I need that, Dawg!"

"You need that dog? What dog? Can you even have dogs in your—fuck it, I don't want to know. Dammit, are you even listening to me? My brother has been caged like a rabid skunk, and my best friend appears somewhat distracted! More so than usual!"

"Cathie, I'm sorry, it's just—it's just a crazy time right now." Understatement. "I'm taking this seriously, I promise."

"Okay, granted, you usually have about eight hundred crises to deal with at a given time, but I'm calling in the best-friend marker. That's gotta count for something, Cadence, so it's on the table today. I am cashing the best-friend chip!" *Please don't cash it. Please don't cash it. Put it back in your purse for another day.* "Just this once, my brother and I have to be the crisis that you put above all your other weird crises *this one time*."

I'd run after Dawg, realizing I was rewarding an overgrown puppy for undesirable behavior, but too short on time and too frazzled to care. I managed to corner her and get the other half of my pair of black flats away from her. Damp, but not chewed. Excellent. Uh, relatively speaking.

"Yep, yep," I was saying, though I'd only caught the end of her rant. "I'll get—" My phone beeped; another call. I took a peek . . . drat it to heck and back! "Oh, Fraggle Rock! That's Michaela."

"No you don't, Cadence Jones, *we* are your crisis *du jour*, we just established that, so you can't—"

"Cathie, she'll have news about Patrick. Whatever it is, I promise, I'll fix it. I *promise*. Hon, I'm sorry, I have to go, somebody might be dead."

"Somebody always is!"

That was true enough. Cringing, I disconnected her. Ohhhh, I was going to pay for that. And pay and pay and pay. And then pay some more.

The last time I'd incurred such Cathie-wrath, she'd painted my front door lime green with wide pastel blue stripes. The colors weren't just awful to look at; people would actually stay away from my door altogether so they didn't have to deal with the sensory input. And that had been over a disagreement about whether or not Van Gogh cut off part of his earlobe for love, or insanity. It wasn't over an incarcerated family member, for gosh's fargin' slimy smelly sakes!

"Michaela?"

"We've got a break. Get here."

"I—"

What? What could I tell her? That I had no idea what had happened, not just with Patrick but with JBJ? That I'd been out of the picture a whole day and had only been back five minutes and oh, by the way, I have a dog now?

And lest we forget: for some reason my boyfriend had been arrested, which Michaela knew all about? Ah, yes, I'm sure *those* facts had nothing at all to do with one another.

How to tell my boss, a woman who frequently waded hip-deep into bureaucratic trouble to keep me licensed/employed/sane that whatever the break was, I cared more about finding and helping Patrick than I did about . . . well . . . anything else right now?

Did that make me a good girlfriend, but a bad agent?

And would going to Michaela right now make me a good agent, but a bad girlfriend?

Max Gallo wouldn't get you in this kind of jam. He'd solve his own problems. Anyone with eyes like his knows all about holding cells.

And just where had that come from? Of all the things *not* to be wondering about right now, Max Gallo's thousand-yard stare was number one on the list.

Honestly, I had a question that wasn't rhetorical: How do people who aren't medicated and/or under psychiatric care handle these day-to-day stressors? *Because I really wanted to know!*

I knew what it felt like to have a psyche pulling me in different directions. To feel mad or glad or sad, but also know that another part of me felt happy or depressed or euphoric about the very same thing.

It was strange but also a known quantity. It was dizzying but familiar, like when you hit the roller coaster when the state fair came to town. You knew it'd leave you with an upset stomach for a good hour, but to *not* ride it was unthinkable.

I'd never known what it was like to have my heart torn—*shredded*—in multiple directions. Not since the day my mother killed my father and I'd split from one to three. For the first time, I truly understood on an emotional level, not just an intellectual one, what a coping process that had been. My brain had tried to protect itself from shattering into a thousand pieces by forcing controlled splitting into three.

Like the man said, "It seemed like a good idea at the time."

I couldn't help but notice, though, that no matter how frazzled and freaked and stressed I got, Shiro wasn't stepping up to help me. Progress? Or a strike? The more tense I got, the more I half expected to wake up and find it was a day later. But I was still here.

That was what a nightmare my day-to-day existence had become: when I was disappointed not to be yanked out of the control room of my own body.

To know that the part of me that lived for solving puzzles and catching bad guys could demand as much of my heart as the part that wanted to drop everything and go to Patrick right now—that was something new and terrible and wonderful.

And Dr. Gallo? Dr. Max Gallo? A mere acquaintance and, worse, the family member of a victim. A man I should think of in purely professional terms . . . and I never had. Not once.

I guess you could say I was having a mental split decision. (Perhaps several.)

"Hmm, well, Dan, I guess the judges are putting their heads together to see if . . . nope, no one's backing off of this one, Dan! We've got a winner, and one of the judges is not *happy about it!"*

Yeah, well. I knew how he felt.

chapter fifty-eight

"I gotta give it to that twitchy son of a bitch," was how George greeted me. "He knows his shit."

"Which?" I gasped. I'd made it to the office in record time, but burned with shame when I thought about all the traffic laws I'd violated to do it. No one was above the law, no matter how many personalities she has. Or boyfriends. Or boyfriend, singular, in jail.

"Which twitchy SOB? Or which shit?"

"George, I haven't been here for about twenty-four hours. Pretend you care, and pretend I'm being fooled by your faux care, and let me know what I missed."

"Well, you missed a lot of the pure simple Awesomeness That Is George Pinkman," he said. Ah. Instead of faux care, it was faux modesty. "And it was pretty great! Like I have to tell *you* that. But what happened was, Paul came away from the crime scene—you remember, Aaron Mickelson, Edina, that weird Dr. Gallo who may yet be my wingman?"

"Yeah, yeah. We didn't think copycat, we thought JBK might be getting a little fed up with his extracurricular activities. We didn't bounce Gallo into a cell because he's related to one of the victims."

"Yeah, I found out that's why he moved here in the first place. Guess his family's taking it pretty har— You're nodding, you already knew that. Fine. Well, after all that, Paul pretty much vanished into whatever geek hell hole he occupies when he's not out in the real world trying to vibrate himself to death. Hours later he pops out, he's got HOAP.1 running and all kinds of new tidbits for us. Me and the New Girl started plowing through it, and—"

"You're back!" Emma Jan had come bustling out of the kitchen—the office kitchen, not Michaela's other office—carrying Cup-a-Soup. Ugh. I'd rather drink Cup-a-Barf. We've got synesthetes designing software that can tell a computer how to think for itself, but instant noodles still tasted like broiled Styrofoam no matter what we did to them? If God was on vacation, I wish he'd finish with the barhopping and get back to running the universe already. "Great! Listen, Shiro, Paul was—"

"That's Cadence." George was looking rumpled, which told me he'd been intrigued by Paul's invention in spite of himself and hadn't gone home in a while. No one here had to worry, though. If he thought he'd worn one of his ties too long, he'd switch it out with one of the fifteen he kept in his lower-left desk drawer. Today's model sported grasshoppers that seemed to be mating. Uh. No. After a closer glance I realized they were cannibalizing each other. Against a peach background.

Whenever I wondered what the dealio was with George's ties, I could almost feel my freaked-out psyche contemplating growing a fourth personality just to deal with all the necktie fallout. So I never thought about them for very long.

"It's Cadence," he was saying. "You can tell because no matter how shitty I am to her, she won't be shitty back. Oh, and her swearing sucks. She's also freaked about keeping Michaela waiting, when Shiro wouldn't give a shit."

"Oh." To my annoyance, Emma Jan looked crestfallen. Crestfallen! Not disappointed. Not mildly annoyed. Not somewhat sad. Crestfallen! The way you feel when something really important—like finding out if you got into your dream college or not—happened! "Sorry, Cadence."

"Sorry *I'm* not who you were expecting." I put every shred of sugar I could into my tone, which, since I repress a lot of rage, was considerable.

There was a short silence while Emma Jan fidgeted. She was wearing the green pantsuit again, but with a black blouse. The gigantic purse was still the same, practically bursting with . . . were those dog treats? Did she know that Behrman didn't have a dog anymore, but I did? Has Shiro been telling her my secrets?

"Listen, uh, don't take this the wrong way—" she began.

"Aw, fuck." George slumped into his chair. "Don't do it, Emma Jan. She'll cry and everything will take longer."

"I will not!"

"I don't, y'know, *care* all that much, I'm just curious . . . because of the case."

"Because of the case, what?" I asked.

She shrugged and met my gaze. "I just wanted to know if you knew when Shiro would be back." She turned to George. "What, is that not cool etiquette with these three? Look, if Shiro was a real person, Cadence wouldn't be mad if I wanted to know when someone who wasn't her was gonna be around, right?"

George leaned back in his chair and stared at the ceiling. "Oh, fuck me twice, here we go."

"Not a real person?" I noticed for the first time I sort of towered over her. Especially when I was ticked off. Especially when I'd been quietly moving closer to her while she babbled about why I shouldn't be offended if she didn't want me around. "Shiro's as real as you are, Emma Jan Thyme! As real as I am! Or do you think I'm not real, either?"

"And me without popcorn."

"Shut up, George." Hmm. New Girl was catching on fast. Sort of. "Listen, don't get mad, Cadence. There's just a bunch of new stuff about JBK I think Shiro's gonna need to know about."

"*And she will.* When she comes *back.* Until then, you're stuck with me. So . . . so just *be* stuck with me!"

"Toldya. She can't even muster a 'damn.' If she tried for 'shit' she'd blow up. Seriously. The stress would shred her tiny mind like shrapnel."

"Shut up, George!" I whirled back to my prey. "It's amazing to me that someone who thinks their *reflection* is out to get them has the nerve to decide what part of *my* psyche is real and what's just . . . what? Made up so I can get more attention? That tends to be an assumption made by idiots who don't know what they're talking about, and don't care to do a little research to find out."

"I can't help it," Emma Jan forced through gritted teeth, "if no one believes me about Her."

"You know intellectually none of it is real," I raged. "It's been explained to you your whole life! So just cough up and swallow it down emotionally and your life—and ours!—will get a lot easier."

"How's she supposed to cough up and swallow at the same—"

"Shut up, George!" we screamed. Then, from Emma Jan: "Oh, that's nice, white bread!"

" 'White bread'? Is that supposed to be some sort of racial—"

"Who the hell cares? This isn't about race, it's about attitude. But as long as we're giving each other advice on how to stop being a pain in the other's ass, *you* might consider the fact that since Shiro and Adrienne are parts of your mind, they're no more real than you think the Mirror Bitch is! After all, you understand it *intellectually*. It's been explained to you your whole life, right?"

"I'm having," George said, peeking into his pants, "the biggest hard-on of my life."

"You're about to understand a broken nose intellectually," I promised in a rage. I could feel my pulse beating away like mad from the middle of my brain. Was that normal? *Was* there a pulse in the middle of my brain? And why was I asking myself a question I had no hope of being able to answer? "If you're lucky, *maybe* she'll be satisfied with that."

"She? Oh yeah? You gonna sic one of your imaginary friends on me? S'matter, Cadence, you're not up to taking care of your own business?"

"Oh no she *dih* uhnt," George chanted, then threw his arms in front of his face. "Okay, okay! I'm shutting up."

I couldn't remember ever being this ticked. I mean, ever. Okay, there was the repressed rage thing, sure, that would account for a lot of would-be fights that never happened, but still. Maybe the pressure of the job was getting to me? Maybe wondering why Patrick was locked up? And what Dr. Gallo had to do with any of this? He had something to do with this, right?

"You're gonna get soooo messed up." Yeah! After Adrienne showed up (she should be here any second . . . in fact, why hadn't she been here ten seconds ago?), Emma Jan Thyme wouldn't *ever* wish one of my personalities was here instead of me. Ha!

That would teach her to wish me gone. At my own desk, she wished me gone! Just stood there and wished I was somebody else, someone she *liked*. I almost envied Adrienne getting to bring on the beat-down. "Don't worry, though. I'll come visit you in the hospital. I'm great at post-Adrienne apologetic flower bouquet drop-offs."

"Just like I thought. God forbid you stick around and actually see something all the way through to the end. You just like the easy part. You just like bringing flowers."

George let out a squeak of terror, clutched the arms of his office chair, and shoved with his feet, hard enough to make his chair zoom several feet to the left.

Oooooh, that did it! I stopped circling and stood still, confidently expecting Adrienne to jump into the driver's seat and kick some serious patootey.

chapter fifty-nine

Wait. Why was I still here?

"Why am I still me?" I asked aloud.

George came out of his cringe. Emma Jan took a step closer.

I couldn't believe it. The one time, the *one time* I actually wanted that redheaded maniac to catapult herself into my life like a neutron bomb, *she* couldn't be bothered.

"Dammit!"

"Holy God, Cadence, was that an actual epithet to part your virgin l—"

"Shut *up*!" I practically screamed. I rounded on Emma Jan. "This doesn't change anything."

"Really?" She smiled. "That's good, because I don't really care which of us gets the beat-down, as long as somebody gets smacked."

"Your cheap rayon blouse is about to get wrecked."

"Bring it, white bread! And it's a silk *blend*. I've been wanting to smack the shit out of *someone* in this medicine chest of a department, and any one of the yous who live in your head will do fine! Do you ever actually catch bad guys, or just talk about catchin' bad guys?"

"Your accent gets thicker when you're mad!"

"I know!"

"But you'll be punching Shiro's face, too," George began, holding his hands up like a referee. "So would that qualify as a lover's—"

"Shut up!" Emma Jan was shrugging out of her jacket. Hmm, that was pretty smart. Decreased the chance of the jacket getting trashed, and increased mobility. I started taking off mine, too. "I figured it'd be *him,* that smirking sumbitch, he seems the type who needs his ass regularly kicked—"

"Oh, ladies, that is so unfair. Wherever I roam, I am misunderstood."

"—but smacking around your smug face will be a pretty great substitute."

"Smug? I'm never smug!"

"Yeah, you're wrong on that one, because you're sorta the poster child for smug," George began. Then, when we glared at him with the bloodred intensity of recently awakened volcanoes, he mimed zipping his lips shut, locking said lips, and tossing the key over his shoulder.

Jacket-free, we circled each other like sharks looking for the best place to bite. "Shiro has a boyfriend, you know. She's dating *my* boyfriend."

"No, I *don't* know, and it's none of my business anyway, because we're not dating, and I think we might be friends—someday—and . . . what? You think I'm trying to steal her away from you?"

Yes. "No!"

"You think I'm gonna try and start a romantic relationship with someone I work with 'fore I've even turned in my rental car slip?"

Yes. "No!"

"What, Shiro can't make a friend unless Cadence signs off on it? Do you use a form, or is it more a verbal OK?"

Well, there was never a need for an actual *paper* form before all this . . . aw, darn it to the furthest reaches of heck! "Stop trying to distract me with your silly questions. You just don't want to get *punched* in your stupid *face*."

"That's what this is really about, isn't it, Ms. Get-Along Girl? You don't like Shiro being her own person. You don't like me . . . so Shiro can't like me, neither."

"Either."

"That's pretty threatening to you, huh?"

"Proper English?"

"Chickenshit." If she'd been younger, she probably would have spit on the floor. It had been spat on before, unfortunately. "Sure, make it about grammar, *that'll* help."

She was correct to sneer—and rats! I forced myself back to the actual problem. "You yourself reminded me that we're all the *same* person!"

"Yeah, except when it's inconvenient. Like now. You were really pissed when your other self, the fighting self, didn't get you out of this, weren't you?"

"No, I was glad." A tiny white lie. "Okay, I was surprised at first, but then I was glad because she's very disruptive and . . . Wait. Is this about Adrienne and me, or you and Shiro, or me and Shiro, or you and me? Because there are a lot of things for me to keep track of in this fight."

"Well, shoot." She puffed a breath, making her bangs tremble (but in a block, not as individual hairs; she used a lot of gel). "If we haveta start thinking about what it's about, I'm gonna lose my mad-on."

I laughed. I couldn't help it. "Your mad-on? Is that what that is? No wonder you don't want to lose it." I was losing mine, too. Emma Jan was right. Why'd we let what was probably going to be a satisfying fight get screwed up with thinking?

"It's swell you two kissed and made up," George said, dismayed, "but now I have to go into the bathroom and beat off. Dammit! A perfectly good hard-on, and no chick-fight follow-up. You two really let me down."

"Awwwww." Emma Jan almost sounded contrite and everything. I snickered.

"Look!" he practically screamed. "You were getting down to it—finally. You were supposed to kick and scratch and spit—"

"Spitting isn't my style," Emma Jan said, a smirk still playing around her lips.

"Gross," I added.

"—and rip each other's clothes, but during the fight you'd realize you were both super-horny, so you'd go from the spitting and the scratching to tenderly helping each other out of your lacy bras and delicate pastel silk panties—"

"It's laundry day. I'm rocking granny panties right now," Emma Jan confessed.

George's groan of dismay almost made the whole silly argument worthwhile. "You can't beat 'em for comfort," I agreed, now forever loyal to Emma Jan's granny panties. Wait. I had best rephrase that . . . "Besides, she and Shiro are friends, not lovers. Right? Not lovers? So her panties are irrelevant."

"Shut up!" George demanded. Was that . . . was that a tear in the corner of his eye? "Then, after you made sweet-yet-nasty love on this disgusting lab experiment of a carpet, you'd decide to adjourn to the steam room—"

"We don't have a—"

"And instead, *this*." George made a gesture encompassing the two of us, and from the disgust in his voice it was a poor substitute to what he'd hoped for.

"Guess you'll just have to stick to your feverish imagination."

"Don't tell him that," I cautioned. "He will, and his imagination is something to be feared."

"No, I *won't*. I don't *want* to have to use my imagination! That's what *you* two were supposed to do. Right in front of me! Now I've got this useless hard-on while you two are practically ready to exchange recipes. I'd be psyched you were going to kiss and make up, except you won't even kiss! I should have known, Cadence, I should have *fucking* known. You can screw up anything with your weird stupid niceness."

"I have been *waiting*."

Ulp. Michaela's voice.

"Hard-on's gone," George said, going at least two shades paler.

chapter sixty

"So," Michaela began. "Updates." *Thwackthwack-thwack!* "If it isn't too much trouble."

We had assembled in her other office, and she was attacking a pile of celery stalks stacked so high, they looked like pale green firewood.

George plunged ahead, and for once I was grateful. Something had Michaela in a mood, and I wasn't certain it was just the JBJ update.

"Tell you this: Paul took *one* look at the crime scene and figured out that the pattern was way, way off. He's been twitching and jerking and practically having seizures since he got back from the Mickelson place."

"Poor guy."

George and I shook our heads. "Genius guy," I said. "It sounds mean, but the more like that Paul gets, the better for BOFFO. The stuff he's come up with, Emma Jan . . . you wouldn't believe it. He's not just a synesthete. His savantism—"

Emma Jan leaned forward, cupping her elbows in her hands. She wriggled on the bar stool—some people had trouble getting comfortable on them, especially in work situations. "We were talking about that earlier."

"Right."

"Don't call me Rainman." Ah! The man himself. Paul stumbled into the kitchen, looking at the reams and reams of data in his hands instead of where he was going. His shirt was untucked; his shoes were untied. I jumped off my stool and went to help him. "That stopped being funny being funny a good ten years ago does anybody smell blue?"

"Here. Ack! Be careful, Paul," I scolded as he stumbled. "Your glasses are filthy! How can you see anything? And it would help if you actually looked where you were—be *careful,* I said! You're not much good to us with a shattered skull."

"Don't tease," George sighed.

Thwack! Thwack! The sharp sound of four hundred-dollar German steel hitting a heavy cutting board brought Paul's head out of his data in a hurry. "You must smell blue if you're doing all that," he told Michaela.

"Just bring everyone up to speed," she ordered, thwacking so hard she had bits of celery in her eyebrows.

"The pattern the pattern was wrong, but HOAP.1 was able to find it. HOAP.1 can smell blue now. It couldn't before. Then I saw the body. So now it can."

We all stared at him. He looked back, calmly enough. He'd been stared at since birth, I figured . . . he *remembered* toilet training. Can you imagine?

He was usually carefully dressed, but he was a mess this morning. His shirt was dirty and both sleeves were unbuttoned. He'd obviously meant to roll them up to his elbows, but either it didn't take or he got distracted between unbuttoning the cuffs and rolling up the sleeves. So his sleeves were flapping and grimy. His shirt was untucked. His glasses were smeared with what looked like . . . axle grease? But that was impossible. Where would Paul get axle grease? And why was my mind obsessing over the least important details in this meeting?

Because I didn't want to hear what Paul was going to tell us. If HOAP.1 could smell blue, that meant there were more bodies out there than we knew. I didn't want to know that.

I didn't want to smell blue.

Even George seemed moved by Paul's state, because he helped me help Paul to the empty bar stool, and stacked the papers on the counter in front of us.

I gently took his glasses off his face, breathed on them, then vigorously rubbed with a nearby Kleenex—*not* the lotion kind. Ah! Much better. Now they were actually clear. Ish. Clear-ish?

"From what my man was telling me before you got here, Cadence, he said these killings have been going on much, much longer than seven years."

I sighed. "I was afraid of that. So how long? Ten years? Twelve?"

"Try fifty-six."

Silence, broken by *thwack! Thwack!* I felt like doing a little thwacking myself.

"That's impossible," Emma Jan said, her eyes enormous in her dark face. She looked frightened and exhilarated, a look—and feeling—I knew well. She felt bad about the deaths. And wanted to get the bad guy really, really bad. Sometimes I hated my job. Hated that to feel completion and joy in my work, a bunch of people had to die first.

"The JBJ killer has been active for over fifty years?" Emma Jan shook her head. "But that's wrong. How can that be?"

I was rubbing my eyes. "I'll tell you how. But we've gotta get rid of the stereotypes in our head first."

"'Our' head?" Michaela asked, arching a brow as she dumped decimated celery into a large green bowl.

"We've been looking for a . . . a boogeyman, I guess, for want of a better name. Our heads haven't really been in the game."

"That's because you can't smell blue," Paul said, not looking up. He was stacking and restacking the paperwork George had tried to put in order for him. "It's not not not your fault."

It was, though. Not only could I not smell blue, I was breaking in a new partner who liked *one* of me but not *all* of me. Something had happened to my boyfriend, and I couldn't get Max Gallo out of my head. Except I was wondering if that was *why* I couldn't get him out of my head. The more personal crap I had to wade through, the less time I had to feel guilty I couldn't smell blue.

"We've been looking at this all wrong." I wasn't sure what I was going to say . . . I wasn't sure why I'd even opened my mouth. But what I was saying . . . it felt right. So I sort of explored it while I was thinking about it, and then talking about it. "White kids in the summer. For over fifty years. It might as well have been the boogeyman, because we weren't going to be able to see the truth."

"What are you talking about?" George asked, and Emma Jan nodded in agreement. They were both staring at me like I'd grown a fourth personality. Ack! I shouldn't even joke about that . . .

"Serial killers don't often come across as drooling psychopaths. Well. Except for the psychopath part. We all *know* that. Intellectually, we know it. But what about Ted Bundy, Mr. Clean Cut? Yikes, what about Dorothea Puente? A little old lady serial killer! She looks like everybody's grandma. If I had ever met my grandma, either of them—"

"Now *there's* a horrifying thought," George said, eyes wide. He knew some of my family history, and was right to be afraid.

"—I'm sure they would have looked a lot like Dorothea Puente.

The jury couldn't believe it! Jeepers creepers peepers, I've read the file a zillion times and *I* couldn't believe it. But that sweet little old lady killed at least nine people and buried them in her garden. For *money*."

"Don't get her started on money," George whispered to Emma Jan. "Oh, wait. That's Shiro. Just play it safe and don't get either of 'em started on money."

"George: *shut up*." His astonished stare was a wonderful reward. I hated to be rude, but some days . . . I'd never told George to shut up in my life, and now, what? Seven times in twenty minutes? It was shaping up to be an interesting day so far.

I took a deep breath. Michaela and Emma Jan were giving me their full attention, at least. "You guys can't look at these unattractive suspects who have priors—like Behrman—and think, even unconsciously—maybe especially unconsciously—'It's gotta be this guy, he sure looks like a serial killer.' "

"I don't think anybody's—"

"No, trust me, we have. We've all done it with this guy, and I'm guilty of it, too. Half the reason I wanted to check out Behrman was because he *looks* like a thug. He looks like the type of buttface jerk who'd get off on killing teenagers on the way to his KKK fund-raiser."

Emma Jan smiled at me, and nodded. "Yup. That's exactly what he looks like."

"This guy, this JBK, is slick. He or she has done a bunch of them and we're no closer to catching him than we were in . . . what? They started in . . ."

"1954," Paul said, his nose almost touching one of his printouts. Michaela slowly shook her head and started cleaning carrots.

"Yes, thank you, 1954, bodies all over the place, all over the country, and we still don't have a handle on this guy, who's probably in his, what? Seventies? Who is going to be on the lookout for a nursing home resident who's also a serial killer? Not anybody *I* know. That's where we've been screwing up. It has to be somebody young, it has to be somebody who looks like a bad guy—it *can't* be someone old enough to be our grandfathers! Except it *is*.

"You think . . . do you guys think, if he looked like what he is, he could have done this so many times? You think, if he looked like what he is, those kids would have let him anywhere *near* them? When he got started? In the fifties? There was child abuse back then and sexual abuse and serial killers, but your average teenager from 1956 wouldn't know any of that. Back then, it was probably a lot easier for him to pick out prey. But these days? With every kid in the country knowing about pictures on milk cartons and watching *Law and Order: SVU*, and a zillion Internet sites devoted to serial killers? It'd be much, much harder for JBK to do his work . . . but he's managing, isn't he? *Because he doesn't look like what he is*. Those poor boys were completely fooled until it was too late."

They were all staring at me.

"What?"

They kept staring. Even Paul.

"Don't do that," I said sharply. "I don't like that."

"Then for Christ's sake," George whispered hoarsely, "don't stare at her, you three. Cadence, nobody wants you to freak out or feel threatened or even get mildly sweaty. Just because Adrienne didn't show up when you planned doesn't mean we want her popping out in this meeting like a redheaded psycho jack-in-the-box. We're not staring! We're . . . uh . . . thinking. While we look at you intently. In fact, I'm going to think—" He cut himself off, and suddenly had the most peculiar look on his face.

"Awwww, shit." George slapped himself on the forehead, hard

enough to leave a white mark that quickly turned pink. "We're fuckin' idiots."

"Elaborate," Michaela ordered, whittling an enormous carrot into a stack of orange coins.

"Of course it's not some elderly desperado, some senior citizen. You guys . . . it's a team."

"Well . . . as he got older, sure . . ." Emma Jan said, brow furrowed as she concentrated on what he'd said.

"Not as he got older. All along. Like the Hillside Stranglers, Bianchi and Buono. Especially like those shitheads Bianchi and Buono. Because what's the first team we're ever a part of? No matter who we are or where we live?"

I had no idea. At all. Luckily, Emma Jan did: "Our family."

"Yeah, that's right," he said, pointing at her. "That's the first team we're all on. And you're either on the team for life or you get traded fast or something in the middle but yeah, gang. It's family, *first.* I'm betting it's family with these guys, too. Don't you get it? The murders have been going on too long for it to be anything *but* a family affair."

"So . . . a family of serial killers. Like in *The Texas Chain Saw Massacre.* Oh, ugh, I can't believe I just referred to a cult horror film in the middle of an FBI investigation."

"This once, we'll let it go," Michaela said, starting on a new carrot.

"Think of all the dysfunction it takes to produce *one* serial killer in a family." Emma Jan was shaking her head so hard, her bangs wiggled. I must find out what kind of gel she used. "Never mind two. What, like . . . Larry and Danny Ranes?"

"Gross," I commented.

"But accurate," Michaela added. "Don't forget about Micajah and Wiley Harpe."

"They called each other brothers, but they were cousins," I said. And, also, gross. They'd killed at least forty men, women, and children over two hundred years ago, until a posse caught up with them and cut off the elder Harpe's head—they liked to make statements with severed heads, did these Old West posses. When they caught up with Harpe the younger, he was tried, then hung. "But it's rare. Thank God."

"Not just a family of serial killers," George said. "Generations of serial killers. You bringing up the Harpes was good shit, Cadence, because they still have descendants around today. But back then, nobody wanted the neighbors to know if you were a Harpe. They changed their names. And like I said, there are Harpes still around today. A rose by any other name is still a fucking loser-ass serial killing jerk-off, or whatever Shakespeare said."

"But . . . why? Generations of serial killers? Why?"

"If we knew why, we'd know who."

"So what next, then?"

"Ah," Michaela said. "Next, you run along and find Mr. Loun and have another chat." *Thwack!*

"And we're doing that, why?" I asked. Loun? What did Behrman's fellow bigot have to do with any of this?

"The parking garage ticket in the Mickelson boy's pocket." George was grinning; clearly, he'd saved the best for last. "It's from a parking ramp in Minneapolis. Guess whose license plate came back? Yup. Philip Loun."

"What was Philip Loun doing parking in the Cities, and who was he doing it with that his parking stub showed up in a murder victim's pocket later that day?" I asked, thoroughly stunned by the new development.

"Don't you wanna go ask him?" George asked, grinning his fuck-it-let's-get-dirty grin.

"Oh, heck yeah."

"Ooooh. I love it when you try, and fail, to talk dirty. C'mon, Emma Jan. Let's see if your mortal enemy is living in my side-view mirror."

chapter sixty-one

After a few phone calls, and reading more of Paul's research (which he told me smelled red), we went back to the grim trailer the three of us agreed we'd seen way too much of. Loun and his buddy Behrman had been discharged from Regions Hospital just that morning.

"Like they needed to be in the hospital for three days for *concussions*," George sneered. "They were . . . uh . . . dammit! Tip of my tongue."

"Malingering?" I suggested.

"There you go," he said comfortably. "Malingering. Three days of clean sheets and pretty nurses. Adrienne did them a favor."

Wow. For George, that was almost gushing. He was in a good mood. But then, he lived for the hunt. We all did, or else we'd be driving ice cream trucks or teaching quantum physics.

Actually, Paul was asked to teach just that, but apparently the entire freshman U of M class just about went nuts trying to reach the conclusions he had, and a couple of them had nervous breakdowns and the parents got mad and Paul kept insisting that if they really, really tried, they, too, could smell orange, and then they changed his meds and Paul had to go away for a vacation.

It's wrong that I thought that was funny, right?

"Is it me, or does his yard look like the setting for *Bastard Out of Carolina*?" George bitched.

"I had that exact thought," I told him as we swung into the driveway. "That *exact* thought."

"That's because you're both small-minded Yankees," Emma Jan said. We got out of the car and saw that Behrman hadn't yet gotten a new dog.

And wouldn't. Ever. If he knew what was good for him (though, clearly, he didn't).

"Avon calling!" George said, hammering on the door. "I know you're in there, Behrman and Loun! I can smell your redneckness!"

"Do you two do anything by the book?" Emma Jan asked. It didn't sound sarcastic, more like she really wanted to know.

"Shush," I said.

"You two!" It was Behrman, standing in the doorway as he held the front door open with tented fingers. "Get the hell off my property. You're goddamned lucky I don't sue you, the FBI, and the tinshit American government for what you did to Dawg."

"What *we* did to Dawg?" I could actually feel my eyes bugging out. They did that, you know, for real. It was a fight-or-flight response to increased blood pressure. "Are you serious? All we did to Dawg was feed her and take care of her."

"Wastin' your time. She won't learn."

I thought about how I'd woken up that morning . . . thought about the tinkling of the bell Dawg nudged with her head because she wanted to go out. Sure, I'd been gone a whole day, but that still meant Dawg had toilet trained in about seventy-two hours. Miraculous, what incentive could do. Or the lack thereof.

"So, we're looking for a serial killer who's been killing white boys since 1954," Emma Jan said. "Feel like helping?"

That did it. The one thing (other than "You've just won a million dollars!") that would encourage Behrman to let us in, no questions asked.

George sighed happily and took a last look around the yard. "I've missed this place." Then we went in.

chapter sixty-two

Loun greeted us with, "If this is about our meeting tonight, you can just file that with 'lawful assembly' and head on back down the road."

"Aw. And here I was hoping you'd vote me mascot and introduce me to all the boys." George was looking at the framed mug shots; I knew that amused expression. I didn't think we had to worry about Adrienne showing up and causing trouble. George was the one to keep an eye on.

"We just had some questions about The Good Citizens," Emma Jan said.

Behrman smirked. "I don't think it's your kind of group."

"But I came all this way to get an application." She, too, was studying the mug shots. "So, funny question. My fellow agents and I have been working this pesky case, the JBJ killer? Awful. It's just awful. And we found your parking stub in the pocket of the latest victim."

Loun and Behrman gaped at each other, then me. "You *what*?"

"See, that's what we said. I mean, what are the odds?" I didn't want to think about that, for real. Someone was helping us. We would not have come back to Loun and Behrman if not for that parking stub. And the killer didn't leave it because he was getting sloppy. I hated to think how many more fourteen-year-old kids would have to die if the killer hadn't been inclined to give us a hand. It was maddening, and infuriating. And depressing. Mustn't forget that one. "So we wanted to ask you a few questions."

"Big question number one," George said. He was now studying the mug shot of the white woman. All black males . . . except for the white woman. "Are you the June Boys Jobs killers?"

They nearly fell all over themselves explaining that they were not, not, not in a million years, jeez, they raised a little hell when they were kids, but they'd never, you know, *kill* a white boy! The very thought! The very idea! We had the wrong men!

"Yeah, yeah, calm down. Jesus, Behrman, sit down before you faint." Amused, George actually helped Behrman into an overstuffed chair that was the color of, and gave off the odor of, Cheetos. "We're leaning away from that theory. Maybe. We could still arrest you at any time. Imagine the media fallout: Local Bigots Are Drooling White-Boy Killers."

"Aw, Jesus," Loun said, his face the color of bleached cotton. "You can't—we didn't kill anybody!"

"Okay. But if that's true—"

"It is! It is! Jesus, it's not *us*!"

"Okay, but then . . . the killer knows you. Or you know him."

Them, actually. Loun and Behrman knew *them*. But how? Here was the awful thing: I believed Loun and Behrman knew the killer. But I don't think they knew *how* they knew him/them. So how could we get something out of them, if they didn't know it themselves?

I thought back to what George had said earlier: if we knew why, we'd know who. Did it stand to reason, then, that if we knew how, we'd know who, too? And why was this thought sounding like something Dr. Seuss would come up with?

"You can start by telling us why you parked in the bank ramp the day of the last murder," Emma Jan said.

So they told her. And it sounded good, it sounded legitimate, recruitment meeting for their lame little would-be militia, but it was hard for me to concentrate on what they were saying. I couldn't look away from the mug shots.

A bunch of black men. And the white female. Old mug shots, too . . . from the 1950s, if I had to guess. Why here? Why were they printed and carefully framed and hung in the trailer of a confirmed bigot?

If I asked Behrman, he'd tell me. But I didn't want to know what he would tell me. I wanted to know, for myself, what these pictures had to do with any of this. Because I felt their import, even if I didn't know why.

Black men. One white female. Old. They were old . . . like the JBJ killer was old. The one who'd committed the first murder, anyway. He *had* to be pretty ancient by now. Maybe even dead by now. But when he got his start, he would have been much younger.

And he got his start

(his start)

he got started when when when

I was getting a headache. Or I could smell blue. Maybe that was it. Is this what it was like to smell blue? Because it was *really* aggravating. It felt like my head was going to split

chapter sixty-three

in two.

"What is the significance of these photos?" I asked Behrman, a greasy, twitchy man I had immediately disliked on sight. My second sight of him had not changed my first impression.

At my tone, George swung around in a hurry, looked me in the face, then said to Emma Jan, "Shiro's in the house."

"Very good, George. Tomorrow we will work on your multiplication tables. Mr. Behrman? Answer my question, if you please."

"It's . . . it's just research. Are you okay, Officer? You sound funny."

"I have a touch of DID."

"It's going around," George said, then snickered.

"What, is that like Asian Flu?"

"*Just* like it," I agreed. "Research for what?"

"What do you care? Look, Phil and I aren't your guys. And if you thought we were, we wouldn't be having this talk in my house, we'd be downtown. I don't know why you're really here and I don't care. So why don'cha head out?"

"But we have so many questions," George whined, and I knew he was going to drop the bomb on them. I was *so* pleased I would be there to watch. "Hey, I have an idea. You tell me about the mug shots. And then I'll tell you something about yourself you didn't know."

"What bullshit is this?"

"You'll liiiiike it," George wheedled. This was a gross exaggeration at best, an out-and-out lie at worst.

I had no problem with either. I caught Emma Jan's glance, and grinned. Her eyebrows arched, and the corner of her mouth twitched. I *knew* I was right about her. She liked a fight. Any kind of fight.

"It's okay," Loun said, giving Behrman what George would call a manly shoulder-chuck. "It's nothing to be ashamed of. Hell, they're the government."

"It's true," Emma Jan said, winking at me. "We are." She waved and mouthed, "Hi, Shiro."

Waved? She waved at me? Like she had spotted me in the middle of a parade?

Hmm. That was not the most inappropriate analogy for what was happening . . .

I waved back, making an effort not to roll my eyes. A wave. Good Lord.

"I just meant that maybe it's good that they know how The Good Citizens got started. Then they could spend more time getting the scum off the streets and less time hassling white patriots."

Oh, I loved it. The patriot card. It had been used throughout the ages to justify all sorts of nauseating atrocities. "But we're patriots!" As if that changed anything. As if it justified everything.

I was a patriot, too. America was the finest country on the planet and I was lucky to live here. That does not mean I would use my love of the country to justify serial murder. And I was mystified by those who would.

"Tell you what, these mug shots? These are how The Good Citizens got started. Back in the day, my family lived in South Carolina, where they had a real colored problem."

"Oh, I'm gonna love this story," Emma Jan said dryly. "I can already tell."

"Is a 'colored problem' like a pestilence problem?" I asked, and dropped a wink at Emma Jan. "Or would you say it is more like a plague? Rats, maybe? Mosquitos in summer?"

"Shut up," George said curtly and, surprised, I did. When he focused, when he forced his sexually-obsessed sociopathic me-me-me mind to seize a puzzle and solve it, he could become admirably laser-esque. "Go on, Phil."

"Right. Anyway, my family—these'd be my great-great-grandparents—they were having a colored problem but nobody wanted to do anything about it. They were farmers, they just wanted to be left alone to do their shit." Encouraged by our complete attention, Loun plunged ahead. "But two little white gals were killed by a black buck right around that time—they were eleven and eight, the girls were. Black bastard wanted to cut himself a piece and I guess they fought him, or cried or something, so he beat 'em to death."

Silence. George, Emma Jan, and I were afraid to breathe. Sometimes, when suspects were on a roll like this, you could find out more than you thought because they would say more than they planned.

"That must have been dreadful for your family," I said. I tried to look meltingly sympathetic. Damn. This was a job for Cadence. She could pity a rabid timber wolf who'd devoured premature babies for lunch. "Very very . . . dreadful." Ugh. This sort of thing was not in my skill set.

Loun nodded, his broad face darkening as he recalled the family tragedy. "Yep. Tore my folks up, tell you that right now."

"Your folks back then, or your folks now?"

"My daddy told me the whole story when I was just little, so I'd know life was precious and you can lose someone you love without any warning at all."

"A difficult lesson for a child to understand. It must have been . . ." Dammit! Why could I only think of one word? *Cadence, I never thought I'd say this, but I very much wish you were here right now.* ". . . dreadful?"

He nodded sadly.

Too sadly.

That was when I realized Loun's sorrow was as fake as my sympathy. And it made sense. He had never known the girls; likely he had never known anyone that far back in his family tree. They would have been names in a newspaper clipping to him, all his life. Never more. It was impossible that they should be more.

So why, then, why should he be torn up about their murder, dreadful thought it was? Answer: he was not.

But he could use it to justify bigotry. He could use it to justify all sorts of horrid behavior. So he did. And here we all were.

"The kid that did it—and it was a kid, some black teenager—he got the chair, and back then they didn't fuck around with ten years of appeals."

"Like Bundy," George offered. Ah, George . . . he could be clever when he wished. A shame he was so rarely motivated beyond what he needed in order to embellish his sex life. "You believe that guy? Killed all those poor girls and then the state of Florida got to pay for all his appeals! The best day's work Florida ever did was zapping that guy."

Loun and Behrman brightened. A kindred soul! A man, a white lawman, who understood their rage and pain and loss! Why, perhaps they had misjudged the fellow! "Yeah, man, say it twice," Loun said while Behrman nodded agreement.

"Do you know how much that rat bastard cost the taxpayers?" George was on a brilliant roll. I smirked at Emma Jan when Loun and Behrman could not see. "Over five . . . million . . . dollars! You know what it costs to execute someone? A thousand. A thousand bucks—the new suit, the last meal, all that comes to about a grand. Shee-it, you guys heard of Andrei Chikatilo? That Russian psycho who killed something like forty kids?"

"Fifty-six," Emma Jan added. "Over half were under seventeen."

"Like the lady said," George said with a courteous nod in her direction. "And this fucker's guilty as shit, right? He confessed—"

"So—" I began, but Emma Jan shook her head. "So he did," I said. "Except what happened was, because it was Iron Curtain time in Russia, their law-enforcement methods were a little on the gulag side. Three homosexuals *and* a convicted sex offender were arrested and after a while 'confessed.' Soviet Russia, right? No Miranda rights. They killed themselves after the interrogations, yet dead kids *still* kept piling up."

George remained undaunted in the face of that unpleasant truth. Nothing new about that, either. And no reason to confuse Behrman with unnecessary facts. "Right, Chikatilo confessed *and* knew gory details *and* led them to bodies they hadn't found. Right? Guilty as shit, right?"

We all nodded, possibly the only time the four of us were in agreement on something.

"So get this, boys, they put his psycho ass on trial, they find him guilty, they get all their 'So long, Comrade Psycho' ducks in a row, they take him to a back room and they put a bullet in his ear. You know how much a round for a nine-mil Beretta costs? Twenty-seven cents! Tell me *that's* not a bargain."

"Shit!"

"Goddamned right."

Never had I felt so close to George before. Right now I felt he was . . . was . . . almost human!

He was still doing a wonderful job feigning regret. "Now, come on, boys. Tell me you couldn't find a better way to use five million bucks. Think what The Good Citizens could do with that kind of money."

"See, that's a prime example of the government screwing up, and honest Americans having to pay for that screwup." Loun nodded as he spoke, clearly enchanted with the words of wisdom dripping from his mouth. "But back then, when our girls were murdered, they didn't screw around. The buck who killed them, he fried for it not even three months after he killed them."

"Wow, three months?" Emma Jan asked. She then feigned embarrassment. "Sorry, you probably don't need to hear that from me. It's kind of embarrassing for me, knowing that somebody from my . . . Well. I'm just real sorry about the girls. Maybe I should step outside while you guys finish. . . ?"

Rarely was I surrounded by such superb actors. A definite treat. I could weep in sheer gratitude. Truly.

"Naw, naw," Loun said, moved to generosity by a repentant African American agent for the federal government. "We don't have a problem with you. It's real good that you overcame your background and now you're defending the law."

Ah, yes. Her trauma-ridden childhood spent in the slums of

Tuxedo Road in Atlanta, where she and her family had lived across the street from the mansion once owned by former Coca-Cola president Robert Woodruff. Emma Jan had access to a seven-figure trust fund, and this moron assumed she must have risen in triumph from a crack-whore mother and absentee gangbanger father. I wonder which of her degrees from Harvard would better help her overcome the terrible burden of her wealth?

I worried, sometimes. I worried that we did not apprehend villains because we were so smart, but because they were so stupid. It was a thought to keep anyone up at night.

Emma Jan, meanwhile, was shrugging modestly. "I don't mind telling you, it was a tough road." Yes, indeed. The horror of being accepted at Harvard *and* Yale *and* Princeton. The shame of driving last year's Lamborghini. The terror of relentless harassment from various charities all hoping for a donation. I am amazed she had lived through the nightmare.

Loun was in an expansive mood now that he saw respectful civil servants and a contrite Negress. Negress! Heh. I *never* got to use that word.

"Listen, it's not on you at all. I'll tell you something my daddy explained to me when I was just a kid . . . something that I've noticed holds true again and again. Now, you might not like it, miss, but it's got the ring of truth to it."

This . . . this should be something. This should be spectacular. I felt like jumping up and down.

"One black alone is perfectly okay, a black alone can be a really good guy. You wanna go bowling with him, you don't mind working with him, you have him over for dinner . . . you know. But." He started wagging a stern finger at Emma Jan. "But, you get a bunch of them together? They turn into niggers. That's where that term 'wilding' came from. You get a bunch of blacks together, they can't help but bring out the savage inherent in all of 'em."

My. I had never heard the word "inherent" in the same paragraph as "wanna" and " 'em."

George started cracking up, and Emma Jan joined him. I laid no blame, but did think they might have tried to stay sober just a minute more.

"That's so great!" Emma Jan gasped. "We've been wondering what to call ourselves all this time. It's really been bugging the membership, you know, for our secret enclave meetings? Wait until I tell the Queen!"

"So let's see. Pride of lions." George began to tick them off his fingers. "Flock of geese. Herd of cattle. Murder of crows. Nigger of African Americans. She's right. It's perfect."

Loun was smiling uneasily, not certain if they were mocking him or laughing with him. It was a testament to the man's foul ego that he could even entertain the thought that they might not be mocking him.

"Anyway," Behrman said, clearly annoyed to be left out, "back when this happened, they decided to form a group of like-minded men, *true* men. So The Good Citizens were born."

"Born from the tragedy of what happened many years ago to your relatives? The dead girls?" I had to ask, because George and Emma Jan were still trying to put an end to their Nigger of African Americans hysteria. "That was how this whole thing began?"

"Yeah. Those are pictures of boys who were caught and tried fairly after their disgusting crimes against white girls. And that gal . . ." Pointing to the white woman in the period dress. "That's one of the dead girl's relatives, she's my great-great-great-aunt.

Hmm . . . might only be great-great . . ." He thought about it for a moment, then shrugged.

"That's why we keep their pictures, theirs and hers. To remind ourselves that what happened back then can't be allowed to happen again, ever. And her picture to remind us how it started, and how one woman with a heart full of love can change things. She's the one who got us all started on the path. She never forgot her murdered kin. She never forgot that justice can be swift if you want it badly enough."

"Her heart was full," I agreed, "but I doubt it was full of love. Let's not debate." I held up a hand to forestall his protest. "Let us instead talk about how you can assist us with the JBJ killer."

"I told you," Behrman said, "I told you the last two times you was here, I didn't have anything to do with those white boys showing up killed."

"You did, actually, but it was nothing you consciously planned. That is the good news."

"The bad news," George wheezed, wiping his eyes. "Whoo! Wow, I needed that. Nigger of African Americans. Good one, Loun. The bad news is, there's a link between The Good Citizens and these crimes. You just don't see it. But you can help us find the killer."

"I don't see how. And we're staying out of the government's business. I'm real sorry those boys got killed, but that's your job and your worry, not mine. We learned not to cooperate with the government 'round about when blacks started getting away with murdering white girls."

"You think that sort of thing is limited to the segregation-filled South of a few decades ago? People have been killing people for no good reason since the Dawn of Man. The Good Citizens are not special. They only think they are."

"Yeah, insultin' our white brothers is gonna get you what you need," Behrman sneered. "Rookie mistake, right?"

"Are you *sure* you want Mr. Loun to hear this?" George asked. "Because it does not look good for you."

"He's my white brother. Anything you say to me you say to him."

"That . . . is . . . excellent. And don't cry about it later, don't pretend I didn't warn you."

"About *what*?"

"Did you know your DNA was on the dog?"

"What d—oh. You mean Dawg?"

"Yup. I don't know if you were kicking her with bare feet or if you licked her or what, but we got some of your DNA off of her."

"Sneaky government agents, shoulda seen that coming." Loun's voice was laced with contempt.

"Yup. You shoulda. Anyway, we were running it to see if it'd help us with the JBJ murders. And it did, just not the way we thought."

"Are you gonna tell us, or keep talking without saying anything?"

"Your great-grandmother was black," George said pleasantly.

Behrman flushed brick red to his eyebrows. I watched with interest; I had never seen anyone have a rage-induced stroke before. He looked at Behrman, startled, then replied, "Don't even start that fuckin' shit, I—"

"Be careful, dumbass." George was still sounding perfectly pleasant, but there was something wrong with his face. His eyes. His eyes were wrong. "It's extremely provable."

I would never tell him, but George sometimes made me nervous.

"You . . . you fuckin' liar, you—the goddamned government makes all this shit up, and losers like you swallow it whole, and—"

"So drop some urine and prove me wrong." He grinned. Well. Showed his teeth. "Or introduce your dick to a Dixie Cup. We've got all *sorts* of DNA to test you against. Except we aren't the ones who need convincing. We *know* you're a match to a black relative. You're the one who needs convincing. You and alllll your buddies."

"Hey, you can just suck it through a hose, okay? I'm not . . . you can't . . . I know my rights."

"Oh, boy." Emma Jan shook her head. "You shouldn't have said that. It's a red flag to that guy; it's a red flag to a bull hopped up on steroids and caffeine."

"She's right, that's the kind of badass I am. You catch on fast, New Girl." Emma Jan waved his pseudo-compliment away. "What can I say, I'm the product of divorce. And since we have all the names of your fellow bigots, we could let them in on your dirty little secret. It'd be a civic duty kind of a thing."

"It's not true. You can't say that, anyway! I know my rights."

"You do, but only when you feel like it. The same umbrella you invoke to justify your poison-spreading nonsense also protects us."

"I'd fucking know if I was black, okay?" Behrman grimaced and I realized he was trying to smile but only baring his teeth. "I'm not. Check the mirror if you don't believe me."

"Sorry, I'm off mirrors for the week," Emma Jan said with faux regret. "Promised my shrink I wouldn't so much as peek, at least until these guys were a little more used to my pecularities. Y'know, back in the day, the child, grandchild, and great-grandchild of a black were considered black. Ever heard of the one-drop rule? People like you thought it up. Well, *some* people like you. People on one side of your family. We know what the other side was up to, don't we? Don't forget about hypodescent—that whole 'children born to mixed mothers and fathers are automatically considered members of the inferior class' thing. Hey, you should be happy you're an African American—"

"Don't you call me that!"

"—in this day and age, where segregation and the like are frowned upon. Your family never told you, right?" She looked almost sympathetic. Almost. "It didn't stop them from teaching hate, but they didn't have the balls to tell you any real truth."

Behrman cracked under the pressure and swung wildly on George. This was a dreadful idea for him to have . . . on top of his other troubles, he could add assaulting a federal agent to the list.

There was a flash of movement and it was likely that only someone with extensive martial arts training could have tracked it. Behrman, unfortunately, didn't have that in his background, and the crunch when George broke his nose was a real eye-opener. Loun, meanwhile, was frozen in place, staring at his "white brother" with horror.

"There's something wrong with you," I commented as George stepped off so Behrman could stagger toward a roll of paper towels. "You do know that, right?"

He looked at me. He had blood on his shirt and his eyes were better, but he still looked desperately unhappy. "There's something wrong with all of us."

chapter sixty-four

"That was fun," Emma Jan said later, "but I'm not sure how it helps us find JBK."

"I am. I just need a computer. And possibly Paul. Is he here?"

"He's off listening to blue, or smelling yellow, or whatever the hell he does when he's not freaking me out. Gah, that guy gives me the creepies."

"I might need him."

"So tell *him*. What am I," George bitched, "your fetcher-of-weirdos?"

"Nice job title," Emma Jan snickered. She had been rummaging through her absurdly large purse while we were talking, and extracted a full-size bag of ripple chips. "*There* you are, honey. Where you been all my life?"

"How long you been carrying around the pleather bottomless pit?" George asked, fascinated in spite of himself.

"Years and years. I don't understand women who walk around with paperback-size purses. How can they function?"

"Are you all right, Emma Jan?"

Crunching, she replied, "Sure, Shiro, why wouldn't I be?"

"I thought Behrman's mirror remark was unkind."

" 'M used to it," she crunched. "World's fulla mirrors. I've spent my life trying to avoid them when I can. It's my Achilles' heel, that fucking Mirror Syndrome. It's the only thing really wrong with me—"

"Besides your weird liking for gigantic purses," George added.

"—but it's a doozy."

"So, you are saying you lead a relatively normal life."

"Yep."

"Except for that one delusion."

She grinned. "Yes, honey, except for that one big, whopping, gigantic, enormous delusion, I'm absolutely fine."

"A minor setback?"

"Right."

I rolled my eyes and she laughed. "Hey, your girl Cadence was gonna give me a beat-down. She thought I was stealing you."

If she had suddenly struck a match and set herself on fire, I could not have been more perplexed. "Stealing me from whom?"

"Her."

"But that is . . ." Foolish. Idiotic. Panicked. Untrue. *Cadence.* That was Cadence.

"So I think we established that you and I aren't dating."

"All right." This emotional chitchat was making me uneasy. So I dealt with it as I always did: "We have work to do."

"Listen, I'm gonna go debrief Michaela." George glanced at his watch and frowned.

"Ah."

"What, 'ah'?"

"It will not work, though you may try."

"What?" Emma Jan was looking from him to me to him again. "What's he gonna try?"

"Michaela takes a dim view of her agents committing assault."

"Which is hilarious," George broke in, "given how often it happens—*right*, Shiro?"

"Correct." What could I say to that? He was correct. "George has decided that a full and fake contrite confession may lessen her ire, as opposed to waiting until she finds out about it."

"At which point she'll unleash her ire all over my delicate ass and a week's suspension with pay could turn into six months without pay. Think how boring that would be!" He seemed horrified at the very prospect. Not the prospect of being low on funds—being kept away from the daily excitement that was working for BOFFO. "Who needs that? Let me know what you guys find out."

"Best of luck, George, and I am sure her ire will not come anywhere near you."

"Oh my God, you are so bad at empathy," George said, rubbing his temples.

"Says the sociopath."

"Yes, but I can fake it convincingly."

"You cannot."

"Can so!"

"You have the moral compass of a moray eel, and it's instantly obvious to anyone who spends more than five minutes with you."

"Ah! But!" He wagged a finger at me, being careful to stay out of arm's reach. Yes, he could be taught. "During those first five minutes, I'm magical."

Despite myself, I laughed and Emma Jan joined me.

The sly bastard had a point.

"I'm not getting this," Emma Jan said, looking over my shoulder. "At all."

"The story Loun told us. The reason he started The Good Citizens. It got me thinking. The death of those two little girls had a profound effect on the family, yes?"

"Sure. They justified starting up their stupid We Hate Blacks Club."

"Remember when he told about the boy who killed them? 'The buck who killed them, he fried for it not even three months after he killed them.' "

"Yeah, that's exactly what he said." She'd pulled up a chair and scooted close to mine so she could see the screen. " 'Fried' meaning electric chair, so the state actually killed the guy within three months of the murders. Wow, they didn't bother with much paperwork back then, did they?"

"Yes, the idea of an investigation, arrest, trial, and execution happening within ninety days simply boggles the mind. But I think that is our lever. That is our answer. Because if we plug in what little we *do* know . . . look what comes up."

I hit a few keys while Emma Jan munched contentedly. "There!"

And there he was. George Stinney: the reason behind the June Boys Jobs. All there in the archives, the puzzle solved if only someone put the pieces together in exactly the right order.

Or if someone could smell blue.

And if I had pulled my head out of my behind, we might have known this earlier and the Mickelson boy would still be alive.

"Oh, Jesus," Emma Jan said, staring at the screen. "Jesus."

"They did it. All those years ago, those two little white girls showed up dead, and the town just went insane.

"They arrested, convicted, tried, and executed George Stinney for murdering the girls. Within three months. The state . . ." I blinked hard but the words did not change. They would never change. "The state executed a child who most likely did not kill anyone." And even if he had . . . even if he had . . . he had been *fourteen.*

Emma Jan and I stared at each other. Her expression was mine: I could feel it, I knew it, looking at her. We were both horrified . . . and glad. Fiercely glad. Because behind any good cop is a puzzle solver . . . and finding the solution to any puzzle, no matter how senseless and awful, is meat and drink to us.

We were thrilled to solve it. It felt better than anything in our lives, solving this. Which begged the question: If I was, say, an accountant, would I ever have been happy? Or did I need the adrenaline of a murder investigation? Did I need a corpse to prompt me to enjoy being alive?

"They executed him . . . he was too little for the electric chair. See? He was too little. Five foot one inch, ninety pounds. They had a hard time with the electrodes. And the adult-size mask did not fit, of course. Nothing fit him. And even that did not stop them from . . ."

I did not want to look at the pictures.

I looked at the pictures. "His family was so afraid, they left the night he was arrested. His father had already been fired. They had to creep out of town and leave their son to his fate. He died surrounded by killers who thought it was fine to electrocute a teenager. He died eighty days after the murder."

I was *seeing* it and I had trouble believing it. *Oh, you bastards. You blind fools, see what your foolishness has brought the world?*

"Sure, makes sense. The murders had to have ramped up tension that had already been there. Racial, political, probably economical, too, and what-have-you. It just . . . fed on itself until it burned out. And it couldn't burn out until somebody paid. George Stinney's family has been making people pay for it ever since," Emma Jan finished. "For generations! They've been . . . my God."

"Pulling a teenage boy—"

"A *white* boy."

"Right, a white boy. Pulling him from the herd. The beatings . . . how the boys died . . . that was how George was supposed to have killed the girls in 1944. They said he beat the girls to death with a railroad spike; their skulls had been broken in four or five places. So the killers have been killing the white teenagers the same way. We thought it was torture-murder at first. The killers have been telling the world the George Stinney story over . . . and over . . . and over. The clothes the boys have been found in . . ."

"Jeans and a striped shirt."

"What George wore to the electric chair. He died in the clothes the state gave him. So the killers dressed them the same way."

It was almost poetic. And grotesque.

"Okay, but George was executed in 1944. Paul proved the murders started in 1954."

"That makes sense if you look at it from the correct perspective. They needed ten years to get some distance. Ten years so people could begin to forget. Ten years for research, maybe even training. An ordinary family suddenly decides they need to get good at murder . . . you do not jump into such a thing without preparation. So they took their time. And after ten years had gone by, they were ready."

She nodded, the chips long forgotten. "It had to have started with one of his surviving family members. So an aunt, or uncle, or maybe even an older sibling. And each generation, one of them . . . what? Loses the coin toss? *Wins* the coin toss? And is taught the killing ritual." She shook her head. "No wonder we didn't see it."

"That is charitable," I said dryly, "because we should have, years ago. I should have."

She snorted, an unlovely sound that was also quite funny. "Right,

Shiro. You should have realized that a murder committed less than two weeks ago was tied to murders starting back in 1954. What a dumbass you are not to have figured that out. You'd better turn in your ID and try to get a job as a crossing guard."

"I should have known earlier." Cadence was not the only one of us capable of mulish stubbornness. "I should have realized it was never about Behrman. It was about Loun. I knew, I *knew* something about the dichotomy of those framed mug shots was going to be our answer. I simply could never . . . quite . . . put my finger on it."

"Now what?"

"Now we tell George and Michaela."

chapter sixty-five

"Are you *shitting* me?" George practically screamed.

"It's not that I doubt you," Michaela said. "I believe every word you said. It's difficult, though, to grasp the years of . . . of poison." She turned and looked at us with haunted eyes. I had never seen Michaela look her age before. "Can you imagine the horror of being born into that family? To know that you will either be the one to kill an innocent child, or that you will be the one to help cover it up? To know that you will grow to adulthood and have children. To know you must teach your son or daughter . . . and they will teach your grandchild. My God!"

George couldn't stand it; he had to jump up and pace. We were in Michaela's actual office, so there was not much room for that. "This is gonna change everything. A whole family of . . . Am I the only one who wants to lock them all up in some secret government lair and then do experiments on them?"

"Yes," Michaela and Emma Jan said in unison.

No.

"Bad enough to be after just some random guy who, even if we didn't catch him—"

"Traitor."

"—we being all cops, not just us, if *all the law enforcement agencies* don't catch a bad guy, it's just him. Nobody worried about Bundy's kid, if he even had one—"

"A daughter."

"Yeah, okay, but nobody's worried she's gonna pick up where Dad left off, right? No one's worried she's gonna flee to Florida and rampage through a sorority house with a goddamned wooden *club*, right?

"But with this guy . . . We don't catch him, and his kid or nephew or whoever takes over . . . and even if *that* guy had gotten nailed, *his* kid was waiting right there in the wings to take up the family business . . . Ugh!" He clapped a hand over his mouth and shook his head. "I just called generations of murder the 'family business.' It's the coolest and most terrible thing I've ever imagined."

"You make an excellent point." Normally I tried not to compliment George. Such things went immediately to his head. "Usually an ugly crime will die with the victim . . . and the killer. But not this time."

"Aw, man, all that? All those kids killed, years and years of it? Parents teaching the hate to their kids and then their grandkids . . . and for what? More death. Like George Stinney even cares, wherever he is, heaven or hell or *nada*, like he cares that his nutso family's been whacking teenagers since he died." He kicked over the garbage can, which couldn't have been very satisfying, as it was for paper, and only had three pieces to spill. "What a waste. Of their lives and our time."

"Do not forget the murdered boys."

"Yep, the victims, too."

"And the murdered girls," Emma Jan added. She looked at Michaela. "Do you think George did that? Killed those girls?"

"I think that their murder was a terrible, heinous crime, and it paved the way for more devastation and death."

"You didn't answer my question, boss."

Michaela shrugged. Click. Closed. She had shown us as much as she would.

"I am not certain George was guilty," I admitted. "Eighty-one days is rather speedy. Sometimes it takes almost that long for jury selection."

"You know what, though? You know what?" Pace, pace. "Even if he did it. Even if he was the killer, killed those two little girls, he *still* got jammed. I don't care if he was slobbering into his chocolate milkshakes and howling at the moon, or if he was just getting an early start in his career as a repressed racially downtrodden serial killer. He was wronged. The system fucked him. It *fucked* him."

I tried to hide my astonishment. To hear this from George Pinkman, of all people. He normally cared nothing for motivation, for the did-he-or-didn't-he game. But he was outraged about this.

"And if he *didn't* do it . . . God!" He raked his fingers through his hair and rubbed his eyes so savagely mine watered in sympathy. "I don't even want to think about all the layers of awful if he was innocent. I can't. Literally can't wrap my mind around it, like Michaela said."

"Well, jeez, buddy, don't hurt yourself." Emma Jan shot me a look, but I could only shrug. I had never seen him like this, either.

"I guess I just don't have the force of imagination to pull it off. Even thinking about trying to face the implications is giving me a migraine. That poor kid." Silence, while he finished pacing and flung himself back into his chair. "So now what?"

"Now we expose JBK to the light of day," Michaela said.

We all stared at her, but it was Emma Jan who broke the silence. "What do you mean, Michaela?"

"We have managed to keep the media out of this, for which I am always grateful. Trust a reporter to ruin a perfectly organized murder investigation, every time. But now we are going to tell the media everything. And then we are going to let the killer come to us."

"Okay, that sounded mysterious and weird, but what, exactly, is the plan?"

She told us. I was not so much surprised as amazed.

chapter sixty-six

Here are various headlines from local papers and news affiliates that prove, once and for all, that Michaela Taro was not the one with whom to fuck. I had no idea how she had put all this together so quickly, and no desire to find out. Some things mortal man was not meant to know. Michaela's Machiavellian practices were quite high on that list.

RACIAL MOTIVATION BEHIND SERIAL KILLINGS: THE TRUTH ABOUT GEORGE STINNEY

GEORGE STINNEY: EXECUTION SPARKS DECADES OF MURDERS. THE KILLING NEVER STOPPED!

THE STINNEY CASE: DEATH OF INNOCENCE?

PROFESSOR DECKLIN COMING TO TWIN CITIES TO LECTURE: STINNEY WAS INNOCENT! WHO REALLY KILLED THE GIRLS?

That one was my favorite. I think it was Michaela's, as well. For one thing, there was no Professor Decklin. For another, there was no proof of Stinney's innocence, as there was no real proof of his guilt.

But the killer wouldn't know that. Even if he did, we didn't think he could stay away.

As it turned out, much to my shock and sorrow later, we were right.

chapter sixty-seven

But that was before my nervous breakdown. My mini-breakdown. Don't judge . . . I was overdue! And I have no idea why it happened just then. It seemed very random to me. As it did (I heard later) from others.

"That's it!" I announced. The buzz of FBI-related activity went on despite my outburst. Of course, I wasn't the first person to suddenly freak out in her cube. Suddenly I wanted out. Out out out!

"That's it," I said again. "I have to . . . have to . . ." What? What could I do? How could I get out of here with a good enough excuse? Where could I go? Oooh! Dr. Gallo! "I have to go donate platelets." Though it might be too early . . . it certainly hadn't been seven days . . .

"No," Michaela began, who'd been on her way to one of her many meetings, but halted when I shrieked. "You have to—"

"No! I have to donate! Platelets! Now!"

All background noise ceased. And I could feel about a thousand eyes on me. For once, literally for *this one time*, I didn't care.

"I get to do *one* normal thing in this weird stupid life/lives of mine, and that's go to the Red Cross and donate platelets! One normal thing! Out of a million-zillion *ab*normal things! Do I ask for *anything* besides that? Huh? Do I?"

George opened his mouth.

"Shut up, George!"

George closed his mouth.

"I read about murder and I hear about murder and I study murder, and when I'm not doing all that I go to murder scenes and look at dead bodies and try to catch murderers, and then I see a shrink or two or five, and then I see more bodies, and then I have a meeting while my boss chops everything in sight into tiny quarter-size pieces while we all pretend that isn't *weird weird weird* and one of my personalities is a motorcycle-obsessed psycho and the other one is a competitive bitch who can't leave the new girl alone for five seconds and now I have a dog even though I can't have a dog and I have a boyfriend and possibly a crush on a man who isn't him and I . . ." I groped behind me, felt something soft, hurled it. "Want . . ." Groped, threw. "To donate . . ." Groped, threw. "Platelets!"

Dead silence.

"So I am *going* and don't you *dare* try to nail me with a Thorazine dart on my way out the *door*!"

"Furthest thing from my mind," a wide-eyed Michaela said. "Though if you could come back straight after . . ."

"Fine! I will! But now, I'm leaving!"

"All right."

"Yeah, chill out," a pale George added.

"It's not like you haven't earned a break," Emma Jan piped up.

"Fine."

"Fine."

"Okay. I'm leaving."

"Okay."

I stomped toward the elevator, fully expecting the sting of a dart, followed by muddy unconsciousness. But it never came. Everybody just watched me go.

I kept the scowl on my face until the doors shut, then couldn't help smile. My! That felt terrific! Should have done it a long time ago.

Then, inevitably, guilt swamped my brain and smashed my joy like a copy of *Gone With the Wind* smashed a bug.

I was the one who returned . . . it really was too soon to donate platelets, so Cadence had merely gone for a walk around the block, enjoying her independence. She could be so cute at times!

There on my desk, waiting for me/us, was a note asking that I see Michaela. Which, after Cadence's tantrum, I expected.

Still, I had to force a pleasant expression when I got to her office. "What can I do for you?"

Michaela had gotten up to close her office door. Now, on her way back around her desk, she sat and looked at me. "Did you know Patrick was in jail?"

Nothing. Silence. The last two words, "in jail" . . . I could almost feel their weight.

No. I had *not* known. But I would get to the bottom of it. Immediately. I stood, only to hear her sharp, "Sit down."

I sat.

"I must apologize; this is literally the first chance I've had to address this. Your boyfriend was arrested late last night. Apparently you and he had a fight—"

"It was not a fight."

"—and Adrienne showed up. She did a great deal of property damage while she was driving the body. For reasons I do not understand, when the authorities showed up in response to the alarm, Patrick took the blame. He confessed to everything Adrienne did. As Adrienne was long gone and he stayed behind to face the music, he was arrested.

"My understanding is that Adrienne went back home and fell asleep. And Cadence woke up a few hours later, and you know the rest."

I could feel my eyes getting bigger and bigger.

"I will be going down there within the hour. He'll be released OR. Trial date will be in a few weeks, unless I can persuade the DA to see things my way. And I can be quite persuasive when I wish."

No doubt.

"It helps that Patrick is willing to pay for the damages. I estimated the damage to be in the low six-figure range, and told him so. He didn't care."

"He's rich," I said through numb lips. Took the blame? Was willing to foot the bill? What . . . who. . . ?

"Yes. I thought you might like to know the situation before I went downtown."

I was as bewildered as I had ever been. I was having to process a lot of information in a very short time. And that was just about George Stinney. "What *is* the situation? And how is it that you know all this?" *And why hadn't I, you treacherous wench?*

"Because I was his phone call."

I was silent, brooding over that one. It was doable. It was even plausible. Patrick and Cadence had recently exchanged address books. He traveled a great deal for work, and wanted the three of us to always be able to reach him. Cadence had felt reciprocation was only polite, and I did not care enough to intervene. So he had Michaela's contact information.

I had to say, I admired his cool head. It had taken some brass ones to call Michaela. Especially when he could afford the finest lawyer in the state.

Especially when he had done nothing wrong, except frighten me. And whose fault was that? Not his. Not this time. I had assumed the worst, and fled, leaving Patrick to face Adrienne in one of her rages.

I was shamed by the nobility of a baker.

"He said something about Adrienne making a mess of the local PetCo being his fault."

I wondered if Adrienne had brought Olive along on her rampage. That poor dog. Having to tolerate *one* of us would be difficult for any animal.

"He said he had done something that had set the entire thing off, and because of that, he felt the blame should lie with him."

The house. His house. He was talking about moving in. He knew I had been upset. He must have realized how upset once he knew Adrienne was coming. So he . . . he . . .

I burst into tears. This was a first. Normally Cadence cried in here. If I had not been so miserable, I would have been still more ashamed.

Michaela, thank all the gods, never changed expression. I might have been discussing her stock options. She wordlessly handed me a box of Kleenex. BOFFO should buy stock; we went through hundreds of boxes a week.

"That fool. That *idiot*. He should not have . . . he . . . fool, fool, oh, Patrick, I am going to *strangle* you!"

"I didn't hear that."

"Good." I ferociously blew my nose. "I did not say it. I did not threaten assault on an innocent man, certainly not where my supervisor would have overheard. I would like to see Patrick."

She smiled, the half-smile I had always found mysterious and charming. "I thought you would. Run along, Shiro. You're no good to me if you're weeping over an incarcerated boyfriend."

Weeping! The horror. I stood. Blew my nose again. Tossed the Kleenex into her garbage can. "Thank you, Michaela. For everything. I know I . . . I know I don't tell you enough. Express enough gratitude for . . . for all that you do for us. I *am* grateful. Even if it's difficult for me to show."

My life was a nightmare. Emma Jan . . . was she right? Did I see Michaela as a mother figure? Did I want to please the only maternal person in my life?

She had brought me here, privately. Told me bad news with subtle kindness. Overlooked my inappropriate behavior. Comforted me . . . in her way. Offered me *Kleenex*.

Soon death would claim me. It had to. This couldn't go on, surely.

"I just . . . cannot thank you enough," I finished, sounding far too watery for my taste.

"I don't know what you're talking about," she yawned. "Run along, Shiro. I desire you to be on the other side of my door, now."

Thankfully, I left. She might be a mother figure, but she would be the *last* to admit it. Which was fine with me. So fine, I might faint from sheer gratitude.

But first things first.

chapter sixty-eight

When they brought him into the room, Patrick looked astonished to see me. Clearly, he had been expecting Michaela.

"What are you doing here?"

"I'm your attorney. Thank you, Officers, I would like some time alone to confer with my client." As they left, I sat across from Patrick, put my briefcase aside, and folded my hands on the table.

Patrick blinked at me in the powerful fluorescent light, then leaned forward and whispered, as if the microphones weren't sensitive enough to pick up someone breaking wind in the vacuum of space, "Shiro, look, I really appreciate this but you can't do this! You can't pretend to be my lawyer."

"Who is pretending? I *am* a lawyer." I pulled the business card out of my left lapel pocket and slid it across the table to him. "In fact, right now I am *your* lawyer."

He stared at me. He was still in his clothes from last night. No blood, thank heavens.

"You—you're my lawyer?"

"I had nothing to do one week so I took the bar."

Patrick slowly lowered his head to the table, then began banging it up and down. I stuck my hands in the way, so he was mashing his face into my palms. "Of course you did. Of *course* you did, it's a perfectly normal thing, someone who doesn't want to be a lawyer hanging around long enough to take the bar exam and passing it and every once in a while being a lawyer." *Thud. Thud. Thud.*

"Stop that; you're going to make my hands numb. And I do not understand your shock. I must say, it wasn't especially difficult. Which really only lowered my general opinion of the legal profession," I confessed. "Besides, once upon a time, all FBI agents had to be lawyers. That is why I took those courses in the first place."

His head jerked up. "Once upon a—yeah, but Cadence isn't."

I snorted.

"And Adrienne isn't."

I laughed out loud.

He bent once more, kissed my palm, then ceased banging, to my great relief. He sat up. "Okay, Counselor. What's the plan?"

"Stop breaking the law."

"Got it. Step two?"

"Stop telling the police you've broken the law when you haven't."

"Oh." He looked abashed. "You know about that, huh?"

"Of course, you hirsute moron."

"I don't shave one morning and here comes the name calling," he complained as he ran a hand over his stubble.

"I also know that you foolishly assumed Adrienne's actions were your fault. I know you foolishly confessed to crimes you did not commit: destruction of property, breaking and entering—"

"Mostly it was just breaking."

"Do not interrupt your attorney. You will be relieved to know I have arranged for your release. And Michaela knows the DA, so there may not be a trial. It was kind of you to offer to pay the damages, but I cannot allow that; I already have to deal with too much shame on this issue, so we shall work something out."

"Shiro, you guys don't have that kind of money and you know I'll never miss it, so—"

"*In the meantime.* It would be a tremendous help if you . . . yes?" I prompted.

"Didn't break the law?" he guessed.

"Correct. And?"

"Didn't say I broke the law when I didn't?"

"An A-plus for my star pupil. Come along, Patrick. You *idiot.*"

He didn't move. "I'm really sorry I scared you. I shouldn't have said anything. I messed it up and . . ." He shook his head. "I couldn't figure out how to make it right."

So in typical Mars fashion (as in, *Men Are from Mars, Women et cetera),* he had tackled the larger problem. The one he knew he could influence.

"I'm really sor—"

"Do *not* apologize for inviting me to move in with you. It was one of the happiest moments of my life."

"And one of the scariest."

"Well. Yes. But that is hardly your fault."

"But the big problem was, I was the coward. Not you. I was the chickenshit."

"What are you talking a—"

He wriggled in his chair; I was betting he wanted to stretch more, or pace, but was forcing himself to sit still and keep eye contact. Interesting.

"When we were talking about dogs. How I knew about dogs. My sister had one when she was little. When she started . . . to get sick. *Really* sick. My parents . . ." He shook his head. "They couldn't handle it. Okay, that's not right . . . they *wouldn't* handle it. Cathie was getting sicker and sicker and at first they said it was just for attention, then they decided it was a learning disability. They grounded her and got her new teachers and tried everything except what she needed, what it was obvious to all of us what she *needed:* a shrink. They never tried therapy, they thought it was something weaklings endured.

"Meantime it was 'Patrick, are you packed for college?' and 'Patrick, have you signed up for Freshman Orientation?' and 'Patrick, are you sure you want to be prelaw?' and that's all they wanted to talk about. Their youngest, something was *very wrong* with their youngest, but they didn't want to talk about that, they wanted to talk about their brilliant oldest, headed for college at seventeen.

"And I kept . . . I kept asking about Cathie, if she was better, maybe she should go to a hospital or something, you know . . . anything, right? And they were all 'don't worry about a thing, she's fine, shouldn't you be packing,' blah-blah. They were lying and I *knew* they were lying and I just . . . just let them take me away."

"Patrick, you were just a kid yourself, and Cathie's mental instability obviously wasn't your fau—"

"Shut up, I can only say this once." He made a slashing gesture with his hand I had never seen, which went with the tight, hard tone of voice I had never heard, and though I mentally raised my eyebrows I let him continue.

"So after I was gone, after I'd been at school, I found out they committed her. A little kid! They went right to the out-of-sight-out-of-mind option and signed her over to the goddamned institute!"

His hands were fists on the table between us and he was breathing hard. After a long moment I said, "If you are awaiting condemnation, I trust you packed a lunch. Patrick, it was not your fault. Cathie being ill was not, and your parents' cowardice was not, and you wanting to continue your life by leaving for college was not. Do you wish she and I had never met? We might not have, if things had happened another way."

"Of course not." Still he would not look at me. "It's just . . . I went to school and I made a life away from all of them—her included—I just let them shut her away from the world. And when she met you—when I met you—I think I loved you before we met. Because when I found out . . ."

"Found out?" I asked gently.

"When I realized what my parents had done . . . what I had let them do because I let them send me away . . . I could actually feel myself start to go crazy. I could feel . . . I thought, *Yay, I'm going nuts, too, I can keep Cathie company, wheee!* I could . . . actually . . . I could actually feel my sanity sort of . . . teetering." He held me with his dark gaze, where tears shone but did not fall. "Like it was a boat. Like my sanity was a boat on a lake and the lake was in the middle of a storm. I could feel my . . . my *self* tipping and tilting. I could feel my self start to want to split. I could *feel* that.

"And when Cathie told me about you, and I met you, I thought, *Here's someone who had that happen . . . she split into pieces, only she couldn't stop it in time.* It was like . . . when I knew you, it was like I always knew you. All the pieces of you. Not just the ones you thought were safe to show the world."

I realized I had been staring at him, openmouthed. My pretty baker, the boyfriend I assumed I had taken on my terms!

"I have taken you terribly for granted," was all I could say to his extraordinary story. Oh. There *was* one other thing. "And feeling responsible for Cathie's mental illness is not only foolish, it is arrogant and self-serving."

Now *his* mouth was hanging open. "What?"

"In a nice way," I assured him. "With the very best of intentions. You should have a chat with Cathie about just this sort of thing."

"I told Cathie all about it ages ago," he snapped. "We used to talk about it every week in therapy."

"You and Cathie have therapy?"

"Not anymore. But once I got out of college and actually grew a pair, of course I was going to talk to her about . . . about everything. Now my folks are . . . fading, I guess is the polite term, now they want to see her. It's their own fault she doesn't want to see them, but that's—" He shook his head. "I didn't plan for any of this when they told me my lawyer was here."

I laughed. "No doubt! I brought enough of my own baggage; I never dreamed you had some of your own to share. And this," I said grimly, "this is from someone who *does* have all sorts of therapy a week. Patrick, the truth is I was afraid. I was a coward. You were just a boy; I don't even have the excuse of immaturity. You offered me something wonderful and my response was to run away from it. You deserve better." *Yes. So run, Patrick. Run like the wind. I can only offer you more pain.*

He raised dark brows at me, and smiled. "Sure about that?"

"Yes. I . . ." I looked away, then back. "I love your house."

His smile widened. "My house?"

"Yes. And I would love to live in your house. With you. I just do not know how the three of us—"

"Five," he said, his smile widening.

"Sorry?"

"The five of us. You, me, Cadence, Adrienne, and Olive the Dawg."

"Olive the Dawg?"

"Yeah."

I sighed and picked up my briefcase. "We will have to talk about this."

"Uh-huh."

"At length."

"Yep."

"Because it will be tricky. The sleeping issue. The sex issue." Specifically: we weren't having any with Patrick yet. Cadence was still a virgin. I was not, though it had been several months since I had indulged. And I didn't know *what* Adrienne was. No one knew. No one wanted to know. Ever. "We will have to have a plan. *Why* are you smiling?"

"I didn't know one of my girlfriends was a lawyer."

"Yes, yes, a day of surprises."

"And you came right down, didn't you?" He smiled at me, clearly delighted. "I just realized. Michaela didn't tell you until after your super-secret briefing. But once you knew, you came straight away." Then, in a dreadful Sally Field impersonation: "You like me! You really, really like me!"

"I like your Meyer lemon tartlets," I corrected. "Not you."

"Aw." He stood. I stood. "Can I get a kiss from the prettiest lawyer in the room?"

"I am the only lawyer in this room, you idiot."

What the hell. I kissed him. Far be it from me to deny the request of a wrongfully imprisoned millionaire baker carrying long-misplaced guilt who enjoyed clandestine visits to PetCo with Olive the Dawg.

There was not one thing in my life that was uncomplicated. On days like this, I did not mind so much.

chapter sixty-nine

"Yeah? Then what? Come on, Cadence, don't stop now."

"Then Shiro got him out, and Michaela got the charges dropped. And we're all moving in together." I was still a little bewildered by that last one. I hadn't even known there'd been, you know, an invitation. But Shiro had agreed for all of us. (Nice of her!) It was hilarious when I thought about it. What else was I gonna do? Keep my no-dogs-allowed apartment while Shiro lived at Patrick's? "Did I tell you I can't have a dog in my apartment?"

"Yeah, at least three times."

"Kindly drop dead, Emma Jan. So anyway, Patrick closes on his house in another few days, and then we'll all live together. Oh my God, this house. Wait 'til you see it."

"How's that gonna work?" Emma Jan was whispering in my ear as she checked the west side of the building for stragglers. "You guys haven't had sex yet."

"How do *you* . . . oh."

"What? Shiro wanted to hit the range again. It's not my fault if she wants to confide in me."

"It is! She never wants to confide in anybody."

"Well, she confided *in* me. And got her butt whupped. Told her she couldn't beat me with my own gun. Didn't think she'd stop bitching the whole way to dinner . . . wait 'til she has to tell Michaela! Also not my fault," she added.

I was pretty sure it *was* her fault. Shiro had certainly never needed anyone to confide in before this. Nor had she appeared to mind what Michaela thought . . . about anything! Now that Emma Jan was firmly in the Friend category, I was less tense about the two of them hanging out, but it was still new to me, Shiro having a friend who wasn't my friend. And all this running back and forth to Michaela, bragging or bitching about range scores like she was their den mother or something? So so so so so weird.

Emma Jan was growing on me, but I doubted I'd ever find her as fascinating as Shiro did. I had even taken the step of talking to my doctor about it.

To my surprise, Dr. Christopher Nessman made me feel better about the whole thing.

"Not liking someone right away isn't a character flaw, Cadence. It's not indicative of your mental state. It happens to everyone and it's not explainable for the same reason love at first sight isn't explainable . . . sometimes, it just happens that way. For whatever reason, Agent Thyme and Shiro clicked. And for whatever reason, you and she did not. That's nothing to worry about. That's *normal*."

Normal, hmph. No wonder I hadn't recognized it. Here I was so worried Shiro would start dating Emma Jan, when she was actually making arrangements to move in with our boyfriend. Gah. Did *not* see that coming.

"I have no idea how it's gonna work." I was checking the east side. Our fake lecture was tonight. The good doctor was, in fact, a fellow FBI agent, one not affiliated with BOFFO. He had a doctorate in American history, so he knew how to lecture, how to sound like a stuffed shirt, and how to portray befuddled amusement. He was also the local silhouette-shooting champ three years running. A handy fellow to have around.

All the better to arrest you with, my dear.

The audience was liberally salted with local law enforcement and more than a few feds. The trap was set. The bait was dangling. We just had to cross our fingers that the JBJ killer would show up.

Knowing what I now knew about the Stinney family tragedy (which, it appeared, was ongoing), I could almost see our killer. Someone who'd lost the coin toss. Someone who had to take time out from his real life to kill a random white kid. And then teach his kids how to do the same.

I wasn't shocked the killer had left the parking stub in the Mickelson boy's pocket. I was shocked someone hadn't done it earlier. Say, three or four decades ago.

We watched. The good doctor had more eyes on him than a goose

(*geese!*)

had feathers, and we watched and guarded and patrolled and were ready for anything. Even though he'd been asked/ordered/begged to stay away, I was sure Dr. Gallo was in the audience somewhere, too. We couldn't legally do anything to him without tipping our hand, and Dr. Gallo excelled at getting into trouble.

When he wasn't wearing doctor's whites, or his scrubs, he could look like the neighborhood degenerate in his old leather jacket. Certainly most people who saw him the first time tended to think *meth dealer* or *cat burglar* or *student loan officer* long, long before they thought *respected physician.*

Odd, how I barely knew him and yet, *knew* him.

I think that was why he'd been on my mind so much. Somewhere beneath the cool jacket and tattered scrubs, Dr. Gallo was like me. Or Emma Jan. Or even Patrick. There were things there, secret things. But it was all right. There would be time to ferret them out.

Some other time, though. Right now there was work to do, right now we were busy with other things, and like I'd said, we were ready for anything at all.

Except for nothing. We weren't ready for nothing, and that's just what we got.

A whole lot of nothing.

chapter seventy

"That was regrettable." Michaela summed up our feelings in her usual detached way. The place had been crawling with the public, feds, and locals all night, but by now almost all the chickens had gone home.

"Fuckin' pain in the ass is what it was," George said. "I can't believe we didn't pull him in. And that fake lecture! How could that guy make the Stinney legend sound so fucking boring? I was ready to hang myself with my own intestines. I can't *believe* we didn't pull him in!"

"We may have," she corrected. "The doctors suggested the best way to draw JBK would be to make it about George Stinney and the crime perpetrated upon him, not the crimes that happened after. But they never said JBK would show up, wrists out, begging to be taken in. They never said forcing a confrontation would lead to a confession. This was always just another way to get closer to the heart of things. If we're thinking like him, we can catch him. You know all this, George."

"In my mind, though? They did promise all those things. Also in my mind, the mayor gave me the key to the city, and the key to all the ladies' locker rooms at all the Anytime Fitness gyms in town." He sighed. "Look, the lecture's been over for almost two hours, the local cowboys took all their toys and went home, I badly need booze, so why don't we—"

"Could you believe all that stuff about that poor kid?" I asked loudly, startling everyone. I usually used my Outside Voice when I was in the middle of setting a trap. Usually. "I mean, holy old devils, it's just so so awful." I took a deep breath to deepen my "you betcha!" accent. Garrison Keillor had forever tainted Minnesotan culture before the world. It wasn't so bad when he started in the seventies, because Minnesota wasn't thought of as an exciting holiday getaway. People took their kids to Disney World or the Grand Canyon, and honeymooners went to Cancún or Paris . . . like that.

Then he started to write about Lake Wobegon. And of course he did a beautiful job. So gradually, our gorgeous, gorgeous state . . . was outed! And nobody checked to see if we'd wanted to be, least of all Keillor. If we'd been asked, we would have politely told him we liked being in the closet. We liked being in on a terrific, beautiful, unspoiled secret. We *liked* that just about everyone in the country thought August in Minnesota was just too darned chilly.

And then. Then! The movie *Fargo* came out. Now listen: I've got nothing against the story, the actors, all that . . . it's an amazing film. I'm not casting any aspersions on the quality of the work.

But those accents! My God! Not everyone in this part of the country ends every single question with "you betcha!" and "then."

"Sure is cold out here today." "You betcha!" No.

"Soooo, we're gonna go right back there, then." "Yaa!" No.

Our secret is out now, and will be for a long time. Everybody knows, now, about our gorgeous forests, the clear pure lakes and rivers, the fresh air, and the crops. The crops! Corn and sugar beets, wheat and rye, potatoes and millet, sorghum and sunflowers. We fed ourselves and still had so much left, we fed the world, too.

And don't forget the tolerable accents and the generally friendly population. Wikipedia insists the Minnesota Nice thing is an urban myth, but Wikipedia is stupid: it only knows what people tell it. But don't take my admittedly biased word for it—anyone can check the state crime stats. We lag far, far behind places like New York and Miami and Los Angeles. Because we're nice!

Then, out of nowhere: I practically heard the crunch as something hard stabbed into my shin. And I realized with amazement that I'd been completely zoned out during a stakeout.

I glanced up at the clock. Ah. Okay. Gone less than three minutes. Still, that's a long time to stand there and try to get someone to engage, or at least finish her thought.

"Sorry, I was thinking. I'm still thinking."

"Be careful, then. You might sprain something."

"Don't put 'then' at the end of your sentence!" I snapped. Before George could say something nasty, or pistol-whip me, I added, "You know what? Here's what I was thinking: I don't think George Stinney killed those girls. And then the state killed *him*, the poor, poor boy. Why wasn't anything done? Someone should tell his *family*, his poor, poor family. Someone should tell his *family* the state owes them a ginormous apology."

I had seen her out of the corner of my eye. Midforties, African American, nicely dressed in a J.Jill winter coat and slacks. She had stayed on the perimeter of things. She had come in very, very quietly and just looked. She was still tracking water so she hadn't been inside for long—it was snowing out.

I don't know what it was about her . . . maybe the way she was hanging back. Yeah. The look on her face, and the way she was hanging back, I think, tipped me off. Even if I wasn't aware of it consciously, unconsciously all my bells were ringing. This woman I had never seen . . . she didn't just look interested. She looked *invested*.

She looked to me the way people did when they put everything, absolutely everything they had, into a family business. A business everyone in the family made sacrifices for. A business they gave their time and money to. Time they could have spent with their children, time they could have used to have a life, time that went into the business, a business that was never, ever satisfied. A business that was always hungry. The Stinney Vengeance Farm: more stressful than running a Burger King franchise.

The Stinney family business. It had left such a mark on her, I could almost see the stamp on her forehead.

To make matters so much worse, we fumbled it. We'd gone to all these pains to disguise ourselves, to make it look like we were random suburbanites out for a lecture and then maybe a trip to the local Starbucks. None of us were wearing anything that said "government-issue federal agent, note the crisp black suit, please."

But in the way that I looked at her and knew her, she looked at us, and knew us.

She tried a tentative smile. Later, when I found out she was thirty-six, I couldn't believe it. Midforties, I had guessed first. When she'd tried that smile out on us, I had jacked my estimation to late forties.

She took a step closer. I admired that. She came *closer*. Anybody else would be running for their lives. Their freedom. When she spoke, it was thoughtful and melodic. "So you're . . . interested . . . in George Stinney." A calm voice. Too calm. Maybe . . . a dead voice? "You think . . . you think he was wronged, then?"

I had no idea what to do, other than instruct myself not to yell at her about "then."

Thank God Michaela was there. "We don't think anything. We *know* he was wronged, ma'am. And we know what that did to your family. I'm very sorry. But you're under arrest." I cringed inwardly. The last time Michaela had gone into the field to get the bad guy, she'd shot him to death.

But I guess I shouldn't have worried. This time, the smile was real. "Now that it's here, I'm actually relieved to hear you say the words at last. Isn't that a fool thing? I'm *relieved.*"

"Because the family business won't gobble up your son now," I guessed.

"Yes, he's . . . yes! You *do* understand. I hoped you would. I thought I could explain . . . if I could just show you—he's fourteen. He just turned fourteen. How could I expect him to do what . . . what I had to do . . . he's fourteen! Like George! They make us do these things because George never got the chance to live, and they don't see what . . . what a poison pill it all is! My son deserved what they wanted to take. He can have a life!" The June Boys Jobs Killer started to cry.

That's when I disappeared. I was gone for a long time, too, much longer than twenty-four hours. The others had to tell me what happened when I finally made my way back.

chapter seventy-one

It was not the JBK killer's fault. Well, it was in the sense that all the things that flowed from her murders were her fault. But she paid for her betrayal. If it even was a betrayal. She did what she needed to do to save her son from her life. From the family business. I think she was the only Stinney family member who *wasn't* a traitor.

I had not spotted the old man. Small wonder—he had been taught by generations of assassins (for that is how they saw themselves, as opposed to the murderers of helpless children). He had taught *her.* And knew her well, which is why he had also come to our fake lecture. Apparently he had been sensing Luann was having a little trouble practicing the family religion: revenge. When she killed the second boy, he knew somebody was slipping off the res.

No, I did not see the man. I spotted the gleam of light on metal when he went for his weapon. He had held off to discover just what his niece was up to. He had chosen his spot well. He had the high ground—there was a small stairwell just behind where we had all been standing. Not much of one, only six steps, but tactically advantageous. He was at the top, aiming down at his niece. His traitorous niece.

I got moving. And if he had not been such an evil old man, he could have killed me long before I reached him. But he was entirely focused on murdering his niece. I thought of a line from *Moby Dick*: "If his chest had been a mortar, he burst his hot heart's shell upon it."

I have been seeing it a lot. What happened on those stairs. Particularly at night. I have declined the sleeping pills suggested by my doctor.

I want to see it. I want to know all my mistakes, and all hers, poor woman. I want to know so the next time I can be faster, smarter, better. I want what I've wanted since I was old enough to understand the concept. I wanted *everything*.

In my head, everything is happening exactly the way it did, except I have foreknowledge of what will happen. It is a great deal like stepping outside myself and narrating the events of my life.

I see the muzzle flash.

I get Cadence out of harm's way.

I sprint for the steps.

The gun is still coming up.

I run and run, but the steps slow me down.

A flash from the Kahr-K9. An excellent little pistol.

Then I am reaching for him, both arms outstretched. I want to kill him not only for the boys, but for his niece, and for his niece's son.

You think you know pain, you ancient poisonous buzzard? You do not. But you will. I swear you will. I swear on

(poor, poor boys)

all of us.

Another flash, and I wonder if the old man had a baseball bat I could not see.

I wonder how he managed to hit me in the shoulder with an invisible baseball bat.

I fall for a long time.

chapter seventy-two

"Awwwww, fuck! Emma Jan! Get your ass over here, I need pressure on this! Somebody find Gallo, I know that sneaky fuck is around here somewhere!"

George. I would recognize that shrill bitching anywhere.

I opened my eyes. I was at the bottom of those endless steps. The old man was also on the floor. He was lying very still. He was not moving his hands. He was blinking hard and not moving his hands.

He was doing those things because Michaela was standing over him and pointing her gun at him. I could tell he thought the barrel of that gun was his world. The barrel of the gun would appear to be at least twenty meters wide and might also contain his death.

I grinned up at George through monstrous pain. It felt like someone had laid firewood in my shoulder socket and then lit it to see it all go up.

Well. I could not lie around like this all day.

"No you don't, Shiro, I know that look. Lie still. Listen, dumbass, we've got an ambulance on the way, so just sit still until—whoa!"

I sat up. Emma Jan grabbed for me and I used her arms as a ladder to get to my feet. "The woman. The JBK killer. Where—"

George jerked his head to the left. The JBK killer was in a sprawled heap not ten feet from where I was.

"Shiro, George is right, you'd better lie—"

"Don't waste your breath, New Girl. She'll lie down after she passes out from blood loss. Hey, wanna bet on how long it takes? Twenty bucks? No, wait: winner gets Shiro's pain meds."

I swayed on my feet, holding my shoulder. I had to see her. I had to see the niece's face. I had to know if I was right. And if she was right.

I took a tentative step. The room was trying to go dark around the edges

(*do not do not DO NOT black out do not do not black out*)

Good advice.

"Emma Jan. George. Help me." I ignored their shocked traded looks. So what if I had never asked for their help before? I could grow, could learn, could change. *She* had. She gave her life to save her boy. She broke through generations of conditioning, and not for herself. She gave up everything so her son could have something. Maybe even just one thing.

I had to. I *would* see. Nobody saw George Stinney; the whites looked and saw an uppity nigger. His family looked and saw death for them all. And in turn, they didn't see any of the white boys.

One step. Another. Another. It was taking forever. It was taking forever. I would be here for the rest of my life—lungs burning, shoulder screaming, blood running from me like small red rivers. I would never get out. I would die in here and no one would see me, either. Another. And then

(*do not do not DO NOT black out do not do not black out think of the endless teasing you will have to endure from George do not black out do not*)

I was there. I was standing over her. I sighed in relief when I saw her face, when I realized I had been right. I had hoped to see her in life. But seeing her in death was not terrible.

She was smiling. There was a sizable hole in her forehead—the nasty old man had been a dead shot, as I was sure he would be. But she was smiling.

She had known it was over. And she faced it without flinching. She had known she was going to her death, and had dressed nicely for the appointment. As the old man could predict her moves, so she could predict his. She could not be fearless to save herself, but she became so to save her son.

"I will advise you again not to move," Michaela was saying. "It will be the last time I so advise, sir, do you understand?"

"Old man." I did not try to keep the loathing out of my voice. "Look at me, viper."

He did it carefully, slowly, so as not to startle the woman who had him in her sights. A woman who was doubtless praying he would make a move. Any move. Michaela, I had decided, was probably a lioness in a former life. She lived for the kill like plants lived for sunshine.

"Your niece was ten of you, old man. Do you hear me? She was the only warrior you produced. Now do me a favor. Move. Do a handstand. Tap dance. Reach into one of your pockets. Move a *lot*. I promise: the agent drawing down on you will cure your ills."

"Now, now," Michaela said, mildly enough. "Let's not try to goad our suspect into suicide by cop. Do I seem as though I would like more paperwork? Hmmm? And Agent Jones, will you kindly lie down before I shoot *you*?"

"That is really good advice," Dr. Gallo said, materializing from . . . somewhere. He was all dressed up in a clean-but-faded dark denim shirt, clean khakis, and loafers without socks. (In this weather! Frostbite-seeking moron.) His fingers were sinking into my upper arm. "Here we go." He was easing me down on my back. What the hell. I let him. "Nice and easy."

"We knew you were here," I said triumphantly.

"I'm so sorry for what happened to you," he told the killer. One of the killers. He was kind to the dead woman who had killed his nephew. He had nothing to say to the old man, I noticed with inappropriate glee. "I don't forgive you, though."

"That's all right," I said, even though

(*DO NOT*)

he wasn't talking to me.

(*DO NOT black out, idiot!*)

Good advice. And I took it; I did not black out. I vomited instead. Emma Jan would need a new purse.

chapter seventy-three

When a paramedic says, without being asked, that you will be "just fine" (as in, "Oh, hey, you're gonna be *just fine*") within the first three seconds of wound assessment, it means you are going to die.

So I laughed at the boyishly earnest EMT (he had freckles, of all the silliest things) when he lied to my face. I had lost too much blood. I felt chilled, and sleepy. I would sleep and then I would die. Maybe it was the shock talking, but I was at peace with it. All of it. If George Stinney's great-great-great-aunt (or whatever she had been to that long-ago executed child) could face death with a smile and her nicest outfit, could I do less?

Never!

"All right, let's get her set up with—ow!"

George, for some strange reason, had insisted on riding with me to the hospital. The stressful day was getting to him; he seemed frazzled and unkempt. He had sacrificed his tie (bees stinging babies against a background of jack-o'-lantern orange) to try to control my bleeding. I could not help but observe that he and Dr. Gallo did little but get in each other's way.

When the EMT, dodging both of them, tried to give me an injection, George grabbed the boy's wrist.

"Don't you lay a hand on her, pusbag. How long have you been an EMT? Are you even qualified to touch her? Show me your driver's license; if you're old enough to vote I'll kiss you on the mouth. And if you're not I'll kill you and sink your body in Lake Calhoun. This is a federal agent! Why isn't the boss EMT along for this ride? Gallo, will you for Christ's sake do something?"

"B-b-because nobody told us any of that stuff," the poor child stammered, terrified. "We just rolled when they told us we had a Code One. Please don't sink me in Lake Calhoun. I can legally vote next month."

"George, release him at once," I ordered while Dr. Gallo seized the radio and told an unseen person on the other end just what to expect. I noticed he did not mention George, which was just as well.

"Hey, I don't want just anybody messing with you. Enough shit's gone on without something happening to you, too."

Perhaps I was hallucinating from blood loss. I had never seen George evince concern for any living being save himself.

"George, everything is fine." Enormous lie. "Let the boy work. Ouch!" I glared at the boy, who went even paler. "And I must say, I cannot help but be touched."

"If you think I'm breaking in another partner the same year I had to get a prostate exam, you're out of your fucking mind, Shiro Jones!"

"And now, I am not." I had never wished so urgently to pass out from blood loss as I did just then. I was delighted when my body obliged me.

* * *

As it turned out, the EMT had been correct. I did not die. Though it was a bit of a trial, recuperating from a gunshot wound and forcing down hospital food. It was a while before I was back to myself. Pardon me . . . before the three of us were back to ourselves. My sisters and I.

In the meantime, I needed answers. And owed them to someone else.

chapter seventy-four

It took a long, long time, but finally they left me alone. Michaela was gone, and so were Emma Jan and George (the latter had been "escorted" off the premises). My wounds had been treated—fortunately, I needed no surgery this time. I had been checked and checked and checked again, and had even managed to grab a nap between bouts of unconsciousness.

Now. I had twenty-seven minutes before the nurse came back to check my vitals. It would only be harder to find Max Gallo and tell him things he thought he needed to know. During first shift, there would always be too many people, both on my floor and in his blood bank. During third shift, I would be too exhausted.

Now. It had to be now: the middle of shift change, 10:55 P.M. The nurses were giving their reports at the station; people were focused on leaving, or arriving. It was as chaotic as it ever got.

I slowly sat up, and carefully untangled and straightened the many tubes running out of or into my body. I would have to bring the IV pole; ugh. Hated, *hated* the benighted things. Like being on a leash. A leash that continually dripped things into my bloodstream.

I swung my legs over the side. Took a deep breath. Stood.

All right. All right! This . . . this wasn't terrible. I was sore, yes, but it was distant soreness. I must be on a morphine drip, or still riding a shot. And I was in the sweet spot, too—pain was distant, but I wasn't too fog-headed.

After I'd shuffled about twenty feet, I decided I had been wrong, entirely wrong: there was not enough morphine in my system for my midshift jaunt. Not by half.

Ah, well. Nobody said the life of an MPD-suffering, gunshot FBI agent with a dog and a baker boyfriend and stacks of paperwork would be an easy one.

I made it to the elevator without incident—it helped that it wouldn't occur to the staff that I'd get the urge for a pre-midnight stroll. And even if I were spotted, I would be in no real trouble.

It made me think of Aldo Raine—Brad Pitt's character from *Inglourious Basterds.* When Col. Landa snivels, "You'll be shot for this!", Raine says, just as calm as you please, "No, I don't think so. More like chewed out. I've been chewed out before."

The urgency of this mission was of my own making. If I were caught, I would not be shot, just scolded and escorted back to my room. But I owed Gallo an explanation. Barring that (could anything like this ever truly be explained?), I owed him the full story. I did not trust BOFFO to tell it. So I, Shiro Jones, temporary civilian, would tell him. If found out, I would not be shot. And I, too, had been chewed out before.

Of course, that was all contingent on my reaching the blood bank—assuming Gallo was even there at this time of night. I was making steady progress, but the hallway had started slowly pitching and yawing up and down, back and forth. I could navigate, but was spending an awful lot of time bumping into walls. When had they moved the hospital onto a cruise ship in the middle of a hurricane? Normally I was one to notice things like that.

Ah! There. There at the end of a seventy-mile-long hallway were the doors to the torture chamber/blood bank place. I was supposed to find someone there. I was supposed to tell them a sad story. I was supposed to make them feel worse about a situation they could never, ever change. And then I was supposed to go back to my life. Who had given me this terrible assignment? Someone with no heart. Someone who had been chewed out before.

I shoved against the doors; they remained stubbornly shut. Locked! No. Wait. I had the strength of a febrile grasshopper; I should make another attempt before being chewed out.

So, in my cleverness, I fell against the doors.

chapter seventy-five

I opened my eyes and saw Dr. Gallo's black ones staring at me from a distance of less than a foot. "Ha!" I crowed. "My plan worked."

"You're insane," he informed me, trying to take my pulse through all sorts of bandages.

"And you are drunk." He was. As I had collapsed through the swinging doors, I caught a glimpse of him sitting bleary-eyed at his desk, a half-empty bottle of rum at his left elbow. In one of those odd moments in time that seem to take hours but are only microseconds, I'd seen his eyes widen, seen him clutch the side of his desk with whitened fingers, seen him vault the desk like a leather-wearing gymnast, and race to me in just enough time to catch me as my knees went. If I had not been groggy and dizzy and sweaty and racked with blinding pain, I would have complimented the man on his fine reflexes. He did *that,* drunk? What could he do when sober?

"Adrienne, what the *fuck*? How did you even get off the ward?"

"That is not my name." *Shhhh! That's a secret!* Shut up, inner voices. "The ward, phagh! I could have left anytime." This was a lie. "I am a trained federal agent and they are overworked, underpaid, taken-for-granted hospital employees who are forever six steps behind me."

"Good point. Now stay put," he added, easing me off his lap. I was sorry to go. "I'm gonna call the—"

I clutched his bony wrist and squeezed in the right spot; he whitened, but said nothing, and nothing changed in his face. In that moment, I admired him greatly. In that moment, I may have fallen in love. Later, I could never be sure. The entire encounter had the quality of a fever dream.

"Wait," I begged in a voice I had never, *ever* used with anyone else. "Wait. I have to tell you. I have to tell you about George and Luann, and all the dead boys in between. I can only tell you right now. Later I'll be very official again. Later won't be now."

His eyebrows arched and the corner of his mouth twitched. "You realize, hon, you're half out of your head with blood loss, among other things?"

"Of course. That's why I had to come now."

Now he was smiling; he looked delighted and clearly did not care if I saw that. "Now? When you're half-dead from blood loss and half-doped on morphine? And dripping from sweat and you've torn several stitches, and I'm drunk off my ass on Captain Morgan's and wondering if this is some sort of booze-induced hallucination and thinking very inappropriate thoughts about the helpless hottie in my lap? Now?"

"I am never helpless." Then I laughed up at him. I shouldn't have felt at all comfortable, cradled in his lap like I was, but I did. "Yes, now."

"Fine." He rubbed his eyes, reached in his pocket for a Kleenex, offered it to me, and when I waved it away, put it back in his pocket.

"The *quick* version. And the second you pass out, I'm calling the ward."

"All right." I closed my eyes. Thought for a moment. Said, without opening them, "I have not passed out; I am gathering my thoughts." He grunted, but did not comment. His hands were everywhere, but it did not feel inappropriate. He was smoothing and examining and even absently patting. I was the inappropriate one; I was dizzy, in pain, weak, thirsty, had a crushing headache . . . and was now sexually aroused. If I could have spared the breath to groan at my self-indulgence, I would have.

"Once upon a time, there was a boy named George Stinney who was legally murdered by the state of South Carolina on June 16, 1944." As beginnings went, it was not exceptional. I was fortunate, though: I had a captive audience. Even if he had been willing to risk dumping my gunshot self off his lap to find a phone or gauze, he was as captivated by George Stinney as I had been.

"Then Luann died smiling," I finished several days later. (To be fair, my sense of time might have been skewed.) "And that is all. There is no more."

"Sure there is," Max said. He was still deathly pale, still had breath that smelled like rum and coconut, but a lone tear had tracked from one eye down the side of his face, and I think he was unaware. "Why'd you tell me this? You could have told me the government-sanitized version and I never would have known."

"*I* would have known. Besides . . ." Things were getting dark around the edges. The blood bank was suffering a gradual blackout, or I was close to passing out. "Besides, you took me flying. Your Honda . . . it's like a storm cloud on wheels."

"Oh, my. A poetic FBI thug." He smirked, but did so in a way that made it impossible to take offense. Then the smile fell from his face and he bent and brushed a quick kiss across my forehead.

"I'm in your debt forever. Not just for telling me about George. For getting them. Both of them. You need a favor, you come and see me first."

I could hear rapid footsteps down the corridor. "I sense my imminent rescue. I suppose they were eventually going to notice my absence."

He laughed, and held up his left hand to show me his cell. "I kind of called them when you weren't looking."

"You . . . sneaky . . ." I couldn't finish. I was too annoyed. And too filled with admiration. Max Gallo: a man who, in another life without MPD, could have been the love of my life. "Sneaky . . . treacherous . . . wonderful . . ."

Fortunately for my pride, I passed out. Who knows what other insanity might have escaped my lips?

chapter seventy-six

Patrick whistled when he saw me in the hospital bed the next morning. "Oh, man! Cadence is gonna be pissed."

"Do not," I sighed, aware I felt more guilt than gladness to see him, "add to my troubles."

He set the cake box down without looking and rushed over to my bed. "Jesus! What happened? You know what? Never mind. I know what happened. You took a bullet for somebody, didn't you? Don't answer that. Agghh!" He had plunged his hands into his thick red hair and they had locked into fists. "I can't believe this! My God, is there gonna be permanent damage? You can't go back to that apartment alone!"

"Calm down. Stop screaming. I will be fine. The prognosis is full recovery." Gallo hadn't fallen to pieces when I'd lurched through the blood bank doors like a blood-spattered Frankenstein.

Not fair, I told myself. Gallo was a doctor. He was used to mayhem.

"Full, painful recovery plagued by far too many visits from physical therapists. Oh, and there is nonsense about a medal. I won't show up for it and that is all there is to it. How is Olive?"

"She's with me," he said absently. "After George told me you'd be laid up for a few days I went and got her. And there was a doctor in the hall who gave me this . . . he said he forgot to give it to you earlier. I think he was a doctor. He looked like a real hard-ass. Thin, dark?"

Gallo had come to visit me! "Oh, I must have missed him," I politely told the man I no longer loved. Maybe . . . had never loved?

Patrick handed me a catalog of the latest Honda motorcycles. Ah! My reward for foiling evil and surviving the gunshot and then stumbling to him in the middle of the night to vomit up everything I knew about JBK. Fortunately I had a bank account Cadence did not know about. I opened the brochure and a small folded note fell out. I pretended to ignore it.

"They said that guy's from the blood bank . . . you've been getting your own blood."

"Yes, ironically, Cadence once again donated for me, though she did not know it at the time. I suppose her silly urge to donate platelets or what-have-you is good for something." In fact, if not for her silly urge, I might never have . . .

Been in the mess I am now. It was *not* a blessing.

"And that doctor thinks your name is Adrienne."

"Yes, that's how Michaela set it up," I replied absently. "Fret not, Patrick, I have thrown in my lot with you." Truer words, as they say, have never been spoken.

"Well, good, because that skinny guy with the catalogue was kind of cute." There was a dark glint of something in Patrick's eyes—jealousy? Anxiety? "But like I said, I've got her, so don't worry about Olive."

"Got her where?" Patrick lived in a hotel when he was in town. It was one of the many reasons he wished to buy a home. And his own closing was still a day or two off.

"Cathie's."

Oh, dear. That was bad. Cathie, Patrick's sister and Cadence's best friend, had OCD. A shedding dog would likely drive her over the edge into the red rage of madness.

For the first time in my life, I was relieved to find I would be in a hospital for the next few days. I had zero interest in calming Cathie out of one of her volcanic OCD-fueled rages. And zero interest in changing my living situation.

Because it would change. I had not lied; I had thrown in my lot with the baker. I was selfish, and I loved driving the body, but I would not ruin Cadence's chance at happiness, nor Adrienne's chance at acceptance. Patrick was willing to take us all; I was willing to go along with all that entailed.

I would not turn my back on a good man because I was intrigued by one who was complex.

I would not cheat Cadence out of the family she had sought since before I was "born."

And I would not break the baker's heart because I sensed something deeply interesting in a man I hardly knew, a man who took me for a motorcycle ride on a whim and, though he would never know, snatched my love before I realized I was holding it out to him.

"You're coming home with me," the baker was insisting. "I close on the house next week. Shit! There's no furniture. I'll buy you a bed. I'll buy you a hospital bed. I'll hire a nurse to—"

"You will not."

"Shiro, will you be reasonable for once? You can't take care of yourself. A nurse will just—"

"Be shot on sight."

"Agghh! Okay, okay, a fight for another time."

Ha! That was what *he* thought. As my personal hero Stewie

Gilligan Griffin would say, victory was mine. I would live with him and lay with him, but I would not tolerate a home nurse.

He collapsed into the chair beside my bed. Rested his head in his hands. Groaned into them. "I was so worried," he said to his palms. "I was so afraid you were going to die."

"As your lawyer, I can tell you it was foolish to fret. I was very far from dying."

"I gotta get used to this stuff, I gotta get a handle on it, I get it. But I am never gonna like it. I guess you wouldn't be you if you weren't charging after gunmen. But you got him? The bad guy who killed all those kids?"

"Yes." For I held it to be true that the evil old man had been as responsible as any Stinney through the decades for the deaths. They could have stopped at any time. They chose not to. It took one of their own to turn, to understand, for the killings to finally, mercifully come to an end. "The killings are over." *Those* killings, I should have said. But why destroy the mood?

"That's good. I just wish you could have stopped them without getting hurt."

"It was a small enough price to pay."

It was true. I had a wound from which I would recover. I still had my friends, my family. I was loved, though was no longer certain I could return that love. Comparably speaking, I had everything.

She had nothing. Just a drawer in the morgue, poor thing.

I was no longer a child, so I would not waste my breath with "It's not fair!"

Sometimes, though, the cost seemed too high. For all of us.

chapter seventy-seven

"Opus didn't have clearance," George told me a day later, "but the guy was a fucking genius with a fucking psycho-genius brother and sister. He was able to hack our system, no problem. Because he'd never had clearance, after Michaela killed his ass we never thought to revoke something that had never existed."

"Terrific," I grumbled.

"Here's the part you'll really hate, Shiro. Right up until last week they had access to all our shit. All the files. HOAP, VI-CAP—everything we could electronically access, they could, too."

"You were correct, George. I really hate this part."

"Yep. Now we've got IT weenies crawling over everything in the office. Nobody can find shit. I'm tempted to ask Emma Jan to shoot me in the shoulder so I can have a nice relaxing week in a hospital."

"I will oblige you whenever you wish."

"Yeah. So, good news, nobody's peeking over our shoulders anymore. Bad news, they were able to look for a long time. They saw all the JBJ stuff and drew their own crazy brilliant conclusions. Watch for another letter, Shiro. They like writing to you, I bet. They'll do it again."

George was correct. I, too, was certain I would hear from Two of the ThreeFer. And soon.

"The old guy was her uncle. His dad had taught him, and he taught Luann. And he tells us he's always had doubts about her, he always kept a special eye on her."

"He has confessed this?"

"He won't shut up about it. There's all kinds of misplaced pride there." George paused. Looked at me, doubtless gauging how I would take the news. "Her kid came to see him. The old man. Emma Jan explained it to him. What was coming. What his mom did. How she got him out of it. And the price she paid for all that shit and more."

"How . . . how did that go?"

"He's ready for a fucking straitjacket," George said flatly. "Maybe someday he'll get it. Right now, he's seriously fucked up." He sighed.

"Do you know what distresses me the most?"

George crossed his arms behind his head and leaned back. Two of the chair legs left the floor as he rocked beside my bed. "Not being able to gaze upon my hot bod?"

"Yes, of course, but I am working through that. What upsets me is that there was no question that TwoFer of the ThreeFer helped us. Thanks to their mocking letter, we were able to look at JBK in a new light. And let us not forget an inanimate software program did some of the thinking for us. Without HOAP.1, we may never have solved it. Remember, too, the niece—"

"Luann Stennen. That's the name she was using, anyway. We're tracking down every single blood relative of hers we can find. The old man, he's bragging about family loyalty and not giving us shit. I can hear the jury already: 'But he's so old!' If he walks, I swear I'm gonna find him and make him eat a gun."

"A fine plan. But remember, Luann wanted to be caught. She

wanted an end to it, she wanted her son out of it. We solved a case *after* the killer left clues, *after* other killers gave us tips, *after* Paul revamped his software program.

"There it is. The thing that haunts me. Would we have been able to solve it without their help? How can we pat ourselves on the backs for putting an end to all this when *we* actually did not?"

"Shiro, you know what? Honest to God, I love the collar as much as you do, but in this case? I'll take 'em any way they come. Luann's dead. The next generation's safe. Dr. Gallo even got closure—how often does *that* happen? You know, Michaela must have briefed him already, he knows all about it. He's kind of cool, for a vampire. So don't be greedy. That's . . ." George trailed off and stared into space for a long moment. "That's gotta be enough for now."

"Why, George. You sounded very close to human just then."

"Yeah, I need some coffee, I'm feeling pretty light-headed. This isn't like me at all. Maybe I'm catching the flu? Uh . . ."

"Yes?"

"Will you flash me your tits before I go? That hospital gown is really doin' it for me. And can we get one of those nurses in here to give you a sponge bath? Me likey."

"Ah. *There* you are. The real George Pinkman has joined us at last."

"And the real George Pinkman is getting the hell out of here. My TiVo isn't gonna set itself." He frowned. "Although it ought to be able to by now. I should reread the manual. They're afraid to send any more cable guys to my apartment. And you should sleep. You look like hammered shit."

"I still have questions. I shall sleep when I am dead," I lied, with a tough attitude I faked.

"At least you have a plan," George said dryly. He gave me a two-fingered wave, and sauntered out the door.

I pulled the note from beneath my pillow. I had read it twenty-seven times. I had memorized it. Still, I liked looking at the ink scrawled on the paper, and would allow myself this one last indulgence: *Next time you want to go flying, call me.—Max G. 439–0263*

I crumpled the note and tossed it toward the wastebasket across the room. I did not miss.

I never missed.

chapter seventy-eight

"Dumbest thing I ever saw." Emma Jan had brought me sushi from Byerly's, which would do in a pinch. "Who charges a gunman? You've been watching too much *Law and Order.*"

"I loathe *Law and Order.*"

"Cadence is gonna be pissed," she added, eyeing my heavily bandaged shoulder.

"Why do you think I have remained? I should like to put that off as long as I can. Thank you for the sushi."

"No big. Listen, I went to the range last night. Dan was asking about you; I told him you'd be out in a day or two. He said he's got some Tec-22s for you to try when you make it back."

I gasped happily. "Really? Wonderful."

She laughed. She had a new purse slung over one shoulder—I still felt a bit guilty about ruining her other one—and it was stuffed with napkins and chopsticks. "You sounded just like a little kid just now. A little kid on Christmas morning."

"Yes, but . . . Tec-22s, Emma Jan!"

"Yes, great, calm down. If you tear another stitch, Michaela will probably tear something in me. Did they really find you on the other end of the hospital? Were you sleepwalking, or did you have a fever?"

"A fever," I agreed. One that was unlikely to go down soon.

"Well, thank God you didn't hurt yourself worse. You're a *tad* behind on paperwork, so Michaela doesn't want your return delayed."

"No doubt."

She didn't say anything else, just struggled to get comfortable in an uncomfortable chair. I said nothing, as well; I was thinking about Luann. I could not recall being comfortable enough with another person to just . . . just sit there with them. And not talk.

"Emma Jan, why do you think she did it? Why now, after all the murders, all the decades of the family business?"

She looked surprised that I would ask, and stopped rooting around in her new big purse. "It's pretty simple, Shiro. Her family, all they ever did, they did for hate. It might have started off as this noble vengeance-killing thing, but after a while, it wasn't even about revenge anymore. It was about keeping the hate alive for years to come. They did that, all that, for hate. Luann did what she did for love."

"For love." I tasted the word, musing. "It sounds overly simplified."

"Yeah, Shiro. I know it sounds stupid, or oversimplified if you will, but sometimes, things just *are*. That's all it is. There isn't any more, so don't keep looking."

Good advice.

"I am tired, my friend. I think I will leave for a bit. Get some rest."

Her eyes widened. "You mean . . . you're gonna let . . ."

"Yes."

She leaned forward and put her hand on mine. "*Thank you* for giving me some warning. Feel better soon; I'll come back tomorrow and bring you more sushi. But I gotta get the hell out of here now. Talk to you later." She brushed a distracted kiss on my forehead, then rapidly vacated. I could actually hear her running footsteps in the hospital corridor.

Well! Enough malingering. The time had come.

Epilogue

I opened my eyes, astonished to find I was in . . . was this a . . . yes! It was a hospital room. An all-too-familiar sight, yet I was always amazed to find myself in these places. Which proved what a slow learner I was. But never mind the slow learning, what the heckfire was I doing in a fargin' hospital room with a . . . a . . .

I clutched my shoulder, then nearly shrieked as the torn muscles reproached me for moving too quickly.

What had *happened*? What day was it? Where was JBK? Had I missed Christmas? If I missed Christmas, somebody was going to pay and pay and pay. What—who—?

Oh, someone was gonna *die* for this one. They were going to see an ugly side of Cadence Jones. They would rue the day they messed with me. I hated to be such a meanie, but punishment needed to be doled out. They were . . . *off the Christmas card list*!

I threw back my head, opened my mouth, and shrieked, *"Oh, come on!"* at the ceiling.

addendum

A friend of mine looked over the manuscript and made an interesting comment. “When that local cop is all pissed because they brought BOFFO in on the JBK case,” she said, “and he couldn’t figure out why crazy people were getting all that money from the government? And Cadence says, ‘Well, it’s the government.’ That seemed overly simple to me.”

I thought that was hilarious. “But it’s the government” overly simple? Unrealistic, even? The federal government would never fund a department full of gun-toting psychotics; the very idea is absurd?

Well, maybe. But below is a list of things the government *has* funded. So check it out, and draw your own conclusions.

In 1976, the National Institute on Drug Abuse funded a six-figure project to develop “objective evidence concerning marijuana’s effect on sexual arousal by exposing groups of male pot smokers to pornographic films and measuring their responses by means of sensors attached to their penises.”

In 1978, the Office of Education spent six figures on a package designed to teach college students how to watch television.

The United States Postal Service spent millions on a campaign to encourage Americans to write more letters to each other.

The Justice Department conducted a study on why prisoners want to get out of jail.

In 1978, the National Institute of Mental Health studied a Peruvian brothel.

In 1975, the Federal Aviation Administration did a study on the measurements of 432 flight attendants, paying extra attention to the "length of the buttocks."

In 2010, the Oregon Department of Corrections spent almost a million dollars on free satellite television service for prisoners (its second Golden Fleece Award, two years in a row).

In 1975, the National Institute on Alcohol Abuse and Alcoholism spent millions to find out if drunk fish are more aggressive than sober fish.

In 1995, the Health Care Financing Administration cost taxpayers $45 million by letting Medicare "foot the bill," heh-heh, for cutting toenails.

The worst part, readers? I could go on. And on. And on.